THE NELSON SCANDAL

A Maryvale Cozy Mystery

Book Two

Jackie Griffey

Cover and eBook design by eBook Prep
www.ebookprep.com

October, 2016
ISBN: 978-1-61417-689-3

ePublishing Works!
www.epublishingworks.com

CHAPTER 1

"**T**his one's not going to make it."

In the OR of Maryvale's General Hospital in Pine County, Tennessee, the young intern announced it solemnly as he gazed down at the head injury that had just been admitted to their care.

"Might as well go on and call it in as a homicide so they can find out 'who done it' as the private eyes say."

"That's not in my job description." The nurse shrugged. "Or it wouldn't be if all this was written down somewhere."

She looked with compassion at the patient. "Someone sure dealt him a mortal blow with something, so I'm sure you're right. But he's hanging in there." The nurse shook her head, sympathetic eyes still on the patient. "Anyway, he's not in pain. Hasn't been since whatever it was crashed into his brain."

"No, it was all over for him then. Good thing. There's more damage there than one blow could have caused, too."

He glanced at her, "Didn't a relative or someone come in with him?"

"His father and a neighbor, I think."

The nurse straightened the sheet, averting her eyes. "You voted yet?"

The intern shook his head, welcoming the change of subject. "I'm going to run down to the courthouse soon as I get a few minutes and vote for Cas Larkin for Sheriff and Tim Carpenter for Judge."

He eyed the unconscious patient again, drawn by the terrible wounds inflicted. "Wonder if this might be connected in some way with the election?"

"You've got this mixed up with the full moon." The nurse let out a small laugh at the thought someone had tried to change the man's vote with a blunt instrument.

"This election's got a lot of those full moon aspects to it," the intern argued. "Cas Larkin is unopposed as Sheriff and only one of the candidates running for judge wants the job."

"I know. Everybody I know is voting for Tim Carpenter for Pine County Judge."

"Me too. You say this fellow's people were with him?"

"Yes, I saw them come in."

He gestured at the patient, "You notice these needle marks on his arms?"

"Yeah, he's a user. That probably had more to do with what happened to him than the election or the phase of the moon. I'll go find his people, give them an update on his being admitted and where he is."

The Pine County courthouse was full of voters and the waiting line was every bit as long as most of them had been dreading. The place was buzzing with conversation, shuffling feet, and crowd noises as people waited, complained or greeted each other.

"Hannah! Hannah McLaughlin!" A cheerful voice rang out. Miss Mayme Anderson's smiling face appeared on the other side of the heavyset man in line in front of Hannah McLaughlin.

Hannah smiled at Miss Mayme and her friend, realizing at once who the friend must be. She was Sheriff Cas Larkin's wife, Connie! She quickly looked away.

"I wonder if she knows," was Hannah's first thought. She quickly hid her worry behind a smile as Miss Mayme turned to her.

"This is Connie Larkin," Miss Mayme introduced them. "Hannah McLaughlin."

Connie and Hannah shook hands, reaching around the man between them.

The man made himself as small as possible, looking embarrassed and hugging the wall behind him.

Connie paused, looking thoughtfully at Hannah. "I, somehow I feel as if I've met you before." She murmured, trying to place the pretty face framed in red hair.

"Hannah works at the library," Miss Mayme explained.

"Oh, that's it! I've seen you at the library." Connie's friendly smile accompanied her handshake.

"I remember seeing you, too." Hannah smiled back. "But I didn't know who you were then. That you're the sheriff's wife, I mean. I'm here to vote for your husband," Hannah added with another friendly smile.

"Thank you. We both thank you," Connie corrected herself.

"I know he's unopposed but he will know people support him and appreciate his work." Hannah looked around at the crowd waiting to vote.

"You're right about that, and we do both appreciate your vote. It's nice to meet you. I'll be seeing you again at the library."

Hannah nodded.

Up ahead of Hannah, Miss Mayme craned her neck to look toward the door. "The line's down to the walk now," she observed.

"Good thing you and Miss Minnie decided to come one at a time," Connie commented. "The flower shop would have been closed a long time!"

Hannah relaxed, no longer listening to the noisy conversations around her. She glanced at Connie's back as she waited in line.

"She doesn't know." Hannah relaxed at the thought. "Her husband didn't tell her I'm psychic, and she seems like such a nice, friendly person. She's his wife, I guess I couldn't have blamed him if he told her I'm a psychic, but I'm sure glad he didn't." Hannah smiled to herself, she was very much afraid of being thought not normal or even by some in Fort Craig, a witch of some kind.

"We're closer to the portrait of Mary Lou Nelson here," Connie commented to Miss Mayme. "We can look at her and imagine what it would be like having to wear clothes like that today." She gazed up at the portrait of a beautiful southern belle which graced the wall where everyone entering the courthouse could see it.

"Definitely not wash and wear." Miss Mayme's smile widened as they admired the rich color and style of the dress in the painting.

Connie's expression was wistful, admiring the lovely old-fashioned dress and the delicate beauty of the face above it.

"No, not wash and wear, but they sure were pretty and so was she." Connie tilted her head as she gazed up at the picture. "She looks like Scarlet O'Hara, doesn't she?"

Miss Mayme was a teacher and had taught English and Art before she retired. She gave the portrait her attention now, studying it critically.

"She's certainly as pretty. A beautiful belle of the time. But Scarlet was supposed to have had green eyes. I think. It would be hard to imagine eyes any bluer than those."

Connie ignored the small difference. "Can you imagine having a town named after you?" Her eyes lingered, dreaming of the era the portrait represented.

"Humpf," Miss Mayme looked away from the spellbinding portrait. "It helps, I'm sure, if your father donates the land for the courthouse. Or that's what Minnie says. She's more of a history buff than I am."

She paused, trying to recall something else her sister Minnie had said. Connie simply stood, her mind and imagination romantically traveling back in time.

"But it must not all have been tea cakes and roses." Miss Mayme's voice interrupted her dreams. "There was some sort of trouble or scandal or something attached to the family name."

That got Connie's attention. Miss Mayme's pleasant face almost frowned in concentration. "Maybe about their donating the land, I don't remember. Ask Minnie or you can probably check at the library."

People ahead of her shuffled forward and Connie tore her eyes away from the portrait to move on as the people ahead of them went in to cast their votes. Intrigued by the implied mystery, she put her curiosity to rest by promising herself to find out more about the Nelsons and the beautiful belle of Maryvale.

At dinner that night Cas and Connie were both glad to get home.

"It's always a relief when election day is over." Cas heaved a tired sigh. "I feel like I need therapy for my smile muscles, not that I'm not grateful. I'm just glad it's over."

"Me too. For different reasons, I guess. Had to stand in a long line to vote. Just think, if it's this much trouble to run when you're unopposed wouldn't it be something to have to get out and go from door to door asking for votes and introducing yourself and all the other things you'd have to do? That we'd both have to do, come to think of it."

She wrinkled her nose. "I scared myself just thinking about it!" She quickly added, "But it would be worth it if we had to."

"Yes, it would. I should know better than to gripe when I've got a good thing going. I like my job."

"Liking your job is something we talked about in line at the courthouse today. About Tim Carpenter and Laurence Fields. Fields is as qualified as anyone in the county, a brilliant lawyer. But he's told everyone he knows he doesn't want to be judge, he likes what he's doing. Do you think they'll elect him anyway?"

Cas reached for a roll, thinking that over. "It's hard to say. If he's told enough people how he feels and word's gotten around. But we won't know until the votes are counted. I'd like to see Tim Carpenter elected, though."

"Me too. Oh, and I met someone today. While we were standing in line I was talking to Miss Mayme about all the new faces here and how Maryvale is growing, and she introduced me to a Hannah McLaughlin. She works in the library. She seems like a nice person, or maybe I just thought so because she said she was voting for you."

Cas paused as he helped himself to potatoes and gravy but made no comment.

"Tim Carpenter or Laurence Fields both being lawyers and so well qualified, either one would make an honest and capable judge. And it certainly is time for a new judge," Connie pointed it out a little too emphatically.

"Judge Spruce did some good things before he got to thinking he owned the county," Cas shrugged. "But he would not have been reelected. He was right to retire when he did."

"I suppose you're right. I'll try to remember the good things he did for the county. Speaking of scandals and such, Miss Mayme was just ahead of me in line today and we were looking at that lovely old portrait of Mary Lou Nelson while we were waiting to vote. Wasn't there some sort of tragedy or something in her life?"

Cas gave it some thought. "Umm, yes. There was. I think Nelson committed suicide. I never paid much attention to the old tales and rumors, so I'm not sure."

"Suicide. I could tell from Miss Mayme's expression it must have been something bad. How awful, that our beautiful belle of Maryvale's father killed himself! Do any of those old tales or rumors tell why, or anything about it?"

His mouth full, Cas simply shook his head.

"I guess I'm going to have to give you nosy lessons! Why, some of the old tales and rumors might help in your work sometime, Cas! Who knows?"

Cas shook his head. "I usually get my cases closed or shifted to some other venue before a hundred years roll by." He set her straight as he reached for another roll.

"Yeah," she nodded, looking thoughtful again. "Seems to me I remember you telling me there's no statute of limitations on murder."

"How did we get from old tales and suicide rumors to murder?" Cas rested his fork in mid air.

"Well, every time there's a suicide or accident you have to make sure there was no foul play involved. But, just never mind. I'm going to do some work for Tim Carpenter. I'll ask him if he knows of any old records or anything about it. There should be something in the library, since Nelson donated his mansion for it."

"Probably so." Cas was more interested in this week's news than what happened a hundred years ago. "Let's get through and have our dessert in the den. I'll turn on the election news."

"Go on. I'll be with you in a little bit," Connie promised. "I hate to leave the dishes."

Settled in the den they finished the pot of coffee, sometimes watching the activity as one candidate pulled ahead of the other and sometimes other television programs interrupted by one of them suddenly pulling ahead of the other again as the votes were counted. It seemed by bedtime, that Tim Carpenter would win the judgeship. But all the votes hadn't been counted.

It was the next day before Cas and Connie knew for certain Tim had won the election by a good margin.

The early news showed Attorney Laurence Fields gracefully bowing out and saying Tim Carpenter was a good man who would serve the county well as the new Pine County Judge. This interview was before Tim had many votes ahead of him in the tally. The news reporter said Laurence looked happier than Tim and laughed as the camera focused on the beaming face of the loser.

"Well, good! Now it's official." Cas warmed up his coffee looking pleased.

"There will be so many people calling Tim this morning, I'll wait until I go in to work to tell him how glad we are for him."

"Good idea. That will be tomorrow, won't it?"

"Yes, today's excitement will be cleaning house."

"Yeah, I've got some exciting paperwork to do, too." He gave her a quick kiss as he reached for the door then he was gone.

"Eating seems to be such a nasty habit once your hunger is satisfied," Connie grumbled to the breakfast dishes.

Connie met two or three people coming out of the courthouse as she approached Tim's tiny office the next day. He was still getting congratulations from everyone who had voted for him as well as some Connie suspected hadn't voted for him for some reason, but wanted to.

After Tim outlined the things he wanted typed up Connie asked him about the records on the courthouse and about Nelson donating the land for it.

"I'm curious about the Nelson family after spending so much time with Mary Lou's portrait while I was waiting to vote," Connie explained her interest.

"Then Miss Mayme said there was some kind of trouble or scandal involved and it made me even more curious about it. I know they gave their mansion to the city for the library. Do you know anything about where I might look for information? Some possible sources?"

"None besides the library, but I'll ask around and see what I can come up with. I'll report back this afternoon. How's that?"

He looked happy as a little boy on Christmas morning and might have looked up Santa's north pole address had she asked for it.

"Thank you, your honor." Connie made him a little bow.

Tim was embarrassed, but left grinning.

Connie got to work, noting that in addition to his routine business letters concerning his move from the small office as Public Defender, there were some thank you notes and a list of things he wanted to do before or after his move to the county office.

She was happy for him and felt he would do a good job as County Judge. She managed to get all his correspondence done. Everything including the have to do and mere hope to do lists had been done per instructions. Only a few envelopes were left when Tim returned from court.

"Just a few addresses left, won't take long." She glanced up and assured him as he came in and stood looking over the finished work on his desk.

"Good. It looks good. I'm still grateful for your showing up to rescue me from having to ask for help from the high school typing teacher." He sat down to write her a check. "It was a lucky thing for me you decided to quit your job in Fort Craig and freelance here in Maryvale."

"Oh, you'd have made it all right."

"Thanks for the confidence but I was desperate," he insisted as she laid the last of the envelopes on the desk.

"It was lucky for me, too, don't forget. I was afraid I'd not get any work here in Maryvale."

She put her check in her pocket, getting ready to leave. "Any luck finding out anything about the Nelson family and the land and mansion they donated?"

"Yes, some," he closed the desk drawer. "I didn't find any actual facts, but I talked to a bailiff who's been here since year one. I got my hopes up just hearing how long he's been here, but he was about as little help as I've been. He said Nelson donated the land on which this courthouse is built as well as his mansion across the street, which everybody knows. That's why Mary Lou Nelson's picture is hanging in the front where everyone who comes in can see it. And as everyone also knows, the city was named after Mary Lou. All that is official. Common knowledge from first grade on up and you'll find the facts, dry dates and statistics on all of it officially noted in the records at the library. But off the record, the bailiff's sure Nelson did commit suicide. The good bailiff is one of those who only states facts and he wouldn't make any guesses about why."

Connie nodded, disappointed. Hopes for something more interesting than dry statistics looked dim. But Tim wasn't finished.

"Unofficially, and all the older people tell this for the truth so it probably is: Mary Lou fell in love and ran off with a Frenchman her father didn't approve of and Nelson shot himself."

Tim sat back in his chair looking pleased with himself. "I got that from one of the older clerks with less scruples and more imagination than the bailiff," he grinned.

"So that was the scandal, or at least the rumor. But he really did commit suicide?" Connie shook her head at such despair.

"Yes. Cas told me he too thought he committed suicide. So that's why Nelson left his home to the county, I guess. He didn't want to leave it to the man he didn't approve of and there wasn't anyone else he wanted to have it. Then, too," she added thoughtfully. "He must have been a very civic minded man. Interested in seeing the city and county prosper, since he also gave them the land for the courthouse."

Tim's eyes held a dubious gleam. "I thought so too after I talked to the clerk. She had heard me ask about the Nelsons and told me the rumors after the bailiff left. So just on a hunch, I looked back in some of the old records the silver fish haven't eaten, where there are the bare bones of real estate transactions and dates, you know...."

Connie tilted her head, his expression was sly as if he were telling a secret.

"He's supposed to have killed himself the night Mary Lou eloped, according to the rumors. But he had already willed the mansion to the city at that time. When the will was read, according to the date, it had already been done and dated well before they are supposed to have run off together."

Connie didn't answer, thinking about the way things were supposed to have happened. She wondered as Tim did, about the seeming conflict of dates. And there weren't, evidently, any actual witnesses or concrete facts about what happened.

Tim shrugged. "Oh, well. You will probably find out more about it in the records at the library. But it may be just a theory about the elopement. I don't see how anyone could know for sure. The bailiff and the clerk both said all the old people know about the land donation and all that and the rumors too, from their grandparents. So it's evidently one of those things that's a combination of truth and rumor and been told so long it's accepted as true whether there's much truth in it or not."

"Gracious! It's a good thing you separated the official from the unofficial for me, I think. Now I want to ask more questions than I did before."

Tim laughed at himself. "That's a habit with me, separating the official from the unofficial things. The official ones are not flexible enough to argue about in a court of law."

"I suppose not. Well, anyway, thank you for asking about it for me. I'm going to see what I can find out at the library. And thanks for the work, too."

As she left, Connie saw the Closed sign was already in the window at Anderson's flower shop.

She had missed her chance for a brief visit with Miss Mayme and Miss Minnie who owned it, but there was still light at the library. "I'll stop by the library a minute before they close. No use planning to come up here and look if there aren't any records available."

"You just barely caught me," the elderly librarian looked up and smiled as Connie went into the library.

Her fragile frame and halo of white hair made her the picture of an efficient librarian with patience as an added bonus. There was no annoyance in her voice at the late hour.

"Do you want to check out something in particular or just browse through the fiction? I'll be glad to help you."

"As a matter of fact," Connie glanced at the reading tables. "I want to come and find something about the early times here in Maryvale. About the Nelson family." She added.

Jo Beth Wilson touched her name plate and her smile broadened. "I've been here longer than most of the books, what is it you're looking for?"

"Something about this house, the Nelson Mansion. I stopped by today to see if there are some records. If there are, I'll come back tomorrow and look at them."

The librarian gestured across the reading area. "There's a reference book over there that gives the facts about Mr. Nelson donating the land the courthouse is built on, and that he donated this house to the county to be used as needed. He also left a trust fund so we'd have a small income to run it and take care of it."

"Fine. I'll come back tomorrow then. Is," Connie hesitated, not knowing exactly how to ask.

"Might there be any more records anywhere? Something more personal, like maybe newspaper articles or write-ups about social events and things about the Nelson family?" Her brows drew together, making her pretty face look worried. "Perhaps some of their and Maryvale's social events around that time?"

Jo Beth's eyes twinkled, belying her sixty years. "You want to know about the scandal, don't you?"

Connie flushed. "Yes. If there was one. Is there some sort of reference or family letters, or just anything about the family? I've heard some of the stories handed down. Have you heard them, and do you know if they are true?"

"I guess my whole generation has heard them. And yours too, the ones interested enough to listen or ask about it. Nelson's name was Edgar Timberlake Nelson. He was a planter and also an attorney. He married Mirelle Ethel Cates and her people were as wealthy as his. Cotton money. They had one child, Mary Lou. I'm sure you've seen her portrait at the courthouse."

Connie nodded, waiting to hear more. She listened avidly, feeling she'd found someone who knew as much of the facts about the Nelsons as anyone she could find.

"Mary Lou was the belle of the city even before she was old enough to be called a belle. Her parents and about everyone else doted on her, and the city was named after her when it was chartered. She was loved and popular. There were always adoring beaus around to escort and entertain her."

Connie wondered how many times Jo Beth Wilson had recounted this. It sounded as if she'd memorized what she knew about the Nelsons and the library, or maybe it was more of a tour guide's recitation? That didn't make a dent in Connie's fascination as she drank it in.

"But of all the young men who courted her," Jo Beth continued. "Mary Lou fell in love with Louis DeVille."

Connie noted the French name and her imagination was already painting tall, dark, and handsome pictures in her mind.

"He didn't have any family here, and in France he was only the third son of a more historical than moneyed family. So he didn't have much in the way of property or prospects. Besides that, Nelson took a decided dislike to him."

She glanced at Connie and explained, "Mirelle had died when Mary Lou was a little girl and Mary Lou was all the family Nelson had. Whatever the reason, Nelson made no secret of his disapproval. He more than likely wouldn't have approved of any man she chose," Jo Beth wound up with one eye on the clock.

"Anyway, it was common knowledge they say, that Mary Lou threatened at one time to run off with DeVille. Nelson evidently shot himself when they did run off, and his will left the house to the city and county."

All this conjured up fairy tale romance plots in Connie's vivid imagination of a dashing young Frenchman handsome enough to catch the eye of the belle of the town, and the disapproval of a powerful man like Nelson. All that romance and conflict was heightened by the background of that turbulent and exciting era.

Jo Beth's voice broke into her thoughts. "I doubt they, the city and county I mean, would have taken the house if Mary Lou had wanted it or claimed it. But she didn't. They never came back or asked about it. So I guess everybody was right in thinking Mary Lou went back to France with her Louie. That's what she's supposed to have called him," she added with a smile at Connie. "Louie DeVille."

"Louie DeVille," Connie repeated softly.

Jo Beth sighed, closing the drawer in front of her. "And that's the scandal that's been handed down all these years about the Nelsons."

"How sad." Connie murmured softly, rousing herself from the pictures her imagination painted. "And Mary Lou didn't know if she ran off. About her father, I mean."

Her eyes met Jo Beth's. "Maybe having gone to France, she couldn't afford to come back," Connie worried aloud. "That was one of Nelson's objections, you said, that Louie had no money to take care of Mary Lou."

Jo Beth patted her hand sympathetically and shrugged. "Well, it's not anything official. It's the scandal or rather, the talk that went around. Back then the story was evidently just fleshed out from the will Nelson left and the little that was known about the situation at the time. Nelson was close lipped about his own affairs, so the will and hearsay were all they had to go on."

As they talked, Jo Beth's hands were busy putting her desk in order. She grinned, picking up her purse. "I guess this is the tale they thought would fit the few facts they knew. Anyway, Nelson's property went to the city and county and Mary Lou and her Louie were gone. And they never claimed the house," she pointed out again.

"I see. Well, thanks for taking the time to tell me about it." Connie turned to leave. "I'll come back tomorrow then and read what it says in the reference books. But, are there any old papers," Connie asked hopefully. "Newspapers or other things? This was their home and they were very prominent people. So perhaps there are newspapers with news about their entertaining or events in their lives or some other kind of family records?"

Jo Beth nodded. "I'm pretty sure there are, down in the basement. You can go down and look if you want to."

"I do. Oh, I definitely do. Thank you again for taking time to talk to me so late. I'll see you tomorrow."

Connie felt good driving home. Good about the election, good about her work, and excited about her stop by the library. She could hardly wait to get at the old newspapers the librarian had told her were in the basement.

It had also been a good day financially. Connie touched the check from Tim she had in her jacket pocket. She had her pay with the promise of more work and felt sure now she would be able to stay in Maryvale to enjoy being home. To catch up on gardening, reading and the other things the long trip to work in Fort Craig every day had made impossible.

Reading and the library returned her thoughts to the rumors she had just heard from Jo Beth about the Nelsons. It was obvious the scandal involved a lot of pure guess work on the part of the townspeople. It was such a tragic situation Connie wondered how much of it was actually true, if Mary Lou and her Louie had simply turned their backs on Maryvale or had really gone to live happily ever after in France. It was like reading a romance with the last chapter missing.

She frowned, remembering the dates Tim had found that seemed to conflict with the handed down version of the facts. Well, no matter. She would take Jo Beth Wilson up on her offer to explore that forgotten treasure trove of information in the library basement.

Cas would laugh at her characteristic optimism about finding anything helpful in the basement's old records but she couldn't wait to tell him all she had learned as soon as he got home.

At home, she hurried in to check on preparations she had planned. But after everything for dinner was done, she reluctantly left it in the warming oven.

She glanced at the clock again. Cas was late and it wasn't like him not to have called and told her why he would be a little late.

Realizing she was pacing the small kitchen, she stopped before the window that looked out on the drive way. Still no Cas. She turned and cast a worried look at the clock, fighting the urge to call the office.

CHAPTER 2

"Anything you need before I go?" Sheriff Cas Larkin was properly grateful for his secretary's efficiency and smiled at her thoughtfulness.

"No, thank you. Goodnight, Gladys."

Cas finished the memo he was writing and cleared off his desk.

"Some time I think I'll say yes, just to break the monotony. But I guess the rest of us are about as set in our routine as Gladys is. It must be in the Pine County genes."

Gladys left and the phone rang before Cas could get his jacket on. He picked it up, hoping it would be a wrong number. His mind was already on home and dinner. But it was Senior Deputy Rhodes Cromwell calling in.

"Cas," Rhodes's voice sounded tired. "I've got to change a tire. It won't take long but I thought I'd better let you know where I am."

"Tough luck," Cas frowned. "I know those tires are in bad shape. We'll get some new ones for the front and rotate the others till the budget will stand the price of a couple more."

"Good. We need to do something. This is the one on the left rear. Again."

"We'll do it tomorrow and look into getting some more. Since I'm here, I'll go make the swing out by Peaceful Ridge and Martin's place before I go home. You come on in when you get the tire changed. I hope it's a quiet night."

"Me too. And thanks. See you tomorrow."

"Gets dark early this time of year," Cas thought as he drove out of the parking lot. It was dark before he'd gone very far out of town and he drove carefully. "Got to tell someone the white line at the edge of the road needs to be repainted."

Just as he sighted the bridge on the near side of Peaceful Ridge Cemetery ahead of him, a dark colored van approached and passed him going at a high rate of speed.

"Smart aleck! Doing ninety-five according to the radar. If a ticket doesn't scare him into slowing down it will at least cut into his gas money for a while."

Cas turned on his lights and started in pursuit. As he started up the incline to the bridge he heard a motor behind him. At the same moment he saw a movement in his mirror. The looming dark shape was a pick-up truck without lights. Startled, it was mere seconds before it slammed into his car, pushing him over the side of the rise.

The impact sent his car off into space then down toward the water below. Airborne and out of control, his lights looked like heat lightning flashes as the car descended hitting rocks and scraggy undergrowth on the way down. The car came to rest at a precarious angle on the rocks just above the swift current of the river.

On the road above, the dark pick-up truck accelerated after the impact, following the van.

Quiet settled again on the county road. The only sign of life in the darkness was the car's rotating light sending its shaft of colors up from its resting place to the deserted stretch of road above it.

* * *

Whistling, shifting a sack to his other hand, Rhodes unlocked the door to the office and touched the light switch.

"It was good of Cas to go make that last patrol for me. Now I can enjoy my coffee in peace."

He put the sack with the Danish and coffee in it on Cas's desk and went to make sure Gladys had hooked up the office phone.

With his tall, rangy body warm and comfortable. Rhodes was full of coffee and his sweet tooth satisfied. He reached for the sack, rummaging in it for napkins. As he wiped sugar off his lips and fingers he chuckled when his stomach made a gurgling sound.

"Guess that hit the spot. Now all I have to do is put a hex on the phone so it won't ring." He frowned at the ring. "Too late!"

He picked up the ringing phone, pushing the sack out of the way with his other hand. Before he could say anything he heard a woman's anxious voice.

"The sheriff's car is off the road, down under the bridge by the cemetery! I can't tell if he's hurt. Hurry!"

Rhodes felt the adrenaline pump and his mouth opened. But there was no longer anyone there to ask anything.

"She hung up! Excited and scared, I guess."

Rhodes grabbed his jacket, running for the door. He locked up but left the lights on, his mind on Cas.

"God! Let Cas be all right!"

In the car he called an ambulance then picked up as much speed as he safely could, still praying for his friend.

"I should have gone out there." his conscience tortured him.

"Wait a minute!" His hands tightened on the wheel. "That woman didn't even tell me who she is. What if that was someone wanting to get rid of me for some reason? Fine time to think of that!"

But in his heart, Rhodes believed that voice. Whether it made sense or not, he believed her.

His eyes covered everything ahead of his car and around him. There was no traffic, nothing moving but him. He picked up his cell and dialed Cas and Connie's home phone number.

"If Cas answers, I'll know I've been had." But it was a vain hope he had no faith in as he listened to the distant ring.

Connie's worried voice confirmed what he already knew, his gut feeling that the caller's voice spoke the truth. He tried to sound calm.

"Connie, is Cas there? This is Rhodes."

"No, Cas hasn't got home yet. I was about to call you. It's not like him not to call if he's going to be late. Do you know if he had to stop somewhere?"

"He went on one of our rounds on the way home. I'm going to check on him now. He may have had a flat or something. I'll call you back, don't worry."

Rhodes had made record time and was getting closer to the bridge. He pictured it and the road as he hurtled through the dark, lights and siren heralding his approach.

He saw the lights first and gripped the steering wheel hard enough to hurt. He slowed as he pulled off the road. He stopped to look down at the car. The open door stirred a faint hope, but there was no movement or sign of anyone there. Thankful the lights were still on, he half climbed, half skidded down to the car, holding to the tough underbrush and outcroppings of rock to ease his descent.

His heart leaped. "I see him! He's still in there."

Rhodes managed to get to the open door and carefully touched the still figure in the driver's seat. He was rewarded with a weak moan.

Rhodes bent his head at the sound. "Thank God! He's alive, just knocked out. Must have got a pretty good lick on the head."

Blood oozing down from Cas's hairline gave Rhodes a twinge as he felt his pulse. But the pulse was strong, reassuring. His eyes took in the rest of the damage.

Cas's arm was bent at an unnatural angle and blood was showing through his uniform pants at one knee but the seat belt was still holding him in place as Rhodes loosened the seat belt a little.

Cas seemed to be coming around as Rhodes cautiously looked him over.

"Don't try to move. This is Rhodes, can you hear me?"

"Yes, I hear you. I think my ears are the only things that aren't broke, the way I'm beginning to feel."

Cas tried to move his left arm. He couldn't, and winced at the effort.

"Lie still. Don't try to move. An ambulance is on its way. You've got a lick on the head and your arm's broken but from what I can see that's the worst of it. You're going to be all right. Did the lady tell you her name?"

"Lady? What lady? You're the one who's delirious! Do you see any lady here?"

Rhodes's face was puzzled in the eerie lights and shadows. "A lady called and told me your car had gone off the bridge incline. That's how I knew to come looking for you."

"Oh. Well, sorry to be so grumpy. Must have been someone passing by."

The ambulance crew arrived and got Cas safely strapped to a stretcher before they started back up to the road.

It was slow going. Rhodes went ahead to light their way with his flashlight. He would call Connie as soon as they could get Cas on the way to the hospital.

Connie was as worried as he pictured her, sitting on a kitchen chair waiting to hear from him. She sat a while, then jumped up to pace some more. She grabbed the phone when it rang.

"Rhodes?"

"Yes, it's me. There's been an accident…."

"An accident," Connie's heart plummeted into her stomach. "Is, is it bad?" she managed.

"No. He's going to be all right. He's got a knot on his head and a broken arm. Maybe a few scratches and bruises, too. But he's going to be all right. He's already in the ambulance and they're heading for St. Anthony's now."

"I'm on my way." Connie turned off the oven and ran out, forgetting her coat and everything else except where Cas was, holding onto Rhodes's voice saying he would be all right.

Rhodes met Connie in the emergency room as she came in.

"He's conscious and they will be putting him in a room pretty soon. As soon as they can get him cleaned up and his arm set. I've got to get back to the office. If he needs blood or there's anything else we don't know about, you call me. In fact, call me anyway as soon as he's in a room."

"I will."

"I'm sorry, I have to go."

"I know you're on duty, Rhodes. I'll call you, I promise. As soon as he's settled and I've seen the doctor."

As Connie sat waiting in the hall the nurses going back and forth kept her posted on things going on with Cas and the doctor. It seemed to break the monotony for them, and they could see how worried she was.

After a few informative and humorous bulletins, one of the nurses told her, "He objected so much to the neck brace the doctor told him he doesn't have to wear it." She grinned at Connie, "Of course, that may hurt the lawsuit!"

Connie shook her head, unable to smile yet. "No, we won't have to worry about that, there's nobody to sue. Whoever did this just went on. But I don't blame him about the neck brace. They do look uncomfortable, and I'm glad there's not sufficient reason for him to have to wear it."

"The way he's talking, he's going to get up and go right on to work," one of the nurses smiled.

"He probably would try it all right but he'll have to stay here a while, won't he?"

"Probably not for long. The worst problem he's got right now is the arm will be in a cast. He's lucky it's the left one. But," she warned. "People are usually a lot more sore all over the next day or two than they are right after an accident."

"I've heard that's true," Connie nodded. "I'm thankful it was no worse than it was."

A little while later the doctor came out to talk to Connie. "Mrs. Larkin?"

"Yes," Connie stood up. Held her breath.

"He's got a goose egg and a few stitches on his head but no concussion. His left arm is broken and there are some bruises and abrasions, but none of them too serious."

He smiled, "He's already started healing. Everything, including his disposition, will be better in a few days," he concluded with a sympathetic smile.

"Um-hum. I heard about the difference of opinion over the neck brace."

"It's more of a precaution at this point than a need. He's going to be fine. They have him in a room now so you can go up and talk to him. I didn't tell him to go to sleep like a good boy, because I gave him a shot that will see to that. Talk fast if you want to ask him anything." The young doctor grinned at her and turned to go back to work.

Connie found Cas sitting up in bed, gingerly feeling around the knot on his head.

"Must be a beaut the way it feels," he grumbled.

"It's not so big, and you're all right. That's all I care about. What in the world happened?"

"Rhodes had a flat, so I was making the patrol out by Caleb Martin's place when a speeder passed me. I was watching him ahead of me when a pick-up truck running dark came up behind me. It was out there at the bridge just before you get to Peaceful Ridge. I didn't see him till he was right on me and he knocked me off the incline. I should have kept a better watch, is what it boils down to."

"You're aggravated because you were in a vulnerable position? Hogwash! You couldn't have seen the truck coming up on you with no lights on. I know how dark it is out there."

"It's dark out there all right. It was hard to see that dark colored van I was chasing." He dimly remembered looking back but he'd only looked back because the truck was close enough by that time for him to hear the motor. Then he had glimpsed the movement in his mirror. He went over it again in his mind, his thoughts getting fuzzy.

Connie could see the doctor's shot taking effect. Cas's eyelids were drooping. She got him settled as comfortably as possible, his arm on an extra pillow, before his eyes closed completely.

"I'll see you in the morning," Connie murmured, kissing his forehead as he relaxed and drifted off to sleep. She stopped downstairs and called Rhodes before going home.

The next morning at the hospital Connie quietly opened the hospital room door and peeped in.

Breakfast had evidently been served and Cas had eaten all of it he thought was worth the wear and tear on his digestive tract. He was eyeing a hard looking little biscuit when he looked up and saw her.

"What? No English muffins? I just happen to have one, still warm, with lots of orange marmalade and butter in it."

"Then I'm glad to see you for two reasons!" Cas tossed the hard little biscuit into the trash can and reached for the tidy paper towel package she held out.

She bent and kissed him, giving him a careful hug. "How are you feeling? Neck still sore?"

"Not much. It lets me know when I try to turn it. I'm definitely ready to get out of here. The nurse said the doctor would be in soon. He'll probably tell me then I can go."

"I was going to work for Tim Carpenter half a day. Do you suppose he will let you out before twelve o'clock? I can call Tim from here…."

"No, I wouldn't. If the doctor came in now and told me I can go, the paperwork would take till noon. I'll call you at Tim's office when I know for sure, how's that?"

"That's fine." She started to leave but turned at the door. "But Cas, if he does want you to stay for some reason?" Her expression gave him the message to cooperate.

"I know, I know. But he won't. The cast on my arm and the bandage on my head is all I need at this point. No need taking up space in a hospital." He waved her away. "I'll call you as soon as I hear what he has to say."

"All right. And if I haven't heard I'll be back when I leave Tim's."

"I hope he doesn't give me any arguments about staying here," Cas worried as the door had closed behind her. "Lucky Rhodes got there and it wasn't any worse. That reminds me," he pushed the tray back with his good hand and reached for the phone to dial the library's number.

"County Library, Hannah McLaughlin speaking."

"Hi, I just called to say thanks. It was you who called Rhodes, wasn't it?"

"Yes, I called."

"Did you see it happen?"

"I saw it just as it happened but I knew the hospital wouldn't listen to me. So I called whoever was on duty that night."

"It was Rhodes, Hannah. He thinks it must have been someone passing by who called."

"Good," Hannah gave a sigh of relief. "I knew whoever was there would go and check on you whether they believed me or not. I was at home getting ready to put something in the microwave when I saw it. I saw that truck hit you out there in the dark. Are you all right?"

"My left arm is broken and I've got a knot on my hard head. But the knot and the arm and the car are all being taken care of by experts and I wanted to thank you."

"I'm glad you're getting healed up all right and you're welcome. By the way, I met Connie in the voting line on election day."

"I know. She told me about it."

"Thanks for keeping my secret. I like her, and she's your wife, I really couldn't have blamed you for telling her about me and my so-called gift."

"Yes, you would," Cas grinned into the phone. "I'm not psychic like you, but I know that. And I didn't want you to feel uncomfortable."

"Anyway, thanks. And another thing, that truck, Cas. It was intentional, It deliberately knocked you off the road. It was not an accident."

"Seemed that way to me, too. There was room on the road if he'd only wanted to get by. Did you see what kind of truck it was? Or better yet, see the driver? Could you see a silhouette or anything to identify him?"

"No, it was too dark. But the angle and the speed were obvious. He ran right at you. It had to be intentional."

"Okay then. If you do think of anything let me know. And thank you, Hannah." Cas carefully replaced the phone on the table beside the bed.

"My hunch, my first impression, was right. Whoever was in that truck pushed me off the road on purpose. A pick-up truck running without lights at a high rate of speed that deliberately hit a police car. Wonder what he was up to?"

"Business as usual?" The call from the door interrupted his thoughts.

Cas looked up at the sound of the doctor's cheerful voice.

"I saw you put down the phone. Neck giving you any trouble?"

"No." Cas winced as the doctor touched the bandage on his head, then tapped the muscle he was concerned about.

"I can go home today, can't I? Don't see any reason to stay here."

"By home you mean back to work, don't you?"

"No reason not to, is there?" Cas evaded the question.

"I guess not. The stress of having to stay in here would probably be worse for you than a little physical exertion."

The doctor smiled. "I'm assuming you've got sense enough not to hurt yourself and take it easy a few days. If your neck hurts, lay your head back and rest a little. And I'd not put a hat over that bandage for a while. Come into the office in two or three days and I'll change the bandage for you."

Cas agreed to all that, wishing he had another cup of coffee. "When can I go? About noon? I'd like to eat lunch somewhere else. No offense," Cas grinned.

"None taken. I'm going elsewhere too. Yes, about noon we'll have you out of here. Take care."

"I'll do it." Cas reached for the phone again before the door closed and dialed his office.

"Gladys? Is Rhodes around there or has he gone?"

"He's here but he's on the phone in your office. Give me the number there and I'll give it to him as soon as he gets off. How are you doing?"

Cas read the number off the phone. "I'm doing fine. I'll be leaving here about noon."

"Leaving about noon? So soon?"

"No reason to stay. Got a bandage on my head and a cast on my arm which, face it, is all they can do. And I'm not in any danger. Hospitals are for sick people, Gladys."

Gladys smiled, his voice sounded reassuring. "I can ring Rhodes now, hold on."

"Did I hear something about your getting out of there about noon? I was just going to call you." Rhodes interrupted.

"About noon is right and what were you going to call about?"

"I've got good news about the van you were chasing and the pick-up that hit you. Harlan Glover just called me. That's who I was talking to. They've got both vehicles impounded and the drivers are in the Marble County jail."

CHAPTER 3

Tim Carpenter looked up as Connie entered. "Hi, I wasn't sure if you would be here."

"You've heard about the accident?"

"Small town telegraph," Tim shrugged. "Is Cas all right?" Tim gestured at the papers on his desk, "This can wait, you know."

"He's all right, thank goodness. He's got a sore bump on his head but the doctor says there's no concussion. And his left arm is broken. With the rest of what's wrong, he seems to think of as down in the merely aggravating category. The usual muscle aches and scratches."

"All I heard was that his car went off the road out there by the bridge but that he would be all right."

Connie nodded. "He's going to leave the hospital today, or at least he thinks he is. If he doesn't call me before I leave I'll go to the hospital from here."

"You can do these things some other time if you'd rather. There's nothing pressing about any of it."

"Oh no. We talked about it when I saw him at breakfast this morning. I can go from here and take him home if they do dismiss him."

"All right then. And before I forget, I found a date for you. Nelson donated the land for the courthouse in eighteen sixty-five as I found out yesterday, and the courthouse was finished in eighteen sixty-eight. That's when the portrait of Mary Lou was donated too."

"Thank you. I found out there is some information at the library. I'll go over there and look at it as soon as I can get around to it."

At the hospital, Cas was back on the phone.

"Rhodes, this is Cas. I didn't catch Harlan. I'll have to call him later. What did he tell you about those two vehicles, the van and the pick-up truck? They were together, weren't they?"

"Yeah, that's what he said, and it gets worse. One of his deputies spotted the van speeding and without lights and started after it. Then he noticed the pick-up in back of him. He called for another car and they got them both. They got a lot more than a speeding ticket. The van was full of marijuana and there was marijuana and cocaine in the pick-up truck. Harlan called here to tell you about it and I told him what happened to you. Said he wants to talk to you soon as you get a chance to call."

"I will, that's good news that he got them. I may come in for a little while this afternoon but don't count on it. If not, I'll see you in the morning. I could call Harlan from home, I guess."

"There's nothing going on here, why don't you do that."

Connie heard her husband's voice as soon as she got off the elevator.

"It's my ARM that's broken, not my legs!"

Cas looked with disgust at the wheelchair the nurse had brought in to take him downstairs.

Connie stifled a giggle and went to pour oil on the troubled waters. She talked Cas into sitting in the wheelchair by convincing him she needed his help.

"You can hold these flowers and the extra pillow I brought."

They managed to reach the exit without too many ruffled feathers and they got him settled in the passenger's seat before Connie got in to drive. He was not too happy about that either, but bit back any comment as he looked out the window.

"You know what your problem is? You don't know how to enjoy poor health." Connie told him about a woman she used to work with who always managed to take every bit of the sick pay available using all sorts of inventive tales.

"Where she messed up was she always came back before she would have lost any pay."

Cas was smiling again before they arrived at their driveway. "I thought I'd heard all the excuses!"

"Well, now you have, I guess. Here it is, Sanctuary as you call it. Hang onto the pillow and I'll get the flowers." She came around to open the door for him. "I'll come back and get the odds and ends."

"Okay. I guess I'll use that poor health plea and let you do it. I need to call Harlan Glover."

Connie dumped everything in the kitchen temporarily and started coffee. Cas headed toward the phone in the den where he could get comfortable.

"Cas!" Harlan boomed into the phone. "I'm glad to hear your voice, how are you doing?"

"I'm fine. I just got home from the hospital."

"You're already home? Have they got an epidemic or a rash of accidents? Why did they let you out so soon?"

"Nothing like that. They've done all they could do for me. Got my head bandaged and a cast on my arm and there was no sense in staying any longer."

"Don't you get too rambunctious, Rhodes said something about your neck?"

"They put a brace on it for a little while. More precaution than anything else. It feels like a mild crick, that's all."

"No crick is mild. They're as aggravating as hell and no fun. From what Rhodes said about the car and what I know about that incline out there, Somebody up there must like you. But we've got the trash that did it. Have you talked to Rhodes?"

"Yes, I tried to call you. Just missed you so I waited till I could get here. He said you got the van and the pick-up both. That they had marijuana and cocaine in both vehicles. I didn't see the truck until the second before it hit me. It was out there this side of the bridge before you get to Peaceful Ridge."

"On that side, yeah, I know the place. It's black as a coal hole out there at night. Do you know that crud in the pick-up still didn't have his lights on when he came through here? My deputy saw him under the street lights and called for back-up."

"Lucky he saw him. He was on me before I could even register shock at how close he was."

"Then they were dumb enough to try to run when they got out of the vehicles. I think one of them was sampling his own wares, the pick-up driver that pushed you off the incline. Didn't seem to be touching the ground very often or know much about what was going on. That reminds me, his front damage looks like there might be some paint off your panel where he hit you. If not, the damage will match up. Will you let us have the panel to use as evidence? We're lacing everything up tight on this case."

"Sure. I'll call the garage right now. I'll be back in the office tomorrow. One of our men will meet yours at the Roadhouse and give it to him."

"Thanks, appreciate it. You take it easy now and give yourself a chance to heal up. I'm glad you're all right. Bye."

At that moment Connie peeked around the door. "Coffee's ready."

"I'm ready too." His eyes went to what she carried. "I wanted another cup at breakfast this morning, and it wasn't even good! I'm spoiled to your good coffee."

"And English muffins and marmalade…."

"Could I interest you in a slightly beat, one armed hug?"

* * *

Cas managed to shower the next morning with the cast sticking out around the curtain and let Connie help him get dressed with the sling comfortably in place.

"Lucky it wasn't the right one."

"Uh-huh, so I see. That was very efficient of you to keep one for paperwork," Connie teased him.

Cas saved his breath for dressing.

"I'll drive you to the office. If you're not comfortable driving the truck, I'll come and get you."

"I don't think it will be any trouble but I'll try it out before you leave if it will make you feel better."

"I'm only going over to the library today, since I don't have any work. It won't be any trouble to come and get you."

Connie pulled up beside the truck in the parking lot and waited while Cas went to get the keys to it. She switched off the ignition to wait and see for herself how well he could manage. She noticed someone had washed the truck. "Probably Rhodes," she smiled to herself.

Cas backed the truck out, passed her and went out of the parking lot. He was back in a few minutes and parked the truck where it had been.

Connie rolled her window down. "What do you think?"

"It's all right, I can manage. And I probably won't be going anywhere but home for a couple of days anyway. See you tonight." He bent to kiss her goodbye.

Connie wasn't going far either at the moment. She pulled across the square and parked in the library's parking lot. She could see part of the courthouse lot from there and silently hoped Cas was right and he wouldn't have to do any driving.

Cas was wrong about not having any occasion to drive the truck anywhere but home. About mid-afternoon he got a call from the hospital about a suspicious head injury. Gladys put the call through to his office.

As he listened, he made a note to get a phone brace so he could take notes if he needed to. His neck protested as he held the receiver against his shoulder.

"The injured man is Welemon Lynch? Yes, I know his uncle. Is his Uncle Clarence there, or who brought him in? I see." Cas interrupted the description of the wound, "I'm on my way, you can tell me when I get there."

He paused on his way out. "Gladys, I'll be back soon or I'll call you."

"Hi there," Jo Beth greeted Connie at the library. "I heard about the accident. I'm glad Cas is all right, or will be when his arm heals."

Hannah came from behind a book shelf and added her good wishes for Cas. "Jo Beth told me you were coming in to look at some information on the Nelson family. I'll show you where the references are, if you like."

"Thank you, I'd like to look at them."

"I'm afraid there isn't an awful lot about the family, mostly dry facts and figures. Here, in these two books." Hannah pointed. "And there are some pictures. Those hung on that wall are of this house when the Nelson family lived in it. And the smaller ones on the back wall in the first reading room are pictures of the land the courthouse was built on and some early pictures of it."

"I'm going to put the books on the table to read and look at the pictures first."

Hannah nodded and went back to her work.

Connie carefully studied the pictures. "I would never have known what these were if Hannah hadn't told me. I guess this other picture is how the land looked seen from this house when the Nelsons were living here."

The pictures of the courthouse somehow looked smaller than it was, but the mansion was interesting. There were chairs on the porch, which was not closed in until the library had it done and it looked as if the family lived in it. The front door appeared to be open and a dog lay at the bottom of the steps.

"What a really lovely old house it was," Connie thought as she went back to the books Hannah had shown her.

"Here is the information Jo Beth told me about. Nelson's name was Edgar Timberlake Nelson. He married Mirelle Ethel Cates, and he was a cotton planter and an attorney. He had donated the land for the courthouse in eighteen sixty-five, and the courthouse was finished in eighteen sixty-eight, as Tim told me." All her facts were right so far, there just weren't enough of them.

"Hum, Mirelle must have died during that time or before. There is no mention of her in the brief paragraph about opening the courthouse or the one about hanging the portrait of Mary Lou. And Nelson must have become a county judge around that time, because the later mentions refer to him as Judge Nelson."

Connie could find no reference to his death until in the last reference book, the year of his death was given as eighteen sixty-nine.

"Nothing but the date." Connie closed the book feeling disappointed. "No reference or hint there of what Jo Beth called the scandal at all." She made a few notes and returned the books to the desk.

"Did you find the information all right?" Jo Beth smiled.

"Yes, the dates and the land that was donated for the courthouse," Connie hesitated. "But what I'm really interested in is seeing some articles or write-ups about the social events and people that lived here in the house and in Maryvale around that time. Is that the sort of things that are in the basement?"

Jo Beth seemed uncertain. "I think so. I know there are some old newspapers down there. To tell you the truth it's been so long since anyone looked at them, I can't tell you exactly what is there. It's cold and unpleasant to work down there so it's just dusted off occasionally. But the material? To tell the truth, it's where we stick things that probably won't ever be asked for to get them out of the way. But you're welcome to go down and look through them if you want to."

"Yes, I would. There should be something. If there's some things I want to read more of or look at more closely, may I bring them up to one of the reading rooms?"

"Of course you may." She turned and raised her voice a bit. "Hannah?"

Hannah appeared again from behind the book shelves.

"Would you please open the door to the basement and turn on the light for Mrs. Larkin? She wants to look at some of the old news issues down there."

"I'll be glad to." Hannah took a key from one of the desk drawers and led the way.

Connie smothered a nervous giggle as the door actually gave a loud creak when Hannah opened it. "It sounds like it hurt it to open."

Hannah agreed. "It's certainly old enough to be stiff," she smiled.

The cold breath from the basement reached out to embrace them. Connie shuddered involuntarily, and moved back a step.

"I have a sweater in my desk, Mrs. Larkin."

"Oh, no, I'll be fine. And my name's Connie."

"Jo Beth should have warned you. It's always cold down there. It's probably not a good place for some of that material but it seems to be the only place we have to put it. I don't think anyone goes down there except the cleaning people, and that's not very often."

"It's well lighted anyway, thank you." Connie got a firm grip on the rail as she started down the stairs, her feet and calf muscles strangely reluctant to step down. She blamed the gloomy coldness which seemed to come up to meet her.

In spite of the bright light on a cord, Connie had an eerie feeling as she descended the stairs. She peered warily around as she went, moving slowly and carefully. There was a wealth of books down there, some of them outdated enough to be conversation pieces. She glanced at the titles on the shelves beside the stairway as she went.

About halfway down Connie stifled a nervous, near hysterical laugh. "Shades of Rudolph Valentino, here's The Sheik!"

Reaching the bottom of the stairs she stopped and glanced quickly at the full shelves and tables that went all the way back to the far wall. Her eyes worked their way back and she started looking at the wealth of material. She found novels and fiction first then odds and ends of non-fiction. After reference books, she began to find back issues of old papers with odd sized print and loose papers which didn't seem to be organized at all.

"Even if they'd been in some kind of order once, the cleaning crew probably doesn't waste any time trying to keep them together."

Her teeth began to chatter and she hugged herself, trying to get warmer.

"Just my luck, the oldest and most interesting looking things are at the very back. The wall is only about a yard away here." She looked down on stacks of what appeared to be old newspapers mixed in with other things in no particular order.

She paused, listening. She shivered in the icy cold as she recognized the sound.

"It's crying, someone's crying! I wonder where it's coming from to penetrate down here?"

Just then a black edged paragraph on one of the papers caught her eye. She reached out and picked it up. The print stood out even in the poor light the one bulb cast. She forgot her cold as she read Edgar T. Nelson dies by his own hand!

CHAPTER 4

Connie gasped, holding the paper higher to see it better. "So, it's true! Nelson did kill himself!"

Her hands shook a little as she smoothed the wrinkled paper, trying not to tear the fragile pages. "I knew there had to be some records here."

Holding the paper carefully she read the black edged paragraph. The old fashioned type told about his generosity and some of his community service. It was hard to read. It closed saying Nelson would be greatly missed by all the citizens of Maryvale and Pine County.

She squinted, searching back over what she had so quickly scanned. Her brows drew together. "But, there's not a hint here about what led up to his suicide or even any speculation about it. Nothing. Though I can understand their silence if they weren't sure of the facts. That's all there is here, just the bare facts. Not one thing of any personal nature to give anybody a clue."

Shivering with cold, Connie was again aware of the crying. She felt as depressed and sad as the crying sounded. She carefully folded the paper and placed it on top of the stack nearest her.

"Reading about Nelson's suicide in this cold, dark place must be having an effect on me. But that is someone crying, I know it is. It's so faint it must be coming from somewhere else but it definitely is someone crying."

She chafed her cold hands before looking through more of the old newspapers.

"Here's something. This is more like it," Connie smiled to herself. "This is what I was looking for. Social events and things about what was happening in Maryvale back then. This article is about a ball of some kind." She held the paper carefully.

"And here's a picture!" She held the paper up higher trying to get the light just right. It was not too clear but it was a picture with several people in it. She put it with the other pages she had chosen to take upstairs with her.

The crying was clearer now and brought with it a depression so strong, even after the happiness of finding the picture Connie had to fight to keep from crying along with the sad sound in sympathy. Something was terribly, terribly wrong. She knew it, she felt the pain in her heart.

"This is silly, just plain silly! There's no telling where that sound is coming from. I'm going to get out of here. I'll come back with some boxes."

Connie moved quickly toward the stairs and didn't look back.

Jo Beth was not at the front desk so she asked Hannah for boxes to bring up the material.

"Just a couple of boxes is all I need. I've found some things I want to take up to a reading room to get a closer look at them. I want to finish reading them, and there's a picture I found too. I want to see it better and read about the people in it." She added, "I asked Jo Beth and she said it would be all right to bring them up where I could see them better."

Hannah nodded, a finger tapping her chin as she tried to remember where she'd seen some boxes that would do.

"Wait a minute." Hannah disappeared and was back in no time with two cardboard boxes.

"I'll go with you and carry one of them for you."

"Thanks, I'll take you up on the offer. But I'll take them down and decide what to bring up with me and then call you. That way I can take my time and look for more pictures or things that look interesting, okay?"

"Good idea. Let me know when you're ready."

Connie again descended into the dank basement. "This is not natural," she muttered to herself. "It's too cold." Somehow just the sound of her own voice helped, as if she'd registered a complaint and the crying was not quite as loud, not that it warmed her any.

Her hand tightened on the stair rail. "And there's that sound again, I mean still." She frowned. "Where could it be coming from?"

At the bottom of the stairs she looked around her and up at the ceiling. "Not much telling about the acoustics in a place this old, with all its twists and turns. Must have been a real monster to keep clean."

At the bottom of the stair now, Connie hurried back to where she'd left the old newspapers and busied herself gathering up what she wanted to take with her.

"I'm going to grab everything I see that looks remotely connected to that time. This old type will give me a clue. I want to get away from this cold and this crying as fast as I can no matter where it's coming from. I'm one solid goose bump!"

She had left the door open when she came back down, not that it had warmed up the basement any. She shuddered as she raised her voice, near panic for some unknown reason, just wanting desperately to get out of there.

"HANNAH! Hannah, I'm ready now!"

She listened on the verge of a waking nightmare, fear that no one would come. Then she heard footsteps approaching the door above. Hannah was on her way. She moved back to where she had left the two boxes.

About halfway down the stairs Hannah's quick, light footsteps stopped, then continued more slowly. When she got to Connie, she looked frightened. Her face was pale as she reached out to a shelf to steady herself.

"Hannah," Connie put her hands on Hannah's arms to steady her. "Are you all right? You look faint."

"It's probably the cold. Let's get out of here."

Each of them took a box and moved quickly toward the stairs. It was Connie who stopped to turn off the lights and close the door. Hannah went on back to the reading room.

"It was awfully cold down there," Connie said tentatively. She set her box on the table beside the one Hannah had brought up.

Hannah didn't answer but she looked all right and had got the natural color back in her face.

"You heard it too, didn't you? The crying? I was afraid I'd imagined it." Connie watched Hannah's expression as she spoke.

"Yes, I did. I didn't know if you heard it. You did, then." Hannah's face expressed sympathy or maybe it was pain, "It was so sad."

"I know. I didn't hear it when I first went down, then I just slowly became aware of it. And you're right about it being sad. I felt like crying too."

Hannah only nodded and looked into the box beside her. "These are the newspapers you were looking for?"

"They are. I knew there must be something like them somewhere. I wanted to read about some of the people and the social events back in the Nelson's time. The things that give you a picture of how life was here when the land was donated and the courthouse was built. These seem to be about all that's left of them."

"Well, happy hunting. Let me know if you need anything else. As long as it doesn't involve going back down in that cold basement," Hannah laughed at herself.

"Don't worry. I'm not anxious to go back down there either. Would it be chicken to save this for the cleaning crew to take back?"

"It will take you days to go through all this anyway so they may be back by then. You can leave them there with a note not to disturb them if you want to."

"Good, that will help. Thanks."

* * *

Gladys had put the call from the hospital through to his office.

Cas listened, his neck protesting, and he made a reminder note to get a phone brace as he held the receiver against his shoulder.

"The injured man is Welemon Lynch? Yes, I know his uncle. Is his Uncle Clarence there, or who brought him in? I see." Cas interrupted the description of the wound, "I'm on my way. You can tell me when I get there."

He paused on his way out. "Gladys, I'll be back soon or I'll call you."

At the hospital the doctor was waiting for Cas.

"I'm Doctor Thomas. I had them call you about this head injury. Thought you might want to see him before he goes to the coroner."

"You said his name is—was, Welemon Lynch?"

"According to his uncle. As they told you, he brought him in. Said someone must have attacked him in the back yard. The uncle's back yard, that is. That's where they found him."

The young doctor shook his head, "He was really DOA with that kind of wound. Must have had a strong constitution to hang on this long. He was a user, too."

"He had needle marks?"

"Yes. On his arms. He's in here." He opened the room door for Cas to enter then went over and pulled back the sheet that had been pulled up over the body.

Cas looked at the needle marks. "He's not in as bad a shape as some of them are that use this stuff." He winced at the sight of the injury. "I don't see how he lived until they got him in here with a head wound like that."

"No, I don't either. And the damage you can't see at this angle is even worse. There was no chance at all. Evidently the first blow knocked him out. That was the end of his suffering. He was just big with a strong constitution and held onto life. His suffering was over. I told the relatives that, and that I would have to send him to the coroner's office for an autopsy and notify you. This is the ID he had on him." He held it out.

Cas reached for the plastic rectangle and examined the picture. "I remember him. I think. Been quite a few years, though. I remember a younger kid, yeah, it's been a while."

Cas noted the address given. "This is where his uncle lives. Welemon would have been thirty-six on his birthday according to this."

He put the ID in his pocket. "Thank you for calling me. I'll go by and talk to his uncle and see if I can find out what happened to him."

On the way to the victim's uncle's house Cas drove the truck slowly, looking at house numbers. A few of the neighbors looked with open curiosity when he stopped in front of Clarence Lynch's house. As he climbed the front steps Clarence appeared at the door and held it open for him.

"Come in. Been expecting you."

"I went to the hospital as soon as they called me about Welemon. I was sorry to hear about it. I haven't seen him for quite a while now. Do you know what happened to him?"

"No." Clarence shook his head, speaking softly. "We took him to the hospital when we found him. You know, he was my sister's boy and he stayed with us after his mama got killed in that factory accident."

"I saw he gave your address." Cas handed the ID to Clarence. "But I don't remember seeing him lately," his eyes held the obvious question of his recent whereabouts.

"No, he wasn't really with us. I don't think he had a place of his own. He always would give this as his permanent address. He stayed with us until he got on dope and we couldn't seem to reach him or do anything with him. He would come back once in a while. We'd feed him and take care of him and do the best we could for him. But he just couldn't seem to get away from dope for very long, and he'd leave again."

From the corner of his eye Cas saw an elderly woman enter the back of the room and stand listening to them talk. Cas judged her to be in her late seventies and maybe a little hard of hearing. She tilted her head as if turning her good ear toward them.

"She looks frightened," Cas thought addressing Clarence.

"You say you found Welemon. How did you happen to find him? Did you hear the noise of a fight or see someone run away?"

"No, didn't see or hear anything. I had just started out to the back and I saw him lying there. I called my neighbor to help me. We got him in the car and took him to the hospital, but wasn't nothing they could do." Clarence looked away.

Cas realized with a jolt, "He's lying to me! Clarence? Or maybe just not telling me everything he knows. And that poor lady in the back of the room is scared to death for some reason." He looked into her wide eyes and smiled.

"We have company, Clarence," Cas turned a little more to face the woman as he spoke.

"Come here, Mama," Clarence spoke kindly to her. "Come and meet Cas Larkin. He's the sheriff here."

Clarence held out his arm and the woman reluctantly came and stood beside him, looking warily at Cas.

"How do you do, ma'am. I came by to say how sorry I am about Welemon, and I am going to see if I can find out what happened to him."

"Welemon," she sighed the name. "He at peace now." She seemed calmer but came and held fast to Clarence's arm.

"I won't keep you any longer. Clarence, if you think of anything or hear of anything that might help us find out who did this, give me a call. My home number's in the book. Call any time you need to."

He nodded to the woman. "Glad to have met you, ma'am." Cas turned to go.

Clarence walked him to the door and watched him drive away.

Cas was still worrying at the reason Clarence might have to lie to him when he got back to his office. He glanced inside as Gladys held out a note to him.

"I see the panel is here." Cas commented as he walked around her desk and took the call Gladys handed him.

"Harlan Glover," he said, glancing at the note. "Is Rhodes or Doug around?"

"Doug is outside. He saw the panel and asked about it."

"I'm going to call Harlan now and I may want Doug to take the panel out past the Roadhouse for me. Tell him to wait and talk to me."

He got Harlan and asked, "Got your call. You looking for that rear panel?"

"Yeah," Harlan sounded apologetic. "I know I'm being pushy when you just got back from the hospital with a broken arm and a knot on your head."

Cas chuckled, "Well, Doug's in better shape and he's here. If you want him to, he can meet your man out past the Roadhouse with the panel this afternoon. About five o'clock?"

"That's what I was hoping for."

"Hold on a minute." Cas gave Doug his instructions about the car panel and returned to the phone. "He'll be there at five with the panel. How is the case shaping up?"

Harlan answered gleefully. "So good, the next job they're free to pull, they'll need wheelchairs for their get away or fly away on that stuff they're trying to sell."

"Great. That's good news and two less we have to worry about. I just came back from the hospital. Got a case with a severe head wound and the victim died. Don't know much about it yet, whether it was just high temper and a fight or premeditated murder. And he was a doper."

"That's always bad news, they come in pairs like snakes, you know. Do you know who he was?"

"Yes, he was one of ours. I know the family. They've been here forever like some of our other residents. They're a black family, who knows everybody like the rest of us old folks. Good people. This one got on dope when he was younger and hasn't been around much lately. If we've got some drug pushers trying to move in, I sure want to nip that in the bud. Where were those two in the van and the pick-up going with their weed and cocaine goodies? Any hint?"

"My guess is Atlanta. One of them is wanted there. I haven't got wind of anything to make me think we're having a problem locally, but I'll sure keep my eyes open."

"It was just a thought. In most drug related cases they put a bullet in the back of their heads execution style. This one was hit with something. Happened at his uncle's home. He, the uncle, found him out in his back yard and took him to the hospital. The victim's name is Welemon Lynch. His Uncle Clarence Lynch is the one who found him. He said he didn't hear anything or see anyone running away. He must have got to him as soon as it happened, because Welemon lived to get to the hospital and no one could have lived long after a blow to the head like he got. What worries me is I know Clarence Lynch, have for a long time. Harlan, he's lying to me! I don't have any proof but I know he's lying or holding something back that he knows about this."

"You think he did it?"

"No. I don't. But he's holding out on me, I can tell. He's not a liar and he's not comfortable with it. He gives himself away. Body language, not meeting my eyes when he hedges. I just know."

"The victim was his nephew? This Welemon?"

"Yes. His dead sister's boy. Nearest birthday thirty-six according to his ID. He was big and in better shape than dopers usually are. Probably because he could always go back to his family when he got desperate and hungry."

Cas paused, "He hasn't been around a while. You ever have any trouble with him over there in Marble County?"

"Welemon. Welemon Lynch. Yeah, I did run him in a couple of times. Drunk and disorderly it was. He didn't hurt anyone but himself though, and it was quite a while back. Maybe six or seven years."

"That's about right, his uncle said he's been away awhile and I hadn't seen him either. He didn't have any place of his own to stay evidently, and gave his uncle's address as his. May not ever find out who did this, if it's tied in with his bad habits where he was before he came back here. Unless Clarence decides to tell me whatever it is he's hiding."

"Maybe it'll come out some other way. Things do sometimes when you least expect it."

"We'll see. Keep me posted on the Marble County connection, I'm glad you caught them."

Connie answered the phone in the kitchen and pulled out a chair when she heard Cathy Taylor's voice. She was Missy's boyfriend's mom and a good friend.

"Hi, I was just thinking of calling you."

"I've got news! Our children will be home for Thanksgiving in two weeks. They'll let us know closer to time when they're leaving."

"That's great! I thought they would let us know pretty soon. I'm going to work for Tim Carpenter half a day tomorrow. Then I'll have lunch with Miss Mayme and Miss Minnie and go with them to put up Thanksgiving decorations at the library. You can join us if you want to."

"That sounds like fun, but I'm simply not all that artistic. I admire other people's work. What were you going to call me about?"

"Now that I think it over, maybe I wouldn't have. What I was going to tell you about sounds so strange. You may think it's all my imagination."

"Imagination? Strange? Now I've got to know. What are you talking about?"

"You know I told you I was going to look for some information on the Nelsons and how people lived back in those times when they lived in the mansion?"

"Yes, that must have been an awfully romantic time, judging by the clothes and teas and socials they had. Just looking at the beautiful things they wore is enough to make you envy them. I guess some of their customs would seem strange to us. Did you find very much information?"

"I found dry dates and facts. Tim Carpenter and Jo Beth at the library gave me those. Then I found some other things, some old newspapers. I haven't gone through them yet. It's going to take some time to do that. Some of it's not in very good shape from being stored away down there in the library basement."

Connie's voice dropped a bit, "That's what I was going to tell you about."

"About the basement?" Cathy was puzzled.

"Maybe I'd better just start at the beginning."

"That's a good place," Cathy laughed. "I'm sorry," she giggled. "Go on."

"Tim said Nelson donated his property to the city, that's confirmed in the library's reference books. Hannah showed me some pictures too, of the house when the Nelsons lived in it and of the land the courthouse is built on. The pictures are hanging on the library walls but I would never have realized what they were if she hadn't told me."

"Oh? Does it look very different? The house, I mean?"

"Yes, it does. The picture hanging in the library was taken before the porch was closed in and you can tell that a family lives there. And I asked Jo Beth if there were any newspaper articles or anything like that. You know, about events and everyday things about the people back then. She let me go down and look at the things in the basement. It's full of old books and things so out of date no one seems to be interested in them anymore. Hannah turned on the light for me and I got brave and went down to look around."

"What do you mean, you got brave?"

"Just opening the door was bad enough. When it was opened for me, I just instinctively stepped back. It's so cold down there no one could stay for long. I don't think the cleaning people stay long either from the looks of it."

"Cold. Guess that's because it's deep and probably lined with stone too, that's why. Like a root cellar or something, it's such an old house."

"That's what I thought at first, but it's more than that. It's downright bone chilling, Cathy. And after I'd been down there a while I heard someone crying."

"Crying?" Cathy thought that over. "Are you sure it was crying?"

"Yes. It wasn't very loud, sort of muffled. But it was crying, I'm sure of it. It sounded like a young girl, maybe around Missy's age."

"Hmm, that is strange." Cathy was as puzzled by the way Connie sounded as by what she was saying. It seemed to have had a frightening effect on her.

"You really think it was a young girl and the sound could somehow be heard down there? But how, Connie? From where?"

"That's just it, I don't know. Even if it was someone crying. Even if she were in the building, it couldn't, you would think, be heard down there?"

"Well, you said it wasn't very loud and sounded muffled. And then the cold. Bone chilling, you called it."

Cathy gasped, "CONNIE! Could the library, could it be haunted?"

"I couldn't help but think it might be, no matter how unbelievable that sounds. As far as I know, the sounds are not heard anywhere else or Hannah and Jo Beth would have known about it. And there's another thing about it. About the crying, I mean. It's quiet. It took me a little while to notice it. Like, I don't know, like it's just so miserable, that there's no hope for it. Just resigned, heart broken and crying. Listening to it, it's so sad, so full of despair, it makes you want to cry too."

"That's weird. Connie, even if it's not haunted, someone has to be feeling that sadness to be crying like that. Whoever it is needs help or comforting. But, if it's not coming from somewhere else…."

"Yeah. If not? Think about that! How would you go about comforting a ghost?" Connie shivered, her hand cold on the receiver. Her soft heart was caught between compassion and a fear that was real whether the crying ghost was or not.

"Heavens, I have no idea! But the basement seems to have all the symptoms of haunting, don't you think?"

"I don't know. All I know is I feel like Hannah does. She works at the library, she's the one who opened the door for me. I don't want to go back down there and neither does she."

"She heard it too?"

"Yes. I asked her. I'm going to tell Miss Mayme and Miss Minnie about it tomorrow and see what they think."

"Good idea. And call me after you talk to them. Promise?"

"I will."

CHAPTER 5

Connie drew a relieved breath when she heard the truck in the driveway. Cas was home. She met him at the door.

"Hi, were you very uncomfortable driving home?"

"No, the truck handles easy. I got my chance to get used to it today. Had to go to the hospital about a head wound that turned out to be fatal. You remember the Lynch family?"

"Yes, was it one of them? What happened?"

Cas told her about Welemon and the few facts they had to work with.

"When I talked to Clarence I felt like there was something he wasn't telling me. With nothing more than we know about it right now, we may never find out who did it."

Cas sat down at the table to talk as Connie poured him a cup of coffee.

"Our dinner's ready. All I have to do is take it up. I left a call for Missy to tell her about your accident. She should be calling any minute."

"There was no need to worry her," Cas frowned at his coffee cup.

"Cas...." Connie placed a hand on her hip and Cas resigned himself to what he knew was coming.

"You know very well she'd want to know. And since we've waited till now to call we can tell her you're home and going to be fine. So stop worrying about word getting out you're only flesh and blood." She rolled her eyes at his typical male attitude that nothing could hurt him.

Cas was saved thinking up a proper retort by the ringing phone. He was closer to the wall phone than she was. Certain it was Missy, he got up and beat Connie to it.

"We were just getting ready to eat." He grinned down at Connie. "How are things in general and grades in particular?" Missy's answer made him laugh and he handed the phone to her mother.

Cas sipped his coffee as Connie filled Missy in on the accident. She reached toward him after a few minutes, waving the phone. "Here, she wants to talk to you."

With his ear to the phone, Cas cut his eyes at Connie and chuckled like a conspirator. It was obvious from his brief answers and amused expression Missy was turning the tables and he was getting a lot of the good and caring advice he usually gave her. Finally he said, "I love you, too. Want to say goodbye to your mom?"

Connie didn't miss a beat, having a great respect for long distance and the charges for it.

"I talked to Cathy Taylor, she called me when Casey called her about Thanksgiving. We're glad the holiday is so close. Are you sure Casey's car is running all right?" Connie laughed, "I'll tell Dad. And do be careful like he said. See you soon."

"What was it she wanted to tell me?"

"She said Casey's car is beautiful on the inside. And this trip they will have good insurance," her eyes danced.

"Insurance?"

"Two of the football team will be with them most of the way so there will be plenty of push power if it comes to that."

Cas chuckled, picturing that turn of events. "Casey's car is a little beat on the outside but he does keep it up. He's a good kid. I don't worry about her as much when she's with him."

Picking up the boots he had pushed off his feet under the table, Cas kissed Connie's cheek. "I'm going to find my slippers and wash the hand that still works. Be right back."

"How like him to refer to his good right hand as the one that still works," Connie muttered to herself. "Anyone else would have taken at least a week off!"

Everything was ready when Cas came back and took his seat opposite Connie.

"Looks good, what is it?"

"It's one of those quickie casseroles. They're not much trouble and they're good. Easy to eat, too. And you won't have to cut any of your salad. Even the tomatoes are cut up bite sized. Aren't you lucky?"

"Sure am. I knew that before I got the bite sized tomatoes." He knew how to make points, but instead of an affectionate peck on the cheek he got a puzzling question.

"Cas?" Connie said thoughtfully, "Do you believe in ghosts?"

"Ghosts? You mean like spirits and 'haints' and things that go bump in the night? What brought that on?"

"No fudging. Do you?" Connie was insistent, her eyes serious.

"I don't know. I haven't given it much thought. I certainly never met one and don't know of anyone who has." He took an exaggerated look around the small, cozy kitchen. "Are we not—alone?" He raised his eyebrows.

"Oh, cut it out. I'm serious."

"I'm sticking to my original answer. I don't know. What got you interested in ghosts?" He poured more dressing on his salad.

"Well, I know all the usual things you hear about them. The unnatural coldness in a place that's haunted and spirits that are not at rest for some reason. And what got me thinking about it, is there seems to be something like that at the library. In the basement."

Cas laughed, pure unbridled merriment. "The library basement? You mean it's cold down there?" He scoffed. "What a surprise!"

"Well, it is. It's a clammy cold. It's freezing you to the bone cold."

"Connie, It's cold down there because it's a musty old basement. Why would you think it was anything more than that?"

"Because it's not just cold. It's so cold it makes your teeth chatter, like I said. And—and that's not all."

"And what? Don't tell me you actually saw one?" Cas raised his eyebrows.

"No, I didn't actually see one," Connie readily admitted. "But I may have heard one."

"Heard one?" Cas thought that over. "What did it say?" He raised an eyebrow looking even more suspicious.

"It didn't say anything, Cas. It was crying."

"Crying?" Utter disbelief took charge of his face.

"Yes," Connie insisted, her eyes meeting his. "It's not very loud but you can hear someone crying down there."

Cas had stopped eating and was looking concerned now. Someone crying sounded like someone in trouble, and Connie was serious.

"You're sure it was crying?"

"Yes. I know it was crying. I heard it, and it's not just me. I was looking at some things down there, mostly old newspapers. And Hannah had told me to call her and she would help me bring up the things I wanted to read. And when she came down she heard it too. She looked like she was going to faint when she got back to where I was waiting for her. We picked up the boxes and got out of there as fast as we could. I asked her if she heard the crying, and she did. Cas, she heard too."

"She did. Well," he shrugged. "I'm sure the cold was a natural thing. That basement's probably not opened very often. And the crying, you said it wasn't very loud. Either it was some trick of the acoustics down there or it was some other sound that was so dim it sounded like crying."

Cas picked up his fork. "I wouldn't worry about it. You got the things you wanted to read, didn't you?"

Connie nodded, still not looking convinced. "Jo Beth told me I could leave all the material I brought up in the back reading room until I'd finished with it."

"Good. Don't let it worry you. A house that old, there's no telling how thick those old stone walls are."

"I'm going to have plenty besides unhappy spirits to keep me occupied anyway, it looks like." Connie added. "I'm going to work for Tim half a day tomorrow then go help Miss Mayme and Miss Minnie with the library's Thanksgiving decorations."

Cas listened to her plans, relieved to have the subject changed.

"Their business has really been good. In between other things, they're planning the Christmas decorations for the library too. Now, that will really be a fun and fabulous thing. And good advertisement for the flower shop, too."

"I'll bet that was Miss Minnie's doing. She would get things planned so they could stock the things they will need and get started in plenty of time. They're lucky to be an artist and an organizer."

"They're really two opposites all right. I guess it takes that to take care of all that's needed in a business. I'm sure the Thanksgiving things will be nice, but what I'm really looking forward to are the Christmas decorations." Connie's eyes sparkled as she pictured some of the things Miss Mayme had told her about.

Cas smiled at her enthusiasm. "I'll make it a point to go by and look at the Thanksgiving decorations."

He kept to himself another reason for going by the library as he poured himself another cup of coffee and headed for the den.

Connie's thoughts were on all the things coming up in the next few days as she watched him go. There wasn't going to be much time to worry about ghosts. The real world and its demands would see to that.

* * *

The next day Cas got a call from Harlan Glover. He was out and Gladys stopped him with the call when he got in.

"Harlan Glover said he was on his way out too so you don't need to call him. But he said you could probably pick up the rear panel off your car Monday."

"Okay, thanks. Anything else?"

"No, no calls to return and everyone that's called in is having a regular old routine, boring day," Gladys reported.

"Sounds good to me. Wish we could bottle all this peace and quiet and save some for when the moon is full."

"When you figure out how to do that you know Harlan Glover is going to want the formula," Gladys chuckled.

Cas put his good hand on his hip in mock indignation. "Just when did you start representing Marble County?"

The ringing phone interrupted Gladys's laughter. "Guess we spoke too soon." She sympathized, her hand shielding the phone. "It's Clint at the coroner's office."

"I knew it was too good to last." Cas shook his head and turned toward his office, "Put him through in here."

"Cas?"

"Yes, what can I do for you? And have you found anything else on Welemon Lynch?"

"No. And I don't think we will, to tell the truth. Looks like the next one in is going to have to take a number."

Cas's heart sank at what that implied. He sat down in his chair.

"We've got another body. This one was fished out of the river. Couple of old codgers had been fishing in the river and called us. Spotted a floater and didn't know who else to call."

"Oh, an unlucky fisherman washed up from somewhere?" Cas felt guilty and hoped he didn't sound too relieved. Poor man was dead after all.

"That's what we figured too at first."

Cas gripped the phone harder.

"We don't know what the rest of his story is yet. But we brushed the hair back off his face when we got him in here and he's got a bullet hole between his eyes." Clint paused a second. "Reckon we should suspect foul play?"

"Oh, rats! I guess so. I'm on my way."

Cas passed Gladys with a clipped, "I'll call you," and hurried out. He only paused to favor his arm as he opened the door.

Outside, he glanced between the buildings across the little park and saw Hannah McLaughlin going to the Smithy for coffee. He crossed the park quickly and caught her as she came out with two cartons to go.

Hannah had seen him coming and stopped to wait for him.

He saw her stop, wondering if she already knew what he was going to ask her. He was in awe of Hannah's psychic abilities and at the same time sympathetic to her as a person who must deal with them and the pain they caused her sometimes. He silently vowed to himself again never to reveal her secret or give her any more problems than she already had.

"Hannah," he started as soon as he got to her. "I need to ask you something. It won't take long." He stopped, fishing for words.

She shifted the cartons a bit, holding the top of the sack. "I guess it's about the basement, isn't it?"

"Yes," Cas was glad to have the ice broken for him. "Connie told me about the cold in the library basement. That it's colder than she thinks would be normal for an old basement whether it's deep and lined with stone or not. And there was the sound of crying?"

He was hoping she'd make light of it, that it was nothing. "She told me you heard it too?"

Hannah's eyes met his with no humor in them at all. Knowing Hannah's almost brutal honesty, he knew without a doubt his optimistic hopes were about to be shot down. His faint smile faded away.

"Someone's buried down there, Cas. I don't know who it is or anything else about it. I was only down there long enough to pick up a box and bring it upstairs."

"Yeah, Connie told me about the old newspapers she found. Had you noticed anything unusual before?"

Hannah shook her head. "I don't go down there, only the cleaning people do."

"I see. It's mostly storage then," Cas mused thoughtfully.

"But Cas, there's not any danger. I didn't feel threatened or anything." Hannah seemed to understand his feelings. "I know you'd want to know, since Connie is looking at all that material about the Nelsons. I don't feel any sort of danger there."

"That's what I wanted to hear. And I knew you'd know since she said you were down there too. But, are you sure there's someone buried there?"

"Yes. That's all I am sure of. But yes, there's someone buried there. One and maybe more."

"And maybe more," it came out as a groan. "But there doesn't seem to be any danger?" Cas pressed. "Any sort of danger at all from anything down there?"

"No. No danger. Just a terrible, deep sadness."

"There are probably some old records on it somewhere but I haven't got time to hunt for them or go into it. And I don't want to get something started I can't finish. As long as you don't feel any threat or danger I'll cross it off my worry list for now. Thanks, Hannah."

Hannah watched as Cas hurried back across the tiny park to get on with his business, then walked on.

He dismissed the library basement from his mind. A fleeting memory of pictures of castle crypts and old cathedrals going with it.

"Back to the real world. I wonder who this man is with the bullet between his eyes. This and Welemon makes two murders I've got on my hands. We'd had such a spell of no excitement, with no troubles at all. Darned if they aren't coming in bunches like bananas the way the cattle rustling did last year."

Cas was grateful the truck was so easy to handle as he cleared the lot and headed for the coroner's office.

Clint was waiting for him. "Come on in," he motioned to him. "I'll introduce you to our latest customer."

"Yeah, do. I drove fast, afraid you'd get another one."

"Gripe, gripe, gripe," Clint grinned.

As Clint unveiled the new problem Cas made an inarticulate sound with mental apologies to the latest customer, whoever he turned out to be.

The man looked smaller than the problem he presented as Cas looked at the thin mound he made under the sheet. The sheet was removed to reveal the body of a small, wiry, white man around middle age.

"Who did you say found him? Some fishermen?"

"That's right. A couple of senior citizens spotted him and called us. They were pretty upset. I told them to go talk to you or call in case you wanted to get a statement from them, so they'll be in to see you shortly. One of them had to go by home for some medication he takes. I have their names and phone numbers for you."

"Okay, thanks."

Cas watched Clint fold the covering neatly at the man's feet. "Looks to be about thirty-eight or forty, wouldn't you say?"

Clint nodded. "We haven't done much except get him ready to work on, but that sounds about right to me. And it was probably a rough thirty-eight or forty years. He had nail clippers, but his nails aren't clean and his skin?" Clint shook his head. "He may have been homeless with not much chance to take care of himself. I noticed some insect bites so he may have been sleeping out. The cause of death was certainly easy."

He pointed to the bullet hole. "Unless we find out some sadist poisoned him, drowned him, then shot him," Clint grinned.

"Don't wish that on me." Cas cringed. He eyed the bullet hole, "Little one. Probably a twenty-two."

"Little, but very effectively placed. No burn marks, either. Someone took careful aim and shot him."

"You have the bullet?"

For answer, Clint held up a slug in a plastic sack and dropped it back in a drawer. "I'll show you his things."

Clint went to another room and came back with a box which he set on the desk. Cas came to examine the contents.

"He didn't have a wallet on him or any sort of identification. This is what he had on." Clint gestured at the articles of clothing.

The box contents were sparse. "Worn slacks, cotton sports shirt, jockey shorts. None of it looks too bad to have been sleeping out. But then, it's been in the water," Cas observed. He looked up, "No socks?"

"No. No socks. I don't know what the story is on that. Just these worn down loafers. Pocket contents here." He gave Cas a small plastic sack.

The sack held a five dollar bill, a one, some small change, an orange marble, a cashier's receipt from a convenience store, the nail clippers, and a smaller plastic sack.

"Is this what it looks like?"

"Yeah. It's cocaine. Not much, but he was a user."

Cas went back to the body and lifted the sheet again.

"I know what you're looking for. There are a few needle marks, but not as many as I've seen on most long time users."

"Not a laborer evidently." Cas bent and examined the hand nearest him without touching it. He straightened up glancing at the rest of the body again.

"Probably was homeless as you guessed. That looks like about a two day growth of beard. From the looks of everything else and the two bills in his pockets, the identification may have been taken to keep us from knowing who he is or connecting him with anyone else."

Clint nodded, studying the corpse. "If it was some of his friends they would have taken the bills and the cocaine too. You're probably right, someone doesn't want him identified for some reason."

"I keep wondering if there's some connection between this and Welemon Lynch's death. But so far I don't see anything to link them except the dope." Cas took the other side of the sheet and helped cover the body again. "Let me know when you have an approximate time of death or anything else that might be interesting. If nothing else, the prints will tell us who he was."

"It may take a while to get a match on the prints. We don't know there's a connection here in Maryvale, with nothing but the cocaine to go on. It may be he and whoever killed him were just passing through."

"Yeah. His buddy did this to him then went on. I should get so lucky." Cas was not happy. "We've got us a regular crime wave here."

"Looks like. Two's a lot for a town this size. I may have to move back to the city to hide."

That remark and Clint's comical expression were enough to lift Cas's spirits again. "Yeah, you're going to move to the city about as fast as I am," Cas laughed as he opened the door. "Thanks for the preview, call if you find anything else."

On the way back to the office Cas toyed with the idea of a link between the two recent deaths. He put Welemon's identity aside and thought only of the two bodies. One black, thirty-six, and a user. The other white, thirty-eight or forty, also a user. The only tie-in so far was dope. One was attacked in his own, or his uncle's back yard. The other had been shot and was fished out of the river. There was no similarity at all in the causes of death.

He parked the truck and walked toward the office, no closer to any constructive ideas than he had been when Clint called him.

"The one thing I'm sure of is Clarence knows something he's keeping to himself. I'd bet on it."

He chased around his brain every reason he could think of for Clarence hiding whatever it was he knew and dismissed them all. He finally decided it might be some sort of family thing. Clarence was loyal to his family. "But he's honest, I'd bet on that too."

Preoccupied, when he got back he went straight into his office.

Gladys called after him, "Did it? Was it ah?" She asked timidly, seeing how lost in thought he was.

"Oh." Her words finally penetrated and Cas stopped before he sat down. "It was a stranger, Gladys."

He turned to bring her up to date. "Probably just passing through here. The body was a white man, small build, no identification on him. He was pulled out of the river. Been shot once in the head. His body will be autopsied and his prints sent in to be matched. They'll find out who he is."

"Yes, sir." Gladys nodded and went back to her work glad and a little ashamed of being glad, that the victim was a stranger to Maryvale.

Cas had barely had time to sit down when the outer door opened to admit two men between sixty and seventy. They wore faded jeans and caps with fishing lures pinned to them.

"Must be my senior citizen witnesses here to give statements." Cas got up and went to meet them.

CHAPTER 6

Connie's mind was still full of questions when she went to work for Tim Carpenter and she felt no hesitation about voicing them.

"Haunted?" A smile played around Tim's lips, waiting for the punch line. It took a couple of seconds for it to dawn on him, "You're serious! You think it's haunted."

"Hold on there, counselor. I only said it had the classic symptoms. But if it is, if there really is a spirit there, who do you suppose it could be?"

Tim laughed at the idea. "Can't imagine. Unless it would be Edgar T. Nelson. He was a suicide you remember, or was supposed to have been."

"Oh, I didn't tell you. I found confirmation of that, Tim. That it was a suicide, I mean. In one of the old newspapers. The headline said Edgar T. Nelson dies by his own hand, so he was a suicide all right."

"Well, that makes it official then."

"But it's not him," Connie shook her head. "If it's a spirit, it can't be him. The crying, soft as it is, you can hear it well after you've been down there a little while. And it's a young woman's voice, not a man's."

"That is a mystery then." Tim's brow wrinkled slightly, recalling what facts he had found.

"No one lived in the house after Nelson died. It went directly to the city. There were no other tenants who lived there."

"No one else ever lived there? Maybe there was and there is just no record of it. Maybe when I've read all that material I brought up from the basement I'll find some reference that will give us a clue."

Connie put the idea aside and concentrated on getting all the typing done Tim needed. When she was ready to leave, she was still puzzling over what little she had found.

"It may be Cas is right. He says it could be the old house's tricky acoustics that makes something else sound like crying."

Connie watched as Tim made out her check.

"I found the facts and dates you told me about at the library, and Jo Beth was really nice about letting me bring some newspapers and things up to the back reading room. I'm going to go through them as I have time for it."

"Found anything interesting yet?"

Connie shook her head. "The basement itself is the most interesting thing I've found so far."

"The basement?" Tim turned to look at her, making sure he heard right. "You're really serious about this cold and crying business then? But after all these years, why hasn't someone else discovered it?"

"No one ever goes down there but the cleaning crew and they don't go very often. And I can sure see why they don't."

Tim blotted his signature and thought about reasons. "Maybe it's all just old things no one is interested in or it's not worth spending much time on. Or it could be because it's hard to find anything?" He liked things neat and well organized.

"Worse than that! It's not only that it's cold as ice. You should hear the crying. It's like it doesn't want to be heard, it's so soft. It's not trying to get anyone's attention, it's just miserable. You feel sad and depressed just listening to it." Connie shook her head. "The place has got all the classic symptoms of being haunted. But Cas, my hard headed Cas, you know how hard he is to convince. He thinks it's not really crying, that it's something else."

"That's the one that gets my vote." Tim quickly agreed. "He's probably right," Tim dismissed the crying ghost. "Well, have a good time decorating and tell Miss Mayme and Miss Minnie hello for me."

Cas straightened his back without getting up to stretch. He glanced down at the Welemon Lynch file and laid it aside, frowning at it as he got out a new folder.

In the new file he put the two statements of the elderly men who had found the second body in the river. He held the picture of the victim Clint had given him in his hand wishing it could answer a few questions for him. It showed the unknown gunshot victim's head and shoulders. Nothing spoke to him but the neat round bullet hole in the forehead just above the closed eyes.

He laid the picture inside the scanty file and put in his notes about Clint's comments, the contents of the pitiful little box of belongings including the plastic sack of cocaine too. It didn't take long to get the new file organized. He wished it had more to offer than neatness as he put it away.

The gut feeling there was a connection between the two murders refused to go away and wouldn't let him rest.

Dope is the only tangible thing I've got. Welemon wasn't around much in the past several years and this white man is a stranger, I've never seen him before. He couldn't have been here long or I would have seen him around somewhere. My hunch is they got here about the same time or together, and they're both on drugs. Dope, time of arrival, and God knows, they're both dead. He took the picture back out and put it in his pocket before he left the office.

He drove directly to Clarence Lynch's house. And pulled up in front. He got out and slowly closed the door of the truck. He moved just as slowly and deliberately toward the house, sensing the eyes of the neighbors on him.

"Clarence is probably watching, too. A stranger would be spotted immediately any time, and all of them have surely heard all there is to hear about Welemon by now."

Clarence peered out the small pane of glass set in the door. He opened the door as soon as Cas got to the porch.

"Come in. I saw you drive up."

"I won't keep you but a minute, Clarence. I have a picture I want you to see." Cas stepped inside and handed the picture to Clarence.

Clarence frowned and squinted at it, holding it out far enough to focus on it without his glasses.

"Have you ever seen him before? Did he maybe come by here with Welemon, or have you seen him anywhere else?"

"All I know about him from this picture is he been shot."

Clarence handed the picture back and didn't volunteer anything further in the way of fact or speculation.

Cas was not satisfied with Clarence's answer. He thought, "He didn't say he hasn't seen him, only that's all he could tell from the picture. I'm afraid I'm in for a lot of game-playing here."

"He been killed here too?" Clarence asked, giving the impression he wasn't interested and didn't really want to hear about it.

"Yes, he was. Found him in the river. It was two fishermen who found him, saw him in the water and called to report they'd seen a body. Floaters is what they call them at the coroner's office. That's where I got the call from. Must have given those two senior citizens a shock."

Clarence bowed his head slightly as if he was sorry about the two old men who had found the body. He was careful not to look at Cas but didn't comment.

"No identification was found on him. So of course, the state will have to identify him. Do you remember seeing him with Welemon? Or anywhere else?"

Clarence shook his head, still not meeting Cas's eyes.

Clarence's mother's white head appeared at the door at the back of the room.

"Do you mind if I show the picture to your mother? Maybe she might have seen him somewhere."

"NO! No, don't show that to her." Clarence held out his hand to prevent Cas from walking back to her. "She'd be upset to see that, with the way it's, the forehead." Clarence stammered.

"Oh, of course. I won't, Clarence." Cas soothed him. "I just thought she might recognize him. I don't want to upset her." Cas put the picture back in his pocket, sure now that if Clarence didn't know who the white man was, he had at least seen him and perhaps his mother had too.

Not knowing what Clarence was hiding, Cas puzzled in vain about how to get at what it was he knew. With a glance at the elderly woman, he tried another tack.

"Clarence, let's go outside and you show me again where it was you found Welemon."

"All right."

Outside, Clarence was glad to escape and led him around the house. He pointed across the back yard. "There by the storage shed. That's where he was."

The small storage shed near the back fence was big enough to hold quite a bit of lawn equipment. Cas noticed the double doors were closed.

He walked to the place where Clarence pointed, his boots getting caked with wet mud and clay as he went.

"And when you found him, you didn't see anyone with Welemon? Or anyone leaving?"

"No. Just seen Welemon lying there. And he was bad hurt, bad hurt…."

Clarence's kindly features were sad as he looked at the scene where he found Welemon. Perhaps he was also remembering the wasted life that ended at thirty-six.

Cas gave his shoulder a sympathetic pat and didn't ask anything else. They walked together in silence to the front of the house.

"Let me know if you hear anything you think might help us, Clarence," Cas told him as he turned to leave.

"I will."

Cas was careful of the clay on his boots as he drove away, headed for the coroner's office.

When he got there Clint was busy and he used the waiting time to carefully remove his boots.

Clint came in, his usual jovial self. "Having foot problems? I thought it was just the city police pounding the concrete who have those problems."

"The feet are not the problem, Good Buddy. It's the clay."

Clint looked skeptical, waiting for an explanation.

"This clay came from the place the first victim was killed. Clarence Lynch's back yard. Is there any chance maybe, that there would be any soil samples left on those beat up, water soaked loafers the gunshot victim had on? I'm still trying to connect the two killings."

"Hmm, hang loose a second." Clint disappeared briefly and returned with a sample bag. He carefully filled it with the clay from Cas's boots.

"I doubt we can find enough to be sure. I don't want to get your hopes up, but we'll give it a try. You know it's going to be a while anyway, on the identification?"

"I know. I don't expect miracles. I'm just working any angle that crops up and might conceivably help."

"You're pretty sure these two deaths are the same case, aren't you?"

"Yes. A stranger and someone who hasn't been around a while, both on dope. It's too much of a coincidence not to be connected."

"All right. May not get anywhere, but I'll do my best to get enough to tell if those loafers have been in that yard."

"Thanks. Get me a dust pan and I'll clean up the mess I've made."

Connie admired the pretty things surrounding her in Anderson's flower shop as she went in. "Hi, girls, have you eaten lunch yet?"

"We waited for you," Miss Minnie called from her office. "You got here just in time. Mayme hasn't bitten anybody yet."

Miss Mayme stuck her head out from behind a big spray she was working on.

"The mere mention of food is making my stomach growl. Let's go to the Smithy. It's filling and fast as it says on their window. Minnie's right. I'm ready to eat!"

"Grab the sign then, you're wasting time!" Miss Minnie made a show of slamming her ledger shut, grinning at Connie.

It was only a short walk to the Smithy. Connie left her car in front of the flower shop.

"Isn't Missy coming home for Thanksgiving pretty soon?"

"That's right. She'll only have the long four day weekend, but all of us are really looking forward to it. She'll be here Thursday, I mean a week from Thursday."

"She and Casey Taylor still dating?"

"Yes, they are and we're both glad of it. I like his mother, Cathy, and Cas likes Casey. You remember he met him when he was investigating the Davis case. At least something good came out of all that. Cas and Casey meeting and Judge Spruce retiring."

Miss Minnie nodded. "Have you had time to read many of the old newspapers and things you found about the Nelson family?"

"No, I've hardly scratched the surface. There's a lot, and I want to read it all." She looked away as they got seated.

"What is it you aren't telling us?" Miss Minnie set her tea glass down. "There is something, isn't there?"

Connie started on her stew but decided not to tell them about the basement. She hesitated, thinking it sounded too far out.

"Okay," Miss Mayme broke into her thoughts. "Fess up!"

"You two taught school too long. And I don't know, you might decide to put me in the asylum if I tell you." A giggle trembled on her lips.

"Well, now if you don't tell us we'll wind up there ourselves from curiosity," Miss Mayme pointed out the dilemma.

"I'll tell you only if you're careful about saying anything about it to anyone else. People would think I've lost my mind for sure."

"Oh, I doubt it could be as bad as that." Miss Mayme began to look worried in spite of her reassuring words.

"We promise not to get you committed to the asylum." Miss Minnie tried to keep a straight face. "Now, what is it?"

"It's what happened when I went down in the library basement to look for the old newspaper articles about the Nelsons. I wanted to know something about the family's personal lives. You know, some of the social events, things that tell you how they lived and the things that were important to them. The bare facts and dates, like when the land was donated and all that, those things are in the reference books upstairs. But the old news issues are about the balls and the crops and the people's lives, and they are down in the basement. One piece was about a boy who came back from the war between the states missing an arm."

Connie's excitement rose, "He had a brother who was killed fighting in the Union army. And there's some old pictures, too. I was getting to some interesting things when I had to leave. There was an article about a party or ball of some kind."

"Sounds fairly sane so far," Miss Minnie gently brought her back from the tangent paths.

"Oh, yes. Well, all this stuff, as I said, was in the basement. They told me it was cold down there but I wasn't prepared for such bitter cold. And after I'd been there sorting through things a little while, I realized someone was crying."

"Crying?" Miss Minnie and Miss Mayme exchanged a look, both raising a puzzled brow.

"Are you sure?"

"Yes. Crying. I was so cold by then my teeth were chattering, and there was this crying. It was so sad it made ME sad. I felt like crying, too!"

"Is the basement stone?" Miss Minnie asked.

"Yes, all the walls except the very back where it's concrete."

"And, are you sure it was crying you heard?" Miss Mayme pinned her down on the facts.

Before Connie could answer her, Miss Minnie put in the suggestion that the basement being so far below ground and having stone walls would make it a very cold place. "And it would be damp too, that would make it seem even colder."

She looked at her sister. "Remember when we were little and went to Great Aunt Pearline's house? They told us not to, but we played in the root cellar and the spring house?"

"And we got spanked for our trouble, too. I think the scolding we got stunted my growth," Miss Mayme rolled her eyes. "But, come to think of it, it was awfully cold down there." She turned to Connie, "It would have to have been awfully cold, for me to remember it."

"So the cold is explained," Miss Minnie stuck to the facts. "The root cellar wasn't nearly as big as that basement must be, and it didn't have the stone walls either. Now tell us a little more about the crying."

"As I said, in spite of the cold, I'd been down there for quite a while and I was so excited about finding the things about early Maryvale I didn't realize I was just about to freeze."

She warmed one hand with the other, as if remembering the numbing cold. "Then I lucked up on some really old newspapers. Some of them are so fragile I, or someone, will have to mount or restore them later. Anyway, by that time, I'd got so cold my teeth were chattering like castanets and I realized the crying I was hearing had been going on all the time. It just hadn't cut through the excitement of finding all that information. I'd been so wrapped up in my reading, it just hadn't registered."

"You said it wasn't very loud," Miss Minnie said slowly. "Maybe it was some other kind of sound. Something that after going through those stone walls, might have only sounded like crying?"

"No," Connie said firmly. "I know crying when I hear it. It was crying."

"Did it sound like an older person, or someone younger? Maybe a child?"

"It sounded like a young woman. Maybe as young as Missy or about her age. And it was so terribly sad. That's the thing I remember most, it was just heartbreaking. I can't describe it, but I felt like crying too."

"That does sound strange all right. I don't know, it must have come from somewhere else even if we don't understand how."

Miss Minnie picked up her disposable bowl to throw away and smiled affectionately at Connie. "So, our conclusion has to be, the cold is a root cellar condition, and the crying is coming from somewhere else. And we won't have to have you committed."

"You're all heart, Minnie," Miss Mayme slapped her sister on the back as they got up to follow her.

"Minnie's a skeptic," she whispered to Connie as they left "From what you told us, I'm sure glad we're not decorating that basement!"

CHAPTER 7

"Harlan? About your message about the panel." Cas leaned back in his chair, getting comfortable.

"Well, forget it." Harlan's voice was flat and final, tinged with disgust.

"Are you sending my panel to jail too? You're a hard man, Sheriff Glover." Cas regarded teasing his friend a perk that went with his job.

"Yeah, I come by that naturally anyway. And being held up doesn't soften me up any. The court's dragging its feet, as usual. It may take longer than I thought to get them to move."

"That's no problem. I don't drive any more than I have to anyway right now since it makes Connie nervous. I'm also waiting on an identification from the state."

"What do you mean an identification? Don't tell me you've got another one? November just hasn't been your month, has it?" He paused, "On the other hand, look at the no-goodniks I've had and still got." Harlan paused to reflect on some of them.

"Yeah, there doesn't seem to be any shortage. But don't worry about that panel. Why don't you, when you don't need it any more, stick it in your office. Then I can come by and pick it up whenever I get a chance."

"Sounds good to me. I was trying to get it back as soon as I could is all. I'll do that. Now, what is this about an identification from the state? And has it got anything to do with the other one you got?"

"That was one of my first thoughts, but I don't know. Not yet anyway. This one is a male caucasian. Looked to be at least thirty-eight or forty, small and wiry build. Effects were the clothes he had on, no wallet, no socks. But he had a very small amount of money in his pocket and a little plastic sack, two of them, in fact, containing cocaine."

"What was the cause of death or do you know yet?"

"They fished him out of the river but the cause of death appears to be a small caliber bullet between the eyes."

"That would do it, all right. Neat and efficient."

"Yes, it did the job. I don't think it was any of his drug connections, though. They usually shoot them in the back of the head execution style and don't bother to throw them in the river. They want to make examples of them."

"Another thing, you said it was a small caliber bullet. They can afford cannons and automatics." Harlan added wistfully, "Wouldn't you think you'd died and gone to Heaven if the law had their budgets to work with?"

"It's never going to happen, Harlan. You know the old saying. It rains on the just and the unjust, but mostly on the just because the unjust have stolen their umbrellas."

"Cas, go on back to work and call me when you hear a better one than that." Harlan mumbled, "Talk to you later." He hung up.

Cas grinned at the phone, "Guess he's going to hunt a cup of coffee and rejoin the human race."

At home, Connie sat with the phone to her ear. "Cathy, this is the first chance I've had to call you."

"I've seen your car at Dick Randolph's office and I knew you'd been working for Tim Carpenter too. Did you tell Miss Mayme and Miss Minnie about the cold in the basement?"

"Yes, I did. They're equally divided, and exactly the way you'd expect."

"Don't tell me. Miss Mayme thinks maybe there's a ghost and Miss Minnie says no way. She doesn't believe in ghosts, she insists there's got to be some logical explanation."

"Right the first time. I guess that's why one of them taught art and the other is the mathematical genius. They're such opposites and such dears at the same time. I love them both."

"I know. Everyone who went to school with them loves them. Even Miss Minnie's math students who will never be able to do anything mathematically but multiply." Cathy and Connie laughed together.

"The logical explanation, Miss Minnie feels, is the basement is big and lined with stone and concrete…is why it's so cold. Like a root cellar or something. And the crying, if it is crying, must be coming somehow from somewhere else. I might think that too if I hadn't been down there shivering and hearing for myself how sad it was."

"Did you find much in the newspapers you brought upstairs?"

"Not yet. With the work I have and Missy coming in Thursday, I won't get to do much reading until after the holiday is over. That reminds me, why don't you and Casey come to dinner Thursday night?"

"Only if you let me bring something."

"Well, okay. I've got a turkey and dressing and I've ordered the sesame seed rolls Cas likes."

"I'll bring a vegetable, dessert, and a salad. How's that?"

"Oh, that's too much. I was going to skip salad anyway and just have cranberry sauce with the gravy and dressing."

"Oh, all right. Do you both like green bean casserole with cream of mushroom soup and all that?"

"Yes, it's one of our favorites. And don't go to much trouble about dessert. If it's sweet, we'll eat it. All three of us are sweet freaks. Anything will be fine."

The holiday was what all Thanksgivings should be, even the weather cooperated. The variety of fall leaves in the yard was beautiful and Missy brought in masses of them to decorate the mantel.

"These colors are gorgeous!"

Missy's face reflected the excitement of the season. Her ruddy cheeks and windblown hair above the masses of bright leaves were the hues the old masters used in their paintings.

"I'm glad you invited Casey and his mother," Missy said as she stepped back to examine her arrangement critically. Satisfied with it, she gave her mother an impulsive hug.

"It's no trouble to have them. We'll enjoy being together. It's nice to have a holiday, isn't it?"

"Um-hum, I like Thanksgiving. Fall is my favorite of all the seasons. The trees are so pretty and the weather is still nice. And there are nights cool enough to have a fire in the fireplace." Missy drifted upstairs with some of the red and gold branches in her arms.

Connie sighed happily, feeling the only thing wrong with this holiday was it just wasn't long enough.

"But, Christmas is coming!" She resolutely hummed a carol as she worked, determined not to think of the time when Missy wouldn't be there, but decorating a mantel of her own.

The cooperative Thanksgiving dinner went as well, or maybe better, than some occasions which had a lot more elaborate plans and menus involved. Connie knew love was the secret ingredient, looking fondly at her family around the table.

"Can't remember when I've enjoyed Thanksgiving more." Cas told Connie after everyone had gone.

Casey and Missy had taken Cathy home and had the rest of the evening to themselves. Connie took a dessert tray into the den before the news came on.

"Ah, coffee and pumpkin pie." Cas laid his paper aside. "My cup runneth over."

"I'm going to enjoy it too, but I'll have to do some fasting next week. That old saying about nothing having any calories during Thanksgiving and Christmas doesn't hold true after the thirties," Connie grimaced. "But I'm still glad I can be at home and enjoy all these temptations instead of wondering what the roads are like between here and Fort Craig."

"I'll drink to that," Cas raised his cup.

"Your quitting that job in Fort Craig has worked out well for all of us. You're going to be home while Missy is here for Christmas too, aren't you?"

"A lot of the time, yes. And that reminds me, I've got to start asking people to get their bids in for that time so I can manage to get all they want done finished and not hurt anyone's feelings. I think I've already mentioned it to Tim Carpenter but I'll remind him. Also, I'm to call Lisa Randolph the Monday Missy goes back to school. I'll tell her then. I think Christmas week is enough to take off completely. You and Missy will both be busy doing other things before that."

Cas sipped his coffee, thinking he'd got himself a large helping of crime for Christmas with the two murders on his hands. Aloud he agreed with her.

"You're right. You wouldn't want them to get used to managing without you now that you've built up a pretty fair amount of work."

"Heavens, no! Remember when I first quit my job? I was so worried about not getting anything to do? Christmas week will be enough to take off. There probably won't be all that much to do anyway. It's the first of the year when things will really pick up."

She began counting potential work off on her fingers. "Miss Minnie mentioned they want me to work half a day for them, but they haven't decided when yet. Since it will be typing envelopes to send bills it will probably be a couple of days after Christmas." She stopped, thinking about the flower shop.

"I wouldn't want them to know it but I worried about them when they first opened. I'm glad their business is good, or seems to be."

"I thought they would make it all right, but the volume of business has been surprising even to me. And their displays look good, the things they put in the windows. I don't know that much about it. But the colors and the arrangements really make the most of what's in season."

He smiled, "Not to mention, they both taught school for so long I'm sure they know everybody for miles around."

"Their shop is an asset to the community," Connie pictured it. "One of the most attractive places on the square, the way they have the front fixed. With all those big urns, or pots, or whatever they are on either side of the front door. It looks like a professional job by someone who knows what he's doing. I mean, what she's doing. All around the square everything looks pretty. There's the Nelson mansion and the little park and the shops and the flower shop. Those urns really set it off."

"I've noticed them. Isn't that holly they have in them?"

"Those are an example of Miss Mayme's artistic knack. They put holly bushes out there, then they got so busy they decided to put artificial ones out there that wouldn't have to be cared for or trimmed. She designed and made the artificial hollies in the topiary shapes and decorated the pots with the wide red ribbons for Christmas."

"You know they have to be eye catching for me to notice them. Next time you see her, tell her I admire her efforts."

"You haven't seen the decorations they put in the library have you?"

"No, haven't been over there lately. But I remember you said they were putting some of their things in there to show people who come in. That was a good advertising idea."

"They're still there. If you'd come and get me for lunch you could go in and see the library all prettied up and we could eat at the Smithy. Do you think you might have time?" Connie asked hopefully.

Cas grinned, "I'll make time. I don't get a chance to enjoy poor health very often. I doubt it will hurt my conscience to go to lunch with my wife. Is Missy going to be using the car?"

Connie nodded. "She asked me if she and some of her friends could use it to go shopping. She'll be back in time for dinner."

"Christmas shopping with a lot of looking and socializing mixed in, no doubt. Okay, we'll do that tomorrow. I'll get things all squared away and call when I get ready to leave."

"Good! I'm glad you're going to see the decorations. I think you're really going to be impressed."

"You wouldn't be planning on dragging me down into that cold basement, would you?" Cas looked sideways at her.

"Really! You are so suspicious!" Connie huffed then admitted, "It did cross my mind."

"We'll see. I probably won't have time for anything but a quick look at the decorations and lunch. We'll just play it by ear, shall we?"

"All right," Connie shrugged. "It was just a thought."

Cas noticed the report on the murdered man did not come as he glanced through the office mail. He was not surprised, not really expecting it until the first of the year. Clint had his hands full and the identification was in line. That was all they could do at this point.

Not seeing anything else that was pressing or that interested him he left the mail lying on Gladys's desk.

His office door was open and Cas looked up when he heard Rhodes come in. He was carrying some packages. Cas knew what they were and went to meet him.

"I was hoping you'd be lucky. I'm glad to see you were!"

"All of us that went were lucky. I brought you venison sausage and some steaks for you and Connie. This one's the sausage and this one's the steaks," he gestured at each one in turn. "I'll put them in the refrigerator." He turned and went toward the break room.

"Coffee's made and doughnuts are on the table," Cas called after him.

Rhodes came back coffee in one hand, a doughnut in the other. "Is there anything I need to do or you want to tell me before I go out?" He finished the doughnut in one last big bite and washed it down with the rest of the coffee.

"No, just thanks for the venison. That sausage is really good. I could sure could get spoiled to it in a hurry."

"We like the plum jelly Connie sent us too if we're going to talk about getting spoiled," Rhodes smiled. "Don't guess you've heard from the state about the gunshot wound?"

"No, I looked through the mail first thing but it hasn't come. It takes long enough any time and I'm sure they've got people who saved their personal holidays or their vacation days for this time of the year. It'll get here when they get around to it and there's not much we can do about it but wait."

"I guess not. Well, I'll be calling in."

It seemed that petty crime was taking a holiday in the town of Maryvale. There were no phone calls and no emergencies to contend with. Cas decided to look again at the two murder files before calling Connie to go to lunch.

The known facts on Welemon Lynch made a very thin file. Facts being scarce as hen's teeth, information was limited to the report of how and where he was found. Not a thing that suggested a place to start unraveling what led up to the fatal blow to the head. There was a note about the doctor's comments and Clint's, plus his own observation of the condition of the victim.

"Multiple blows to the head. And poor Clarence. Hurt bad, he said. His sister's boy, and only thirty-six years old." A wave of compassion for both Welemon and Clarence washed over Cas.

He shrugged off the feeling and reached for the phone. Clint's number was on the phone base and he dialed it quickly, the few facts he had playing like a background tape between his ears till Clint answered the phone.

"Clint, it's me again," Cas said hurriedly.

"This about Welemon Lynch, the head injury?"

"Yes. It seems to me from that big bloody area and the damage," he winced, picturing the broken piece of bone protruding. "He must have been hit more than once, though the doctor said the first blow probably ended his suffering."

"Yeah, there was a lot of damage. Whoever did it must have hit him two or three times. Some of the slivered bone was sticking out, as you saw. And it was a big area, too big for just one blow. He was hit at least twice, and hard. But he was past worrying about the second one. The first hard blow and it was all over for him."

"I told his uncle that, that he didn't suffer very long. I don't think Welemon was bad or mean. He just got on dope and there wasn't much his family could do with him."

"I remember your saying you knew the family. It's a shame, all right. There's still nothing from the State on the identification of the other one."

"I didn't expect to hear anything yet with the Christmas season coming up and the backlog they've usually got."

"I know someone up there I could ask and get some unofficial information or whatever they've got at this point, if you want me to."

"I'd appreciate that. I'm getting ready to leave now. But I could call you back, say about two o'clock?"

"Fine. Don't get your hopes up but they sometimes have the information a while before they can get around to getting the reports typed up. I'll try."

"Thanks. I'll call you about two."

He broke the connection and dialed Connie at the library. "I'm on my way if you're ready to go."

"I am, come on."

Cas moved the truck to the library's parking lot with the vague idea of stopping by Clarence's house later. He could look at the decorations and they would walk to the Smithy.

Jo Beth greeted him as he came in, touching both his hands. "Now I know the decorations are spectacular if you came to see them. It's good to know I voted for a man with good taste."

Hannah waved from the other side of Jo Beth's desk, her smile taking in Connie, who had joined him.

"After he's admired the Anderson sisters' talents I'm going to take him downstairs with me to make sure I haven't missed anything on the Nelson family or early Maryvale. If it's all right with you?"

"I guess it's all right, if you don't disturb the resident ghosts down there," Jo Beth's eyes twinkled knowingly.

Cas chuckled, "I've heard about the cold and maybe someone crying. But I'm sure not going to give it anything else to cry about," Cas promised with as straight a face as he could manage.

"Well, that's all right then," Jo Beth moved away with the air of a satisfied school principal and folded her hands primly on her desk.

Cas laughed at her and turned to go with Connie. "Hannah," he called with a grin. "I don't guess you want to go, not being sure about the, what was it Jo Beth called them? The resident spirits?"

"No, not me," Hannah answered from where she was replacing books on a shelf. "As cold as it is down there, I'm going to pass on that. But I'll open the door and turn on the light for you."

"Good enough. We've only got a minute anyway. I took time off to take Connie to lunch today."

"Now I'm really glad I voted for you," Jo Beth looked up from a box of library cards.

"Wait a little about the lights, Hannah. We'll look at the decorations first."

Connie showed him all the decorations and arrangements including the ones in the reading rooms, pointing out special ones here and there.

"Miss Mayme made these and brought them over so people could buy them and take them home to decorate with and enjoy at home."

Cas nodded. "She's really found her calling, and there's about any size or kind you'd want." He looked around as he followed her back to the reading rooms.

"Are these the pictures you told me about?"

Connie nodded, "The land the courthouse is on, and the house when the family lived in it."

"You were right, I wouldn't have known what they were either if you hadn't told me."

Hannah had been watching. As they started that way she came to open the basement door and turn on the hanging light.

Cas went ahead and warned Connie to watch her step. "It is cold down here all right."

When they got downstairs and their eyes got a little better accustomed to the dimmer light, Cas looked around at all the outdated books.

"Smells musty, not any fresh air down here," he muffled a sneeze.

"Back here is where I found the newspaper articles and things I brought up to look at." She led the way to the back.

Cas followed, still looking around curiously.

Connie started shivering and Cas held her close to him a minute. "I see what you mean about the cold. You could hang meat in here. We've got our coats on but they aren't much help."

He looked around at the walls.

"Seems to be a penetrating cold. Must be the stone walls and dampness down here. And it couldn't be good for these books and papers. These loose things here, is this what you're talking about?"

Connie didn't answer. She was listening. Cas paused and listened too. She could tell by his eyes he heard the crying. She raised her eyebrows.

"Yes," he admitted. "I hear it." After a few seconds he commented, "Makes you want to do something for it, doesn't it? Sounds like someone about our Missy's age."

"I think so too. It's definitely a young woman, I could tell that the first time I heard it. And if it's coming from somewhere else I sure don't know how." Connie looked up, regarding the dark ceiling and walls around them.

Cas remembered what Hannah had told him and said brusquely, "Well, look around and make sure there's nothing else you want while we're here."

"This little stack right here is all."

He stood back for her to go ahead of him and looked at the back wall. Concreted over. The other walls being the original stone.

Upstairs, he pushed the door closed with his foot holding onto the papers Connie had given him.

"When you're through reading all this, you let the cleaning crew bring the boxes back down there and set them where they'll be together." Cas said.

"Together—my foot!" Connie thought in surprise. "He doesn't want me to go back down there!"

Her heart warmed at the thought of his being so over protective about something he didn't understand.

"Cas, I've found some interesting things. One of them is a picture of a large group and the best I can tell, it has Nelson, Mary Lou, and some others in it. I'm hoping one of them is Louis DeVille. The picture is of some kind of big party or something they were having. I can't wait to get a better look at it in a good light. I'll put these with the other things. It won't take long."

"All right." He made sure the basement door was closed securely and the light was off.

Coming back by Jo Beth's desk Connie told her, "As I said, there's a picture back there you might want to look at. I'm hoping Louis DeVille is in it. I've been dying to see what he looked like."

"They do say he was a very handsome young man," Jo Beth chuckled. "You're so excited about this, next thing I know you'll be calling in Della Reubens to meet them!"

"Who?" The name was strange to Connie. "Who is Della Reubens? And what do you mean that I might be calling her to meet them?" Connie stood mystified at the thought. "I don't remember hearing the name."

"Della Reubens. She's, I guess you'd call it a medium. Used to hold a séance once in a while. Haven't heard anything about her in a long time. She must be getting up in years now, if she's still with us."

Connie stood drinking in every word till Cas touched her arm.

"Connie, we'd better be on our way. Nice to see you again, Jo Beth." There was no sign of Hannah.

They enjoyed their lunch at the Smithy but Cas was already beginning to feel guilty about taking the time off to look at decorations and such. Connie smiled to herself, recognizing the little signs of being anxious to get back to work.

He went back to his office instead of going on to see Clarence, in case there was anything urgent waiting for him. He had taken longer than he planned.

Gladys knew where he had gone and smiled her approval when he came in. There were no calls for him to return and no excuse for him to feel guilty.

"Who, besides my good hearted, conscientious boss, would insist on coming to work with a broken arm and feel guilty about taking his wife to lunch?" Gladys thought as he passed her.

At his desk he looked at the clock and decided to go on and call Clint. He got out the two murder files just in case there might be something new.

The one on Welemon was depressingly flat and the other one had nothing either but the basics: Description of the body, clothes and effects, the usual. There was also the picture Clint had given him of the body. It was noted, though the first blow was fatal to Welemon, he had been struck again at least once. He added a note about the splintered bone he saw, shuddering a little as he pictured the back of Welemon's head. He looked again at the two pictures, the head and shoulder shots he had of Welemon and the one of the gunshot victim.

He moved the legal pad closer, ready to make any necessary notes. He still had the gut feeling the two deaths were connected. It was possible the white man had been with Welemon. Clarence claimed he didn't see him but that wouldn't account for the way Clarence was acting.

"He's just too evasive, I felt it as soon as I talked to him. There's no way I'd believe Clarence would kill Welemon himself, even if he was on dope. He's his nephew, his dead sister's child. No, he didn't do this, so what the heck could he be hiding?"

It was exactly two o'clock when Cas made his phone call. Clint answered on the first ring.

"Clint, this is Cas. Were you able to get any information on the gunshot victim?"

"Yes. Hold a minute."

Cas heard a drawer open and the rustle of papers, his neck no longer protested holding the receiver against his shoulder as he waited.

"Here it is. You ready?"

"Ready. Pen poised. But I don't take shorthand, remember."

"Okay, here goes. His name's Peder Sellczk. That's S-e-l-l-c-z-k."

"Okay."

"Age forty-one."

"Okay."

"That's unofficial from the State. Ours is he was a little undernourished as you saw, and though there were some needle marks we didn't find anything in his system. They didn't either. He more than likely didn't have the money to buy anything. The report will be more detailed and have the lab results in it typed up with everything else. That's the gist of it for now."

"That's a big help. I appreciate it. At least I've got a name now. I can check and see if he's got a record anywhere for starters."

"Got to have. They get their drug money from petty thievery, usually."

"It's good to have something to go on, I owe you a lunch."

"I'll take you up on it after the holidays. Do you still go over to eat at the Smithy?"

"If I was there any oftener, they'd charge me rent!"

"I forgot how close you are to it. I'll look forward to some of their good stew."

Cas lost no time checking on Peder Sellczk. The record was full of petty thievery; wanted by immigration for not registering; no felony convictions in this country; wanted for questioning in drug related cases in Tennessee and Arkansas, Memphis and Texarkana.

"That well beaten opportunity path, highway forty," Cas mused to himself.

CHAPTER 8

Connie looked critically at her schedule of work days.

"It's a good thing I'm starting now to arrange for Christmas week at home. I've got days for Laurence Fields, Lisa Randolph, and Tim Carpenter. Judge Carpenter." She felt good about that. "And there will be a half day for the Andersons whenever we can work it in. I'll bet there will be a lot of bills to send out, they've been so busy."

Decorating the library had turned out to be a brilliant idea businesswise. Every one of their arrangements on display had sold and more orders for silk arrangements were still coming in. Connie wondered how plans for the Christmas decorations were going.

She paused, her eyes falling on one of the bright leafy decorations on the mantel. "It sure is lonesome around here after Missy's been home a while. Her fall leaf arrangements are beginning to droop. I'll pull out the droopiest ones and keep them as long as I can."

She was admiring her efforts when the phone rang.

"Hi! Are you lost and lonesome as I am after our good visit?"

"Cathy! Hi yourself, and of course I am. I was sunk in a sentimental bog just now. I was straightening up the arrangement Missy put on the mantel. Trying to keep them as long as possible because she put them there. How's that for downright pitiful?"

"Oh, that's not so bad. I'm just as bad off, but I don't think I'll have hit bottom till I get to missing that old car of Casey's." Cathy laughed. "And the Christmas holidays will be here soon. We can look forward to that. Are you real busy?"

"Not today. I called everyone I've worked for and am trying to get everything they want done so I can have all of Christmas week at home. From the list, it's a good thing I started early."

"That was a good idea all right. To take Christmas week and make arrangements for it. I don't suppose you've had much time to spend on the old news issues and things you found in the library basement, have you?"

"No, but I got Cas to go over to see the decorations and he went down in the basement with me to make sure that there wasn't anything about the Nelsons or early times in Maryvale that I'd missed and wanted brought upstairs."

"You sneak!" Cathy chortled, "You wanted to see what he thought of the haunting, didn't you?"

"I did. But I didn't fool him at all. He knew that's one of the main reasons I wanted him to go by there. It's dangerous being married as long as we have. We can almost read each other's minds." Connie giggled.

"Well, anyway, he did go. What did he think? Tell me about it."

"We both had our coats on when we went down in the basement but it was still cold enough to make your teeth chatter back there where I got the old newspapers. He said it was too penetrating for our coats to keep it out because of the damp. And the crying, he heard it too. He said so."

"I guess he tried to explain it away?"

"Yes and no. He thought the sound might be coming from somewhere else because it's so faint. But sometimes what Cas doesn't say is louder than what he does say. When we got back upstairs he told me to do my reading in the reading room and let the cleaning crew take the boxes back down."

"That sounds like a convert to the does believe in ghosts group to me, whether he ever admits it or not. He didn't want you spending any more time down there with whatever caused those unpleasant conditions whether any of us understand it or not."

"That's exactly what I thought. And I did find a couple more things. One of the old newspapers has a picture of a lot of people at some big event and I'm hoping one of them is Louis DeVille. I'm dying to see what he looked like. But I haven't had any time to go back and take a good look at them. I've been so much bother at the library, I'm going to volunteer to mount some of the papers and things or whatever they want done to preserve the old records. Some of the things are so fragile they're about to fall apart. A few of them have."

"I'll bet. Sounds like bad conditions for any kind of paper to me. Connie, do you remember telling me about Jo Beth mentioning that woman named Della Reubens?"

"Della Reubens?"

"You know, Jo Beth said next thing you'd be calling Della Reubens so you could meet some of those people you've been reading about."

"Oh, yes. The one she said was a medium or something. From the way she said it she must be getting up in years, I thought she was probably dead and gone. I didn't think any more about it. Up in years to Jo Beth would more than likely be pretty old, you know." Connie chuckled. "Jo Beth is getting on up there, too."

"Well...." Cathy said slowly, sounding mysterious. "Della Reubens is not dead and she doesn't even sound all that old."

"You mean you've talked to her?"

"Yes, I have." Cathy's breathing was faster, excited. "I found her, Connie. She lives in Lee's Corners. That's so close I don't think it's even a long distance call. It's in our area and she's still listed in the phone book."

"And you called her? You actually called her?"

"I sure did! Do you think I shouldn't have?"

"No. No. I don't think that. I'm just so surprised is all. What did you ask her? Tell me everything she said!"

"I told her my name and where I live, and I asked her if she's the Della Reubens who used to do séances a few years ago. She said she is but she hasn't done anything in quite a while. She sounded, I don't know, like she wasn't too anxious to get involved in anything and I was sort of discouraged."

"Oh," Connie's voice dropped with discouragement at that. "I guess she doesn't want to be bothered anymore."

"Well, in spite of the way she sounded I told her about the cold in the library basement and how terribly cold it was where you found the old newspapers. She didn't say anything, she just listened to what I was telling her. And I told her about the dim sound of someone crying. Also, I told her that you and Hannah had both heard it. Then she asked me if it was a man's voice or a woman's, the one who was crying? And I said no, not a man, it was a young woman's voice. I also told her it made you feel depressed and sad when you heard it."

"She was getting interested, wasn't she?" Connie's voice rose a little, getting excited again.

"I thought so too. I offered to go and get her if she would come, so she could go down in the basement and see what she thought. I didn't know really, what else to suggest."

"Oh! Is she coming?" Connie jumped up, too excited to stay seated, already hoping to meet Della Reubens, a real medium.

"Yes, she said she would. I got the idea from what she said, she wouldn't bother to do anything unless there was really evidence that a spirit is involved."

Connie caught her breath as she listened. "But she is coming to see about it? About the cold and the crying?"

"She said she would, but she can't come this week. She took my number and said she would call me next week.

She'll come over and go down in the basement to see if she can hear the crying too."

Cathy paused, "You don't think Jo Beth will mind, do you? Having gone this far it will sure be embarrassing if we're not allowed to go down into the basement. Or maybe there might be some kind of rule against it or something?"

"Oh," Connie was confident. "I don't think she'll mind. It is a public library, after all. And let me know when you hear from Della Reubens, will you? If I'm not working, I'll go with you and lend moral support. I don't think there will be any problem at all, and I would really like to meet her. A medium. A real medium who's done séances before," Connie marveled.

"Do you think she really is? A medium? That she can make contact or whatever they call it?"

Connie laughed, "You know as much about it as I do. I've never seen one before and only saw a séance once in an old movie. But from what Jo Beth said, she must have had some sort of success. She's actually done this before. Did Della Reubens say anything about anyone she's contacted or had séances for?"

"No, and I didn't ask her anything else. I was afraid to press my luck after she said she'd come."

"You're right. She probably wouldn't have told you anyway or said anything else about the library for that matter, without seeing the place for herself."

"Maybe she'll tell us a little more when she comes, I'll call you when I hear from her."

"Good, I'm glad you called her!"

Cas cudgeled his brains over the two murder files every time he had a spare minute.

"Two murder cases at once; both of the victims on dope. There's a connection here somewhere, it's just a matter of finding it. The times of death are close; both strangers. Welemon hadn't been around for several years and the second one is a stranger; both of them users; and both turn up here in Maryvale at the same time. And Clarence isn't telling all he knows, he's holding something back. But why? And what?"

He thought back to when he showed Clarence the picture of the gunshot victim. What Clarence had said was, "All I know about him from this picture, is he's been shot." Cas frowned. "He didn't say he had never seen the man before." The thought was quickly followed by, "Wait. Yes he did!" Cas frowned. When I asked him point blank, he looked away and said no a little too loud and didn't meet my eyes. That's when I was sure he was lying to me for some reason."

Both files open in front of him, he dialed Clarence Lynch's number.

"Hello?"

"Is that you, Clarence?"

"Yes, Sheriff Larkin, it's me." Clarence sounded weary of hearing his voice. He waited for Cas to speak. He still wasn't going to volunteer anything.

"I've made a little progress since the last time we talked." Cas paused, but Clarence still didn't speak. He was no more willing to talk to Cas now than the last time he'd tried to get at what he knew.

"I've found out the name of the other man that was killed."

"You mean that white man that was shot?"

"Yes. His name was Peder Sellczk. Does that ring any sort of bell? Ever heard Welemon mention him or hear it anywhere else?"

"Peddle—"

"No. Peder. P-E-D-E-R. His name was Peder Sellczk. Do you know if Welemon knew him or anyone who had a name that sounds like that? I may not be pronouncing the last one right."

"No, sir. Never heard any name sounds anything like that."

This time, Clarence's answer had the ring of truth to it. Cas believed him.

"Well, get something and write it down. Peder S E L L C Z K. And let me know if you do hear anything about him. Will you do that?"

"I'll do that," the weary voice conceded.

"All right. You have my number here and at home too, if you think of anything else that will help. Thank you, Clarence."

Cas sat staring at the silent phone.

"I know I'm bugging you, Clarence. But you're not leveling with me and I'm not going to let you alone until you do or I get what I need to solve these two cases some other way."

He sighed, leaning on his good elbow. He hoped when the report came in on Sellczk there might be something that would help. He couldn't shake the feeling the two deaths were connected even if the murder weapons were different.

Connie had a busy week. She worked for Laurence Fields, Tim Carpenter, and had four statements to do for the Randolph law firm sometime before the first of the year whenever she could work them in.

When she went in to work on the statements Lisa told her there would be more. "But these four are the only ones we need by the first of the year."

It was a good day to be inside working on statements. The nice weather seemed to have been used up, and there was a steady downpour of rain at lunch time. The windows framed a depressing gray view. Lisa Randolph volunteered to go to the Smithy for stew and rolls so Connie and Jill took her up on it, ordering Danish too.

"I'll get the Danish if Jill will make us come coffee," Lisa offered.

"Good deal! I'll do it now, and get the gooey ones."

Connie felt the statements were going well but the break was welcome. They had the break-room to themselves since Dick Randolph was in court.

"I doubt they even know it's raining at the courthouse." Lisa commented, reaching for her coat and rain hat.

The bad weather was at least good to keep people off the streets and Lisa was back in no time. The Danish smelled heavenly as they got settled with their coffee.

"How are you doing with your research on the Nelsons and the mansion?" Jill asked Connie.

"And have you been back down there where the ghost is crying?" Jill looked eager for news and though Lisa tried not to be too obvious, she was interested too.

"If there is some logical way to explain it," Lisa did venture. "I for one, would like to hear what it is."

The discussion was put on hold to refill their cups and Lisa announced proudly, "I got the last of the gooey Danishes. Now, where were we in this basement adventure? I haven't missed anything, have I?"

"No, we don't want to miss anything," Jill giggled.

Mouth full, Connie shook her head and sipped her coffee before answering. "No. I haven't been back down there but once to see if there might be something I overlooked when I brought up all the old newspapers and things. But it's still there, whatever it is, and still crying. And it's still cold enough down there to make your teeth chatter. Have either of you ever heard of a Della Reubens?"

Jill looked blank. Her mouth full of pastry, she shook her head.

"I have," Lisa said. "It was some time ago but I think she's a medium or something like that. It seems there was a séance held."

She had their attention trying to remember what she'd heard. "It was in some small town or community around here, but that's all I can remember about it." She smiled, "I only heard about it after it was all over, worse luck. Wouldn't it be interesting to go to one?"

Lisa's eyes widened, staring at Connie. "Wait a minute! Are you saying you've talked to Della Reubens? Do you think she might do a séance to see if the basement has a ghost?"

Lisa and Jill lost interest in their dessert, lips parted, waiting for an answer.

"I ah—well, I don't know yet. I heard her name and told a friend of mine about it. I haven't talked to her myself. Didn't even know she was still around. But my friend called and talked to her. She lives in Lee's Corners."

"Lee's Corners! That's where the séance I heard about was held." Lisa's eyes met Jill's.

"My friend told her about the strange cold and the sounds in the basement and to make a long story short, she's coming to see for herself. She's going to come to the library and tell us what she thinks."

Connie leaned forward, "If it's just a natural cold down there, or—or what?"

"Well," Jill didn't hesitate. "If it turns out she thinks it's something unnatural and holds a séance, I definitely want to go!"

"I do too," Lisa quickly agreed. "You be sure and let us know what she says, will you?"

"I will. But all she's said so far is she will come to the library. So, I won't know anything definite to tell you until she decides."

By Friday, Connie had only a half day's work for Tim Carpenter left to get done before her holiday. She decided she'd skip lunch to go to the library and get a better look at the group picture she'd found.

Hannah had either gone home or was off that day and Connie waved to Jo Beth on her way to the back reading room. In her purse, she had a magnifying glass to get as good a look as she could of the faces in the picture and the names under it. She felt her excitement rising as she draped her coat over a chair and picked up the picture first.

Holding the fragile old paper carefully, Connie peered at the people in the picture.

"Oh, this glass really does bring things out! The clothes they wore! Some of those shirts are as pretty as the frills on the ladies. And here is Mary Lou. She looks happier and more alive than in the portrait. You'd think expressions were against the law or immoral back then, much less any

kind of emotions. This dark, handsome young man must be
her Louie, Louis DeVille. And he's looking back at her and
smiling like she is, as if they are the only two there. They
look like they're in love, all right. And he's really good
looking as they say, if that's Louie. And it is! It is!"

Connie moved her glass down to the caption then back
up to the picture of Louie and Mary Lou. Her heart warmed
to them, Who could blame them for falling in love, he was
so handsome and she was so pretty!

A voice broke into her thoughts. "Looking at some of the
social set in Maryvale, are you? You were smart to bring
that magnifying glass."

"I thought it would help and it sure does. Look how it
brings things out." She handed the glass to Jo Beth who
took it and the picture to look closer.

"I've been dying to see what Louis DeVille looked like.
Mary Lou's Louie, and here he is!"

Connie was delighted and looked up at Jo Beth. "We
can't let these things just deteriorate."

"No, we can't." Jo Beth pulled up another chair and
joined her at the table. "You're right. But it's going to be a
lot of work sorting it all out and figuring out how to
preserve them. For right now, when you get through with a
piece lay it over here. I'll look as you read, to see which
ones we're going to have to do more to than put between
plastic."

"All right. These right here are what I've gone over so
far. I meant to tell you, you've been so nice to let me look
at all these things I'll be glad to help mount them or do
whatever you want done. I'll work it in around my typing
jobs."

"I knew you were working here in Maryvale, freelancing
now. I think you were a smart one to do it, too. The driving
back and forth to Fort Craig is a job in itself."

Jo Beth smiled, "And I appreciate your offer to help. Any
time you get a chance, you can just come in and work with
me here. None of us will probably have much time before
the first of the year and there's no hurry anyway, now that

we've got them up here. I'd be glad to have your help."

"All right, we'll leave it at flexible then." Connie finally relinquished the picture. "This certainly is one of the things that should be mounted." She shook her head, "Some of these other things are in pretty bad shape."

"That's why it's a good thing there's no hurry. We can take our time and do it right."

Connie spent the rest of the afternoon in the sunny back reading room, carefully putting the things she had read aside with a paperweight on them.

"I'm beginning to feel as if I know Mary Lou and Louie DeVille. These old pictures are really something, and I can just imagine how the house must have looked back then."

She sighed. "That reminds me, I'll stop by the flower shop and see when they're going to start on the decorations here for Christmas. The way the fall arrangements sold and brought business in for them, they'll surely want to get started as soon as possible."

Connie admired the front of the flower shop as she walked toward it. It was beautiful and colorful, lending interest and variety as well as adding a prosperous look to the other businesses around the square. She couldn't even remember what the dress shop window had looked like and decided that must have been part of their problem.

She grinned to herself. "Goodness knows, Miss Minnie and Miss Mayme's efforts were never dull. Not even in school, bless them."

Miss Mayme met her at the door with the Closed sign in her hand. "I saw you coming and it's about closing time now anyway. We've got a pot of coffee we need to finish before we leave."

"Sounds good to me. Timed it just right. I skipped lunch and went right over to the library. I'll be ready to bite somebody by dinner time!" She followed Miss Mayme back to the office pulling off her coat as she went.

"How about a slightly dry jelly doughnut? I heard you say you skipped lunch and there are three left." Miss Minnie set the box out and poured their coffee.

"Great! Waste not, want not, as the saying goes. I came by to see when you're going to start on the Christmas decorations at the library. Maybe Monday?"

She sipped her coffee. "I'm not taking any more work till after Christmas. I'd planned on taking all of Christmas week anyway and my customers stopped even earlier. Not that I mind. Are you going to start Monday?"

"Definitely Monday. Mayme has quite a few arrangements she's done and made the general design for the library so we can get started."

Miss Minnie set her cup down. "And we're going to put some things in the courthouse this year. The things we put around the library at Thanksgiving sold like hotcakes. We're hoping the Christmas arrangements will do as well."

"Probably even better!" Connie was optimistic.

"The only thing I'm not sure about is the staircase at the library," Miss Mayme said thoughtfully. "There are so many different and beautiful things you can do with a stair case. Especially one as grand as that. I've got a general idea and we'll just do it as we go." Miss Mayme dusted pieces of icing off her ample bosom.

"Do you have something lined up for Monday, Connie?" Miss Minnie asked tentatively.

"No, that's why I'm being so nosey. I thought maybe I'd come and help decorate, if I can get myself invited."

"You're officially invited then. But why don't you come and work for us half a day to get out the billing for some of the shop windows we've done and the arrangements. Then come help us with the decorations after lunch. We could have lunch at the Smithy if you want to," she raised her eyebrows inquiringly.

"That would be fine. It's a good idea." Connie licked the bits of jelly goo off her lower lip and set down her empty cup. "I think I'll make it till I can get dinner cooked now." She smiled as she got up. "I'll see you at eight o'clock Monday morning, thanks for the vitamins."

She grinned at Miss Mayme who wrinkled her nose at the doughnut box, "Such as they were."

* * *

Cas stopped by Clarence Lynch's house before starting home. He had the picture of Peder Sellczk in his pocket.

"Some days I like my job better than others," he frowned.

As he knew it would, Clarence's door opened before he reached it.

"Afternoon, Sheriff Larkin."

Clarence stood in the open door as Cas came up the steps.

"Clarence, I came by here on my way home for two reasons. One, to tell you I'm sorry Welemon's body hasn't been released yet and I'll let you know as soon as they notify me."

Clarence nodded understanding, no animosity or impatience in his sad face.

"And two, I've got that picture of this Peder Sellczk with me. I'd like to show it to your mother. I don't want to upset her, but she may have seen him with Welemon even if you didn't if they were around here together. We're certainly never going to know if we don't ask her." His eyes asked Clarence not to make him insist on cooperation.

"She's awful nervous," Clarence said slowly. "Let me hold it and ask her. I'll put my thumb over the forehead there."

He looked doubtful as Cas handed him the picture. "But I don't think it will do any good."

Cas stayed where he was and Clarence approached the elderly woman who sat in a rocking chair at the back of the long room. He bent down to her and said something Cas couldn't hear, then brought the picture up into her line of vision. His hand looked like he was holding his thumb over the top part.

Her reaction was pure fear. Cas saw it plainly in her large, dark eyes when she looked at the picture then turned her frightened face to him.

Clarence spoke to her again and she shook her head, her eyes still on Cas.

Clarence brought the picture back and handed it to Cas. "No, she don't know him."

"All right." Cas spoke grimly, meeting Clarence's eyes. He returned the picture to his shirt pocket.

"I'm doing all I can to find out what happened to him and to Welemon too. They were both in this county and both entitled to the best we can do to clear this up."

"I know that," Clarence said just as seriously. "You've always been fair and done the best you could for everybody."

In the ensuing silence, Clarence allowed himself a faint smile. "I voted for you."

"Thanks, Clarence." Cas allowed himself a smile as well. "I hope you'll go on voting for me. You have my card and it's got my home number on the back. Call me if you hear anything or remember anything that might help."

Clarence dropped his eyes but said nothing. He opened the door for Cas, standing silently by as he went out.

Out on the porch where his mother couldn't hear, Cas turned and tried again before Clarence shut the door.

"Clarence, no one's threatened you or anything have they?"

The startled look was an honest reaction.

Cas added, "I have to know all the facts. Maybe things you wouldn't even feel make any difference, to get to the bottom of this. Are you sure there isn't something else you want to tell me?"

"No. No, I don't know that man. He's a stranger to me. And hasn't been anybody around threatening me, or I'd sure tell you that."

Cas left and didn't look back but as he started the truck he remembered the startled look when he asked Clarence about any threats.

"Maybe I gave him something to think about. He may be wondering now, if he did see Sellczk, if there will be some sort of threat to him. Users and suppliers are a bad lot. I may have accidentally done myself some good if it will make him open up. Right now the only thing I can think of is maybe this Sellczk was supplying Wellemon with drugs and Clarence doesn't want to get involved with anything like that. But Sellczk wasn't prosperous looking enough to be a supplier. I guess I'm just going to have to find the truth the best way I can."

The next day Cas picked up his calls and mail from Gladys and ran through it as he sat down at his desk.

"Nothing burning, nobody bleeding to death." He stuck most of them on a spindle and reached for the phone to call Clint.

"Coroner's office."

"Clint, I haven't had a chance to get back with you about the clay samples I brought in. Did you find any dirt or clay on Sellczk's loafers? I know it's a slim chance you'd find enough to compare to the scene where Welemon was found."

"It didn't look like I was going to get enough so I took them apart. It's not as if he's going to be needing them anymore."

"Good for you, I'm down to grasping at straws on this."

"I scraped together enough to send out and I kept a little here to compare myself. They're the same. I hope that's what you wanted to hear."

"It is, I guess. I'm not too happy about the way my suspicions are heading but I've got to get to the bottom line whether I like it or not."

"Well, it's the same. The clay, and there was some grease or something. There were traces of whatever it was in both, on the loafers and what was on your boots. Probably grease he used on his yard equipment."

"Okay. Thanks, Clint."

Cas and Connie enjoyed their weekend. Cas went to the office but came home early, and Connie spent most of the day cleaning house and baking cup cakes. The leaves that hadn't fallen to carpet the ground made bright splashes against the sky as Connie opened the back door for Cas.

"This time of the year always makes me wish I could paint." Connie said it wistfully, gazing at the bright foliage surrounding the house.

"I don't know how you'd work it in." Cas laughed at her, lifting her off her feet with a hug. He kissed her as he set her down.

"You're going to need eight days this week as it is, aren't you?"

She put her arms around him, snuggling. "I wouldn't say that. Some of what I've got to do is supposed to be work, but I like the work I'm doing. And the rest of the things I just want to do. Interesting things I'd never have been able to do if I hadn't decided to quit my job in Fort Craig."

"Yes, I'm glad about that too. Umm, something sure does smell good, is that a muffin pan of banana nut cup cakes?"

"It is, but dinner's ready. We'll have them for our dessert. Cup cakes need coffee."

Over dinner she told him about the picture of Louis DeVille she had found.

"I took the magnifying glass with me. And Cas, he's so handsome! No wonder Mary Lou Nelson fell in love with him. And as interesting as they were, some of those old papers and things are in really bad shape. I'm going to help Jo Beth in mounting and preserving them so they won't be lost or destroyed."

"That's good, I approve the idea. But do you have time to do it?"

"Jo Beth says it's one of those things you don't have to worry about, there not being any deadline. We'll not take them back down to the basement. They'll stay in the back reading room until we can get to them."

Cas looked down to hide the mischief in his eyes. "And are all the ghosts behaving and staying in the basement where they belong? Not traipsing around upstairs?"

"No, wise guy. Or if they are, they've been very quiet about it. And that reminds me, there's a woman coming to check on that soon. She's going down into the basement to see if she thinks the cold and the sounds are really something unnatural."

"Supernatural. But, what woman? Don't tell me there's a company here now that runs service calls on spooks and haunted basements?"

Cas had an uneasy feeling about what she was telling him and in spite of his teasing, it showed on his face.

"Jo Beth mentioned this woman. Her name is Della Reubens. Some time ago she held séances, and she knows about things like this. Cathy got brave and looked her up in the phone book and called her. She didn't sound very interested at first, Della Reubens didn't, I mean. But when Cathy told her about the cold and sound of the crying, she changed her mind. She said she would call Cathy soon and come to see what she thought it might be. You know, to see if it's only naturally cold and the crying can be explained or if it really is something as you said, supernatural."

Cas thought that over, not making any comment.

"I don't know if I'd have done that or not," he sounded dubious. "But I guess it won't hurt to hear what she's got to say."

He gave her a level look, his voice getting firm. "But if she does decide to hold one of those so-called séances, don't plan on going."

Startled at his tone that was flat and final as a slab of marble, Connie asked, "Why shouldn't I? What would be the harm?"

Cas tilted his head and explained patiently. "Would you vote for someone for sheriff whose wife was out trying to raise the dead?"

Connie laughed. "No. Now that you bring that up, I don't suppose I would. I see what you mean."

"You won't feel too underprivileged, will you? And of course, there may not be a spook to raise."

"Well, I don't know, maybe not. Maybe Della Reubens won't think there should be a séance. But I'd probably have gone. I would like to have, I think. But I won't. Besides," she pointed out, eyes dancing, "I know if there is one, I'll hear all about it. Anyway, we may be worrying too soon about a séance since Della Reubens hasn't said she would do one yet."

Cas remembered what Hannah had told him, but kept his apprehensions firmly between his ears and behind his worry lines.

CHAPTER 9

Connie peered into the dark shop as she knocked.

It was eight o'clock. She squinted, trying to see if there was a light back in the office.

The office door opened, silhouetting Miss Mayme's generous proportions as she hurried to let Connie in.

"We're going to put the Closed sign on the door with the return time as one o'clock. That way, no one will be knocking and bothering you," she explained to Connie. "We can meet at the Smithy at twelve then Minnie or I will come back here to keep the shop open this afternoon."

"Sounds like a fine plan to me. Are you about ready to go?"

Miss Minnie joined them. "We're ready. Mayme has a few more things she wants to put in the car. We're going to park in front of the library so we won't have to carry things so far."

Miss Mayme had begun gathering the things she wanted to take and came from the other side of the shop carefully balancing several things she didn't want to crush. She smiled gratefully at Connie as she took two of them to carry for her.

With everything safely loaded, Miss Minnie stuck her head out the driver's window. "The door will lock when you close it, Connie."

"Okay, see you at the Smithy at twelve."

Inside, Connie took the precaution of closing the office door thinking someone might be persistent about banging on the door if they thought there was someone here to help them. She smiled to herself as she glanced back at the outer door, "They're sure getting good use out of that back soon sign they bought."

In the small office she noted with satisfaction the flags in the files where there were bills to be sent out, the supply of envelopes and forms open on the desk top.

At the library, Jo Beth saw Miss Mayme and Miss Minnie coming, their arms full of decorations and the makings for more arrangements. She held the door, looking past them at the other things visible through the van's doors.

Hannah was there also and went out to help bring in the rest of their things.

"Thanks. I think one more trip will do it." Miss Minnie followed the others out again.

Jo Beth paused before returning to her desk, interested in the things the Andersons had brought in.

After all they had loaded in the car had been brought in, Miss Minnie unrolled the paper with some of Miss Mayme's designs on it. "Why don't I start putting the garlands of greenery on the stairs while you put the finishing touches on some of those arrangements?"

"Yes. Good idea. Use the garlands in that box over there and the other big box like it. Remember, it's better to have plenty plus than not enough, and we've got them to spare. It won't take too long to get these arrangements I planned on doing today together then I'll be there to help you."

Jo Beth watched from where she sat at her desk. "I'll just stay out of your way unless you want me to do something." She added hopefully, "I'll be right here."

"Oh, we'll manage. But thanks."

Miss Minnie started pulling the green garlands out of the first box.

By eleven-thirty Miss Mayme had the arrangements set around in eye catching places and the stairway began to look like a green pathway.

Jo Beth joined Miss Minnie and Miss Mayme as they stood admiring the progress they had made.

"It's bringing out my Christmas spirit already!"

Her eyes twinkled as if she had some sort of news bulletin to share. "I was waiting for Connie to get here since she's so interested in the Nelsons, but well, wait a minute. I've got something to show you."

Miss Minnie and Miss Mayme exchanged a puzzled look as Jo Beth hurried toward the back reading room, obviously excited about something.

"She must have found something we can use."

"I hope it's as good as her opinion of it, from the way she looked. And she said Connie would be interested in it too."

Further speculation was cut off by Jo Beth's triumphal return. In her arms she carefully carried a huge red velvet bow. It looked to be a yard wide. Perhaps a bit more, Miss Mayme figured, measuring it with her artist's eyes.

"That's pretty!" She admired it, touching it gingerly. She asked curiously. "Is it part of the decorations the City Beautiful Commission had?"

"No! Better than that," Jo Beth confided. "It's part of the original decorations that were in the house when the Nelsons lived here."

"It is? But, where?"

"Yes, where or how did you find it?"

"It's been up in the attic all this time. We've never been allowed to use the attic, though the key is here with the others." Jo Beth explained.

"Since Connie is so interested in the Nelsons and the way the mansion was then, I called the committee and asked if they had any objections to my looking in the attic to see if there might be anything up there we could use. The woman who answered was all for it. They're hoping there might be some things they will be able to use in the museum they're planning at the back of the courthouse."

"They're going to set up a museum?"

"Must be, I didn't know anything about it either, but that's what she said. I didn't ask what they were going to have in it. But anything about the Nelsons or the house would be Maryvale history, I'd think."

"Were there lots of things up there?"

"There are. Boxes and boxes of things. And a really beautiful old wardrobe. I didn't take time to look at it, just looked around to see if there were any more Christmas decorations saved that we could use. That way we could tell people they're the original things that were used in the mansion when it was a home and the Nelsons were living here."

"This was the only Christmas looking thing, then?"

Jo Beth nodded. "It's all I found. It was probably saved because it's so big and expensive looking. May have been their favorite, or maybe it was a tradition. It could even have been made special for the house."

"As big and beautiful as it is, I'll bet it was made for the stairway," Miss Mayme eyed it thoughtfully. "It must have been, and it will be beautiful there. I'm glad you found it."

Miss Mayme carefully took the bow, holding it up between her and the stairway as if trying to picture where it would look best.

"Connie will be glad to see all the other things you said were up there too, whether they're decorations or not. She's been so interested in the Nelson family and the social life they enjoyed back then. I guess you couldn't tell too much about what kind of things there are up there without opening the boxes, could you?" Miss Mayme asked hopefully.

"Just enough to make me curious. There were only a few things out that I could see. There was an old dress maker's dummy. One of those things you can adjust to make patterns larger or smaller. The thing that caught my eye was that beautiful old wardrobe. It's a beautiful thing, made of pretty, dark wood, it's something to see, a beautiful antique."

"Connie will be here after lunch so you can tell her about the attic then."

"Speaking of that, one of us will have to open the shop. Are you going to go back today?"

"Yes, I'll go. You can stay at the shop tomorrow."

"It's about time to meet Connie," Miss Minnie looked up to catch Jo Beth's attention. "We'll stop back by and get the bow to touch up the gold on the pine cones."

Jo Beth nodded and waved, looking forward to Connie's reaction to her news about the things in the attic.

Out on the sidewalk they saw Connie coming toward them. "Timed it just right, didn't we?" Miss Mayme called.

The conversation centered around the decorations as they walked toward the Smithy. They filled her in on Jo Beth's good news.

"She called and got the commission's permission to look in the attic for Christmas decorations the Nelsons might have kept."

"Oh!" Connie interrupted, stopping in the middle of the sidewalk. "You mean she did find some? Is that the news? Something that belonged to the Nelsons?"

Miss Minnie took her elbow and started walking again. "She found a big velvet bow that Mayme is going to put on the stairway."

"And she said there are other things besides the Christmas bow. Not decorations, but boxes and things. She'll tell you about it when you get there."

"Oh, something original! If I couldn't smell that good stew from here," Connie looked back at the library.

"Come on," Miss Minnie laughed at her. "You've got to eat. As long as those things in the attic have waited I don't think a few more minutes is going to make any difference."

"I never dreamed there would be anything in the attic. It's hard to believe that bow's laid up there all this time and no one's even cared to look at it or the other things."

"But they couldn't. The library personnel were told not to use the attic. That was reason enough not to go up there, I'd think. They must have made that instruction pretty clear. Jo Beth still didn't go up there until she called and asked permission to see if perhaps there might be some Christmas decorations."

"Come to think of it, by the condition of the basement you told us about, no one probably wanted to go up there anyway. Just think, if it hadn't been for the Museum Committee, it still might not have been found."

"Museum Committee?"

"They're going to try and find some things about the Nelsons and Maryvale's history is what Jo Beth was told when she called. After all these years, they said the City Beautiful Commission wants to see what's up there that the Museum Committee can use. I guess some of the same people are on both committees."

"Um-hum, I'll bet most of it will need more restoring than the little gold pine cones we can paint. Don't get your hopes up too much," Miss Minnie warned Connie.

"Oh, I know," Connie was a little embarrassed. "But it seems to me to have been such an interesting, exciting, romantic time. I haven't got over the thrill of finding the newspaper picture of Mary Lou and Louis DeVille yet. And it's part of the town's history, don't forget. You might say it's our civic duty to preserve these things."

Connie tried to look noble and dedicated but grinned instead. "It's only coincidence that it's also so romantic."

"Sure it is," Miss Minnie rolled her eyes. "I guess I'm going to have to see this good looking Frenchman, Mayme. Soon as we get back I want to see that old newspaper you found."

"Heavens to Betsy," Miss Mayme screeched in mock horror. "It's catching! Minnie's got the itch to excavate attics too!"

"Gotcha! You can't excavate an attic!" Miss Minnie jumped at the chance to correct her sister.

"Well, do excuse me! I suppose I'm still wondering about that cold in the basement."

Fortunately for Connie, digestion needed no conscious help from her, leaving her hands free to eat and her imagination free to wonder about the things in the attic and the wonderful old wardrobe Jo Beth described. She finished her lunch and managed to get back to the library without dying of curiosity, but it was a struggle.

After a brief, awestruck look up the back stairs at the attic door and a promise to herself to explore everything as soon as she got a chance, Connie returned to admire the bow and went dutifully back to helping Miss Mayme with the decorating.

The next day Connie had no work scheduled so she was free to spend the day helping with the library's decorations.

"I can't wait to get all this finished and get into those things in the attic." Her mind whirled as she worked with Miss Mayme. "That attic looks like a regular gold mine from what I saw when I glanced in. And Jo Beth is right about that lovely old wardrobe. Why, I wouldn't be surprised if it's handmade!"

Miss Mayme touched her hand, bringing her back to the present.

"I can see your mental wheels racing around that attic while the rest of you decorates. Maybe working from the neck down is the way to go, Minnie will be surprised to see how much we've got done."

Connie set down the box of greenery she was working with and looked around them. "It looks pretty already. But I knew it would be gorgeous," she complimented Miss Mayme as she stood admiring their work.

"It is, isn't it? These old mansions are impressive any time, but decorated for Christmas they're really grand and gracious looking."

Connie nodded, her eyes dreaming of bygone grandeur. "There's magic in Christmas."

"I think the red velvet bow really looks good there at the top of the stair. Everyone should be able to see it up there, don't you think?"

Connie nodded absently, picking up garlands from the greenery box. "I'm going to put some of this around the pictures in the back reading room."

"Good idea. There's plenty of it. I'm going to find a couple more likely places to display as many of our arrangements as I can."

Just before five o'clock Miss Minnie came and joined them. "There was no one in the shop so I closed a little early." She turned toward the decorated stairway. "That red velvet bow looks pretty there."

Miss Mayme followed her sister's gaze. The lovely old velvet bow was on the newel post at the bottom of the stairs. It spread out wide and beautiful, the gold pine cones Minnie had touched up reflecting the light.

"That's not where I put it."

Miss Mayme went to the stairway and reached for the bow, glancing at the wire on the back. She took it back up and fastened it to the greenery around the top of the banister. "There now. It's a shame we'll have to take all this down after the holidays. It's so pretty all decorated like this."

"It makes the house look lived in again." Feeling sentimental, Connie stood lost in admiration. "I can almost hear the music, and the voices singing carols," she sighed.

"Better be careful there, we don't want to hear any more voices in here." Miss Mayme warned, only half teasing as she looked around at the gathering shadows in the far corners.

"That reminds me since we're through now, except for the other arrangements you want to bring over, I'm going to find Jo Beth. I'm anxious to see the other things in the attic. I'd like to come in the morning and go up there to see what we can find in the boxes and things."

As she left them, Miss Mayme was pointing out all the places they could perhaps put one more arrangement, Miss Minnie nodding approval at each one.

"You're the artist, Mayme. The Thanksgiving arrangements certainly did well."

Miss Mayme smiled happily, she and her sister were very close even if they did bicker half the time. "Connie," she called, "We're leaving now."

Connie turned to wave and almost collided with Jo Beth coming from behind a shelf.

"Oops! Were you looking for me?"

"Yes, to tell you the decorations are about done I think, except for a few more arrangements they want to bring over from the shop." She glanced at her watch, knowing Jo Beth was anxious to get started for home too. "And to tell you, if it's all right with you, since it's so late now, I'll come in the morning and we can start going through the things in the attic."

"All right, we'll do it. I'm looking forward to it, too."

"Is there very much? I couldn't tell much by just peeping in, but I'll bet all those boxes and things are just full of all kinds of treasures from that time."

"They probably are. I haven't had a chance to look either. When I got the velvet bow I saw two big old trunks, and of course, there's that beautiful old wardrobe. It and all those boxes must be full of all kinds of things besides clothes. Odds and ends and who knows what. We won't know until we've had a chance to go through them."

"Don't tell me any more! I can't bear to guess. We'll just go up and start exploring together tomorrow. There's no telling what we'll find up there!"

"That about sums it up all right," Jo Beth laughed. "No telling what. And we'll be helping the Museum Committee, too. You know, they must have had to take the doors off that wardrobe to get it up there. It is a beautiful piece of furniture and was a popular thing back then, but hard to get up stairs and through doors. I don't know much about wood, but it looks like something you'd find in one of the better antique stores. It's probably worth too much." She gave a slight shake of her head.

"Worth too much? How could it be worth too much, and why the sad note?"

"The Museum Committee might want to sell it to finance the restoring and displaying of all the other things. It was probably brought over from England, so many fine things were then. It's probably very valuable," Jo Beth finished.

"Oh, I see." Connie felt deflated at the thought they might not be able to keep it. "I'd hate that. Surely they won't sell it, unless there's no other way at all to get the museum up and running without parting with it." She brightened up, encouraged by an idea.

"Most of the cleaning and restoring we can do ourselves. Or maybe we can get people here in Maryvale to donate their services."

"Donate their services?" Jo Beth's doubt showed on her face.

"I mean, if it's a beautiful old dress, or a suit of clothes, we could put a small sign beside it where it's displayed."

Connie pictured it as Jo Beth listened, "Maybe one saying restored by such and such quality cleaning or something like that?"

Jo Beth nodded, "I see what you mean, it would be good advertising for them. I don't know, but we can give it a good try!"

"I'll be here as soon as Cas leaves for the office in the morning. I'll probably dream about it," she giggled.

Jo Beth chuckled with her as she closed the door behind her, amused at Connie's excitement.

CHAPTER 10

The library hadn't been open long when Connie arrived. When she and Jo Beth went upstairs Connie didn't realize she had been holding her breath while Jo Beth unlocked the door to the attic. She let it out with a soft, "Oh," as she looked in.

"The light from that window makes that wardrobe look like it's made of gold!"

She frowned slightly, "Some antique dealer might think so too. I hope the committee doesn't have to sell it. It belongs here, after all."

Jo Beth nodded. "It's a pretty thing all right. I'm sure they will do a lot of thinking and planning before deciding about it. Let's see what else there is here."

The accumulation of things stored in the attic so long ago was all Connie had been hoping for. All of the boxes and chests with carefully stored away things were put here so long ago. A real treasure trove of memorabilia. There were clothes, books, pictures, toys, and personal things that were the stuff of everyday life for their time period.

"That's the very thing that makes them such treasures today," Connie marveled.

With a last admiring glance at the old wardrobe each of

them picked one of the boxes they had opened and started going through it.

"This is like opening presents, not knowing what to expect next."

They carefully examined everything they came to holding up things from time to time for each other to admire.

After going through her box Jo Beth reluctantly got to her feet and stretched her back muscles. She had been kneeling beside a box they felt must have belonged to Mirelle Nelson.

"Some of these dresses can be restored without too much trouble. We won't have to do anything to this old fashioned corset with the whalebone in it." Jo Beth chuckled as she held it up.

"Except maybe explain what it is!"

Connie gave the corset a critical once over. "I've never seen anything with whalebone in it before but I've heard of it."

Jo Beth laid the corset back in the box. "I've got to go back to my desk now. Hannah is down there by herself."

Connie nodded absently, not even turning to watch Jo Beth go as her hand encountered a strange object.

"What's this? It feels like a little book of some kind." She dug through the other things to get to it.

"It's a little old fashioned book, a diary!"

Pleased at her discovery Connie sat back on the floor, getting comfortable before she opened it. Her touch was cautious, fearing the pages might be stuck together. They weren't. It was easy to handle and on the fly leaf she read, "Mary Lou Nelson. Daily Journal."

She leafed through all of it, reading a brief bit here and there until she heard Hannah's voice.

"Hi, I haven't got but a few minutes. I wanted to see what you two had found up here. Jo Beth is still raving about it. Oh, this is it, the wardrobe she carried on so about." Hannah stepped closer to examine the dark wood, admiring the lines of it.

"It does look expensive as Jo Beth said. Must have cost a lot even back then. Look how it's made, and this wood finish shines where it catches the light."

"Looks expensive to me too." Connie sighed regretfully. "Maybe TOO expensive. Jo Beth thinks it would be worth a lot of money to an antique store and that if the committee sold it maybe it would bring in enough to take care of cleaning and restoring all the other things. But I hope they won't have to do that. I'd hate to see them have to part with it. It's the original furniture that was here in the house. That should be considered, wouldn't you think?"

"Seems to me they should. What's in it, or is it locked?"

Connie looked blank. "I don't know. We were so busy looking at the quality of it and the workmanship wondering what it would bring in an antique store, neither one of us tried to open it. We started on the boxes."

She got to her feet and came to stand in front of the wardrobe with Hannah.

"Well, here goes!" Hannah gingerly took hold of the knob on the long door and turned. It didn't give, and they were both disappointed. Hannah tried again, giving it another turn and a strong tug at the same time. It opened suddenly with a loud squeak.

"Goodness, maybe the wardrobe's haunted," Connie giggled at the sound.

Hannah simply stared, pointing.

"Oh!" Connie felt goose bumps rise on the back of her neck. "It's—it's the dress in the portrait, isn't it?"

Neither moved, transfixed at the sight of the dresses. Hanging inside on padded hangers, there were three of them. The one in front that they could see best was the one Mary Lou Nelson had worn when she posed for the portrait at the courthouse.

"They're beautiful!" Connie's breathless reaction matched the awed expression on Hannah's face.

"And this one, it is isn't it? It has to be, surely?"

"It is. It's the one in the portrait." Hannah's wide eyes mirrored the excitement in Connie's. "I'm almost afraid to touch them."

"Maybe we can see what else there is in there without disturbing them."

Very carefully, Connie pressed against the dresses enough to see behind them. She reached inside and drew out two stiff arcs leaning on the wall behind them. A frayed ribbon held the arcs together.

"What do you suppose these are?"

"It must be whalebone. Jo Beth said you found a corset up here with whalebone in it."

As Hannah studied the two pieces Connie handed her, the ribbon fell to pieces.

"It's a hoop, Hannah! That's what it is. See how they must go together? It must be to go in the dresses."

Connie spotted the dressmaker's dummy across the attic and handed Hannah the hoop pieces. "Let's have a look at that contraption over there." She suited action to her suggestion.

"This dress maker's dummy doesn't look so bad considering how long it's been up here." She dusted the upper part with her handkerchief though it didn't seem to need it. Connie glanced around them.

"In fact, nothing up here is all that dusty. The mansion must be well built."

"It would have to be to have survived the years so well," Hannah agreed as she helped manage the thing.

"We're going to have to be awfully careful," she warned when they got the dummy rolled over to the wardrobe.

"We will. Here, hold the dress up so it won't touch the floor." Together they managed to get the dress on the dummy without any visible dust or damage to it.

Connie examined the hem. "Here's where the hoop goes in, this little slit. I guess we should fasten one side of it first."

"I did. They just snap together. "Hannah handed the whalebone hoop to her. She held up the skirt and turned the dummy slowly as Connie worked the hoop through the narrow seam.

"There!" They straightened the skirt and stood back to look at the result. The dress stood alone in regal splendor as if it had a personality of its own, the very picture of old fashioned elegance.

"This will be the highlight of the museum. It will have to be displayed under glass or some way that will protect it. Whoever would have dreamed we'd find this. How to take care of it will take some thought."

"Under glass sounds good to me. I've seen them done that way. And you can walk around them and see them from all sides. But I've got to go back down now. When I tell Jo Beth about this she'll break a leg getting up here." Hannah went out laughing to herself.

In no time at all Jo Beth was back. "I didn't know you could move that fast, Jo Beth," Connie teased her.

"I doubt I could have for anything else," Jo Beth admitted breathlessly. "Isn't this the prettiest thing!" She walked slowly around the dress, tilting her head to admire it from all sides and angles.

All the excitement hadn't kept Connie's back from getting tired. She went to one of the big trunks and leaned carefully against it as Jo Beth admired not only the dress on the dressmaker's dummy but the other two in the wardrobe as well.

"These are priceless, every one of them. And this one, to think it's the very one in the portrait! It will be the best thing in the museum since people can see the portrait then come and see the dress she wore. The museum will be a big success, I know it will. The Museum Committee will be so pleased about this," Jo Beth pictured their reaction to this boost for their project.

"And to think, all these years have gone by and we didn't even know these things were here."

Jo Beth came abruptly back to the present, seeing Connie leaning back against the trunk. "How are you doing with the boxes?"

"All right, I won't be much longer." Connie looked back at the open box she had been going through. "I'm going to look at a few more things in this one before I go."

"Back beginning to complain?"

"A little. I'm glad we can take our time with this and the things from the basement. There certainly is a wealth of things here."

"The Museum Committee will see that it's all done carefully and correctly. The whole town will be proud of this museum. I've got to go back down. Let's leave it as is for now. Just pull the door to firmly when you get ready to come down."

As Connie shut the attic door behind her she heard Jo Beth saying goodnight to Hannah.

"Go on and close up in a few minutes, half an hour at the most. I doubt there will be anyone else by today. They're all busy Christmas shopping."

"I will then. Goodnight, Jo Beth."

When the door closed, Connie called, "I'll be leaving soon too, Hannah."

"Had enough exploring for one day? Me too," Hannah called back. "When you come down just pull the door shut and it will lock. Goodnight."

The few night lights were on when she went downstairs and Connie walked slowly to the back reading room to get her coat. She admired all Miss Mayme's arrangements on the way then turned to look back at the stairway, experiencing a vague feeling something was wrong.

"Oh, no," she stifled a groan. "I guess Jo Beth must have been trying to help us. Well, I'm certainly not going to say anything, bless her heart. I'll just move this back where it belongs."

She took the big red velvet bow from the newel post and put it back at the top of the banister where Miss Mayme had put it.

CHAPTER 11

Cas couldn't keep from laughing out loud he was so pleased with his Christmas gift for Connie.

"I've found it, the perfect present! I've found one this time that will certainly surprise her. No run of the mill shopping for me. Or should I say run of the mall?"

He congratulated himself as he stopped to make sure the nursery men had placed the young shrubs in the truck so they wouldn't fall over and be damaged. He had picked out the two best ones and pictured them as Connie would see them.

"I'll stop by and get Clarence's grandson to plant them for me and surprise her when she gets home. Clarence will be wondering what I want this time." He pictured Clarence watching the street from his window.

Clarence did see him coming and noted the happy look about him as Cas came toward the house.

"Evening, Sheriff Larkin." He greeted him and held the door open. He paused, waiting to see what Cas wanted to tell him or ask him about.

Cas's question was completely unexpected.

"Is that big, strong grandson of yours around here somewhere? I've got a quick job for him if he's available and wants to make a little money."

Cas looked around but saw neither the grandson nor Clarence's mother.

"I'll holler him up for you. What you want him to do?" Clarence asked curiously.

"I've bought two young evergreen bushes for Connie for a Christmas present. But with this broken arm I need someone to dig the holes and plant them for me. I'd like to get it done before she comes home, if possible."

Clarence turned at the back door and bellowed, "Terrence!"

In a short time they heard someone coming up the back steps and he was there, looking askance at his grandfather. He was clad in old jeans and a sweatshirt, his big right hand holding a football.

He saw Cas over his grandfather's shoulder, "Yes, sir, you want me?"

Cas nodded, smiling as Terrence put his arm around his grandfather to give him an impulsive hug.

"If you're interested, I need someone to plant two trees, or rather, bushes, for me. I want to surprise my wife with them when she comes home. Could I get you to do it? I'll bring you back home if you can come with me now," Cas looked hopeful.

"Sure can." Terrence grinned at Clarence and threw the football to him. "I'm ready to go."

"My kind of guy," Cas grinned. "I'll bring him back home in a little while, Clarence."

"Wait a sec! Meet you in the driveway," Clarence said.

Terrence pointed out the back door.

Cas and Terrence went to get the shovel and Terrence took the sausage biscuit Clarence had brought him as he passed.

"I'm glad you have a good shovel. Mine isn't much, and only a hoe for backup."

"No problem. Ours is old too, but it's good to dig with."

Cas was happy with the gift he'd found for Connie and it didn't take too long to get the holes dug in spite of the cold. The soil was loamy and Terrence was young and strong.

He helped Cas straighten out the strings of outside lights and laid them on the steps.

"Thanks, Terrence. I can plug them in and loop them over the trees."

Cas had time to drop Terrence by home and hurry back to get the outside lights in place and turned on before Connie got there. He wasn't disappointed when she saw them. She pulled the car into the open garage then went back to admire the trees as he came out.

"Cas! They're beautiful! Live Christmas trees, they're a present to enjoy all year!" She looked at their reflections in the front windows then pulled him out into the yard to admire them with her. "They're so pretty and full, and they look just perfect there. Thank you!" She put her arms around his neck and kissed his cheek.

When she drew back, he said with a hurt expression. "They're bushes, I think, and there are TWO."

She laughed and kissed him again. "Okay, there's one for each bush. How about one for each light?" She tickled his side.

"Hey! I'm an old man with a broken arm. That's enough gratitude—for now," he added with a leer.

"And I'll throw in a good dinner. There's a roast in the crockpot."

"My nose told me that. And I'm properly grateful," he added quickly, holding the door for her.

Full of excitement about Casey and Missy coming home for the Christmas holidays Cathy called Connie Friday. "I can't believe they'll be here this weekend. Thanksgiving was just too short a holiday. Have you got all your decorating done?"

"Yes, here and at the library too. You'll have to come and see what Miss Mayme and Miss Minnie have done. The stairway is a work of art all by itself. I can't describe it. You'll have to see it. And they have all these lovely arrangements here and there too. It looks so nice. Like the old mansion must have looked when the Nelsons were living in it and decorated it for Christmas."

"I'll sure do that. I intended to come anyway and I have some news. Della Reubens is coming here to Maryvale with her daughter to do some Christmas shopping. She said if it's convenient, she will come Wednesday to look at the library basement. I'm going to call Jo Beth this afternoon to let her know. I don't think she was overjoyed when she first heard about it, but at least she doesn't object."

"Now would be a good time to talk to her. She's in a good humor," Connie said sounding mysterious.

"She is? What was it that brought on this happy condition?"

"We opened the attic in the library. Cathy, it's chock full of absolutely priceless things. Things that just reek of the time when the Nelsons lived in the mansion." Connie's voice was rising with excitement.

"The best thing is the dress in the portrait of Mary Lou. It's there, Cathy!"

"You don't mean the dress in the portrait that's hanging in the courthouse?"

"Oh, yes I do. And it's complete with a hoop!"

"Oh, my stars, as my Granny used to say. A hoop! I've got to see that—if they'll let me. I may be pushing my luck," Cathy sounded uncertain.

"Well, as Cas says about iffy things, we'll play it by ear. There's going to be so much to put in the museum they're trying to get together we may need more space than they've arranged for."

"I'd heard a little about it but this sounds lead-pipe certain now with all this to go in it. Are the things in good condition? They've been up there in that attic for an awfully long time."

"I know, and they're fragile. But the dresses aren't even faded. And I brought home two journals of Mary Lou's. They're in her own handwriting. One she wrote in when she was about ten years old or so, I'd guess. The other doesn't seem to have much in it but I brought it home to read anyway. Oh, and let me tell you something funny."

Connie told her how Miss Mayme had worried over the stairway and designed the decorations just so, and about the red bow Jo Beth had found that started their look around the attic.

"Miss Mayme put the wreath at the top of the stair and every time we leave, Jo Beth puts it back at the bottom of the stair! I'm sure not going to say anything. But it's such a funny situation, I can hardly keep from laughing."

"That is funny. I can just picture it. It's one of those Three Stooges situations where none of them know what the others are up to," Cathy giggled. "Listen, if you don't hear from me to the contrary, I'll be at the library Wednesday as soon as Della Reubens shows up. You're going to be there, aren't you?"

"Oh, I'll be there. You know I wouldn't want to miss that. And it looks like we'll be working all next year on these Nelson family things. Before we found the things in the attic I promised to help preserve, mount, or whatever, all that stuff that I brought up from the basement. And with those and the things from the attic too."

"I get the picture. And you'll be slowed down, no doubt, by good advice from the City Beautiful and the Museum Committee."

"I don't know," Connie sounded doubtful. "I don't know how working with them will be yet. I only know we'll all be at it for a good long while with so much work to do. But back to Della Reubens, I'll definitely be there Wednesday. I can't wait to hear what she will have to say about that basement."

"Me either. To wonder about it and make guesses is one thing, but to have it confirmed by someone who has at least the reputation of knowing about such things, I sort of have mixed feelings about it. Suppose she does say someone is trying to call to us for help? I can't see just leaving it at that, can you?"

"No." Disturbing as it was, Connie agreed. "No, I can't. How could you just walk away from something like that, needing help and so sad. But my husband has already informed me I can't go if there is a séance."

"What? What do you mean, you can't go?"

"He doesn't think I should go, that it won't look good to the people he depends on to vote for him and give him their support to keep things on an even keel in the county. You can see that point of view, can't you?"

"Well," Cathy gave an exasperated sigh, "He's probably right. There are some awfully buttoned down minds here in Maryvale, not that they aren't all good people."

She paused then added, "I just hadn't thought about it in that light."

"But even if I can't go it won't do any harm to ask her about it. Or she may just talk to you about it on her own after she's heard the crying. The others who know about it will want to go if she does hold a séance, I'm sure of that. I'd be there too, if it weren't for the position Cas is in about public opinion and votes."

"We'll have to wait and see what Della Reubens says about a séance when she comes Wednesday. But you know she must be pretty sure there is something unnatural there, to have agreed to come at all. Connie, I'm sorry you won't be able to go."

"Oh, I'll live. Let me brag on Cas, now that I've told you he set his foot down about my going if there's a séance. He surprised me with my Christmas present early, and you'll never guess what it was!"

Cathy refused to be misled by Connie's excitement. "Humpf, men are usually predictable. I found that out when I worked one season at a shop in the mall. They all want to buy either a negligee or a blouse, and none of them know one thing about what size to get."

Cathy giggled, "My guess would be a blouse, a sexy negligee, or if he wanted to play it safe, a handbag. Of course, the blouse and the nightie wouldn't fit, and the handbag would match nothing you've ever owned in your entire life. Am I close?"

"No, you cynic. Not even in the old ballpark! I saw it when I drove in. He bought two beautiful little holly bushes or trees, I don't think he knows either whether they're bushes or trees, so he gave them plenty of room when he planted them. They're about four feet high. He got them from the nursery, had someone plant them, and got the outside lights on them and had them all lit up and looking pretty before I got home. Now, aren't you impressed?"

"I am! All that with a broken arm! My compliments to the Head of the House," Cathy conceded good naturedly.

"He made a good choice. And you're right, it must have been a bother too, to have to get someone to plant them for him with that arm in a cast."

"The more I think about it the more impressed I get. Cas is one of those people who are always there to depend on. You don't stop to think they have bad days along with the hard decisions they have to make like everyone else. I'm looking forward to seeing the new trees soon. It certainly was an original idea. I guess we can forgive him his concern about the voters," her grin was audible.

"That's what I thought when I saw the trees. And I'm depending on you to tell me everything immediately if there is a séance."

"I will, you can count on it. See you Wednesday."

CHAPTER 12

Casey's faithful old heap deposited Missy in the Larkin's driveway, home if only for a brief holiday. She stood a moment after getting out of the car to look at the front windows.

"Don't call mom, I want to surprise her." Casey stuck his head out the window and called, his foot on the clutch as he waved.

Missy nodded and waved back. Inside, she went to the front window and watched as Casey drove out the driveway.

"Welcome home," Connie came to give her a hug. "I thought I heard the car, I was upstairs cleaning."

Missy returned her hug before looking back out the window. "Mom, I knew there was something different out there. It's those two pretty little trees. They're new, aren't they?"

"Yes, aren't they just right there? Dad got them for me for Christmas. He really surprises me sometimes with his good ideas. Come on out and look at them," Connie led the way.

"Real holly trees and loaded with berries! And they've got lights on them. They look just right there and it's getting dark enough for the lights to show up. I'll have to tell Dad tonight how proud I am of him."

She smiled and picked a few small twigs and some longer ones with berries to take into the house.

"I'm going to put these on the table," she decided.

Connie baked cup cakes while Missy chose things for her holly arrangement.

As she looked over the glass assortment on a top shelf Connie reminded her, "There are lots of things you could use in the shelves out in the laundry room. There are some odd vases and all sorts of baskets, and some silk flowers too."

"What about red ones?"

"Yes, there are some red ones you might want to use with the holly."

"I'd forgot you had all those things out there. I'll go see what we have to use. I remember Dad telling you once when you were looking at baskets somewhere that you had more than the shop had on display," Missy laughed at the memory and her mother's weakness for baskets and decorations.

"He teases me about being one rung above pack rat. He has no appreciation of a good sale unless it's on something to go in the freezer." Connie wrinkled her nose.

Missy came back from the laundry room looking pleased. She had a bowl, a basket and two or three silk poinsettias in her arms. "Dad was right," she nodded at her load of things. "But I'm glad. It's nice to have so much to choose from."

"I'll put my cup cakes over here on the counter when I take them out so you can work on the table."

"Thanks." Missy had already spread everything out and set to work concentrating as seriously as Miss Mayme would have. "How is Dad's arm doing, does it bother him very much?"

"No. I mean, it's not painful, only inconvenient sometimes. Like when he's showering."

"Showering. I'll bet it is, I hadn't thought about that."

"He gets all ready, the water just right, then he eases in and holds the arm with the cast on it outside the curtain. I've offered to wash his back if he wanted to get in the tub, but he prefers the shower."

"How is he managing at work?"

"He's driving the truck while his car is in the shop. He says it's easy to handle and he doesn't do all that much driving. It came in handy when he decided to buy the trees, to be in the truck." Connie smiled, "I'm really pleased he thought of getting them."

"I am too." Missy rearranged a couple of the holly sprigs. "I'm looking forward to seeing how they look tonight when it's really dark."

"You'll have to come and see the decorations the Anderson sisters put in the library, too. And do you remember hearing me and Cathy Taylor talking about the cold in the library basement?"

"I don't think so. If I did it didn't register for some reason, I guess. What do you mean it's cold?"

"Just that it's terribly cold down there. Then when you've been there a few minutes, you can hear someone crying."

"Crying?" Missy stopped and turned to Connie. "But, you don't mean—you think it's haunted?" Missy wondered if she had heard wrong or misunderstood.

Connie shrugged. "We don't know. Some of us do wonder. And others that know about it say it's probably something that has a logical explanation."

"What do you think, Mom?" Missy stuck in the last sprig of holly.

"I don't know. But it doesn't seem natural. There's a woman named Della Reubens coming Wednesday to see what she thinks about it. She's what you'd call a medium, she used to hold séances."

"Séances?" Missy's eyebrows rose. "And Dad's got two murders to investigate. My goodness, all this excitement right here in Maryvale! I thought I'd got out into the sophisticated mainstream now that I'm in college, and all the excitement is right here at home!" Missy laughed.

"I'd keep an open mind about all this, mom. Those people that get you all excited about the supernatural are mostly fakes," she cautioned. "But it will be fun to see what she says about it."

"You sound like your Dad. I told him about it and all he's sure of is if there is a séance, I am not to attend. I couldn't imagine why and asked what would be the harm in it. And he told me, in no uncertain terms."

Connie tilted her head as Cas sometimes did when he was making a point, and did a good imitation of his tone of voice. "Would you vote for someone for sheriff whose wife was out trying to raise the dead?"

They both collapsed laughing, elbows on the table.

"Well, I'll tell you right now, I wouldn't!" Missy wiped her eyes. "He's got a point there. But I'm sorry you won't get to go. Talk about something different to do! They can't hang us for wanting to hear about it, can they?"

"Certainly not. And if there is one I'll hear all the details, you can bet on that."

Missy pushed the longest holly sprig down a bit and examined her arrangement with a critical eye. "What do you think?"

"It's lovely. Exactly what we needed to make the table look festive."

"You wouldn't be prejudiced, would you?"

"No. I'm nosy enough to be helping if I thought it needed something. It looks as good as Miss Mayme's things she makes up for their shop. You know," Connie considered the arrangement thoughtfully, "The library is pretty inside with all the decorations. Miss Mayme and Miss Minnie have done so much and they've got eye catching arrangements everywhere. But not being there at night, I hadn't thought about the outside. There's nothing outside except the two wreaths on the double doors. Wouldn't it be nice to have two trees or bushes like ours only smaller for the library? A holly bush on each side of the walk as you go up the steps?"

"It would look gay and Christmassy at night if they had lights on them all right."

"I'll ask the City Beautiful Commission about it. They probably have some money left in their Christmas budget. It won't take all that much."

"I guess you're planning on being there Wednesday when this séance lady comes?" Missy's upper lip twitched.

"I can see that skeptical grin trying to get through," Connie accused. "And yes. I am. I've got enough to do there to keep me busy all the spare time I have anyway."

"That much?" Missy couldn't understand such volume. "I knew you were looking up some of the old news items about the Nelson family."

"That's just it. The old papers are in bad shape. Some will have to be mounted, some preserved between plastic or whatever they want to do. But you haven't heard the latest."

"You've found more? In the basement?"

Connie shook her head. "The attic. There's a lot of things in the attic. It's never been used by the library, but the key is with the other keys they have. Jo Beth called and got permission to go up and look for Christmas decorations and found a lot of stuff that had been left there by the Nelsons."

"Called who? Are we back to the spirit world again?"

"Smarty! She called and got permission from the City Beautiful Commission. There's a museum committee too now. They're the ones who gave her permission."

"You mean after talking about it for so long they're actually getting off the ground with the museum idea?"

"They sure are. It's going to be near the back of the courthouse. They've already got just a few things stored there. We've been going through some of the things in the attic and there seems to be enough there to fill the museum. And Missy, the best thing is we found the dress Mary Lou Nelson was wearing in the portrait of her in the courthouse."

"You didn't!" Missy's eyes sparkled. "As old as it must be, Mom, did it have a hoop skirt?"

Connie nodded. "It was hanging in a lovely old wardrobe with two other dresses. The hoop was there too, and it's whalebone."

"Whalebone!"

"Yes, whalebone. We put the dress on a dressmaker's dummy that's up there and threaded the hoop through the bottom. The dress is not even faded."

"Could I take you to work and use that as an excuse to go in and see the dress? Do you think they would let me?"

"We won't ask so no one will have a chance to say no. When you come in with me I'll take the journal I brought home with me back up there and you can go with me."

"You found a journal? Whose was it?"

"It was Mary Lou Nelson's. She must have written in it when she was about ten years old. That reminds me, I want to ask your Dad about a Lacey Lynch. Several times she's written: Lacey Lynch is coming to play with me today in the journal."

"Wow, she wrote in it all those years ago," Missy turned to gaze out the window.

"I see Dad's truck!" She ran to meet her Dad, old fashioned journals forgotten in the joy of being home.

Connie listened to the glad sounds from both of them as Missy tried to figure out how to give him a hug without hurting his arm. They came in on a wave of laughter and brisk winter air, both talking at once, the catching up and sharing of news enhanced by the special season.

"It seems every time I come home I've been gone for years, and this is the last nice long visit. There will be only weekends until spring."

"By the time you're home for spring break or in June at the latest, surely the museum will be finished and open to the public," Connie consoled her. "So you'll have something to look forward to."

After dinner Missy went with Casey to admire the town's Christmas decorations and Connie took her and Cas's coffee into the den.

"How is everything going on your two cases? Have you found anything else to go on?"

"No. Other than the bare facts I already knew and some early hints from Clint. I still have the feeling Clarence knows more than he's telling me and he knows I know it.

That's what's making him uncomfortable. I'm hoping he'll get worried enough to tell me whatever it is."

Connie paused, concerned. "You surely don't think he, that it was Clarence?"

"No. No, Welemon was his nephew. He'd never have hurt his sister's child. I don't know what it is he's not telling me, but there's something, I'm sure of that."

An idea occurred to him. "Since you're the family worrier, let me ask you something."

Connie smiled at the title of worrier and waited, curious.

"When Clarence found Welemon, he and a neighbor got him up and brought him to the hospital. Clarence said he knew it was too late but he was alive and they tried to get help for him. There's always hope. Then after the doctor told them plainly how bad it was but assured them everything they could do was being done for Welemon, Clarence had his neighbor take him home. That bothers me."

"Maybe the neighbor had to leave."

"No, I've talked to everybody I can connect with this at all, and the neighbor himself said Clarence told him to bring him home."

"Did he not even go back?"

"Yes, he went back later. His grandson drove him. But he had already called the hospital and they told him Welemon was gone, really. He never opened his eyes or spoke. All Clarence could do was see him one last time."

Cas's worry lines deepened. "There's no point in asking you what you and I would have done. If any of us had been there with a family member, we'd have stayed. Clarence's reasons for leaving sound like flimsy excuses to me."

"What exactly does he say?"

"Said he didn't want to keep his neighbor there and he would come back. But the neighbor is a kind man, he'd have stayed or come back for him. What do you think?"

"Sometimes when you don't know what to do, or there's nothing you can do, I can see where he'd get confused. And too, at a time like that, he probably wanted some of his own family with him. Who did you say took him back?"

"His grandson. When they got Welemon to the hospital they let Clarence know how bad his condition was and explained what they had to do in cases like this, that they had to be reported, I mean. And then after talking to the doctor Clarence left. I couldn't understand that. But you may be right. He may have felt better with some of the family with him. I didn't think of that."

"It's hard to tell what you'd do in a case like that. Will you ask him about something for me? It has nothing to do with what happened to Welemon."

"Ask Clarence?"

"Yes. In the journal I brought home, the one Mary Lou Nelson wrote in when she was a child, she mentions a Lacey Lynch. Several times she mentions her name and a lot of the entries end with Lacey Lynch is coming to play with me tomorrow or today. Sometimes it adds while her mother helps with the baking, or different household things."

"Lacey Lynch. And the right age to play with Mary Lou, from what she said. I know the family has been here as long as the town. They go way back as the saying goes."

"And it's spelled the same. L Y N C H, so it must have been someone in his family."

"This restoring the things in the attic and the old papers in the basement is really exciting to you, isn't it?" Cas folded the paper with a curious glance. "Is that Louis DeVille as good looking as you said he was?"

"He was. He could be a movie star today." Connie grinned at the thought and pictured Louie as Rhett Butler. "He's what you think of when you hear someone described as tall, dark, and handsome. They must have made a handsome couple, the portrait of Mary Lou is so pretty. They must have looked like they belonged together."

"Too bad Nelson didn't see it that way." Cas thought about how glad he was Missy was dating Casey Taylor.

"Um-hum, according to everybody, Nelson was dead set against him from the first. The consensus is Nelson shot himself because Mary Lou ran off with DeVille. Some of it's got to be nothing but hearsay, but I found an item in the papers we brought upstairs about his death. It's edged in black and says Nelson died by his own hand. So that part isn't hearsay. It did happen. The young people must have gone to France and may not even have known about it."

"That's one thing that hasn't changed. No one can know all about a situation except the ones who are there and involved in it. There are lots of things we will never know about what happened." Cas shrugged, "But the museum will be a good thing for the town to have. Give it some place in history. Some roots, you might say. And the town was named for Mary Lou."

"The romantic story about handsome and beautiful and powerful people makes it interesting. Romance is popular, that hasn't changed either." She smiled as she got up and stretched. "Want to come upstairs and share my bubble bath? I'll wash your back," she invited.

"I'll take a rain check on it, but you can wash it in my shower later if the offer extends that far?"

"I guess so." On the way out she added, "When I finish I'm going to get comfortable and read the journal Mary Lou wrote in as a young lady."

"There doesn't seem to be much in it." She mused to herself after a quick look at it. "Maybe I'll wait until tomorrow."

CHAPTER 13

"Happy Tuesday, Sheriff Larkin!"

A young male and smiling face appeared at the door facing, feet still waiting outside for an invitation.

"Casey! How good to see you." Cas greeted him, surprised as well as pleased to see him.

"Thanks, same here. If you're too busy right now to visit a little I can stop by another time," Casey began self-consciously.

"Now is fine. Come on in. There's nothing much going on. People are too busy to get into much trouble during the holidays. And before you ask, my arm is making progress as they say at the hospital."

Cas grinned. "In fact, I'm considering keeping the cast to get out of things I don't want to do."

"Might work with the county but you'll need a lot of luck to get by with that at home." Casey solemnly advised.

"Sounds like the voice of experience," Cas chuckled. "Maybe I'd better give it a little more thought." He glanced briefly at the files on his desk.

Casey noticed the look. "Is that the file on Welemon Lynch? And the other one, what was his name?"

"Peder Sellczk."

"Two murder cases," Casey's interest showed. "And close together, too."

Cas nodded. "I'm not having much luck with either one of them. I have the gut feeling they're somehow connected but I can't come up with anything. Aside from their being strangers to Maryvale. Welemon hadn't been around for a while is why I'm calling him a stranger. And both of them were dopers. That's all I've got besides my famous gut feeling about a connection," Cas admitted regretfully.

"What can you do in a case like that, just pray a lot?" Casey looked embarrassed at having asked.

"You sound like you've had experience with hopeless cases. That's about it at this point. I've asked questions of everyone I can think of who might have known or seen either of them and of course, Welemon's family. But something will turn up. It always does. It may take a while, but nobody gets away with murder no matter what you see on television."

Casey was still standing and Cas got up, reaching for his jacket. "I'm going to ride over to Marble County, do you have time to go with me?"

"Sure! I'd like to."

"Okay," Cas stuck the files in a desk drawer and locked it. "I'll tell Gladys and we'll go."

Casey's pleasure at being permitted to go somewhere with Cas was obvious. He had admired him ever since he'd met him on a case he was investigating before he and Missy had started dating in high school.

Cas measured up to what Casey thought a law officer should be. Able to cope with any problem that came up and still retain some compassion for the people he dealt with. He watched Cas drive, admiring his one armed expertise as he handled the truck. He watched the passing scenery and announced happily, "I'll pretend I'm on the payroll."

Cas studied him with a sideways glance. He looked like a little boy playing sheriff, he thought. A wave of affection for the boy whose father had died young caught him off guard.

"This is a good example of the job," Cas said as he watched the road. "Most of it's leg work, paperwork, and plain old routine digging."

"You mean it's not as exciting as the write-ups in the paper?" Casey let an 'aw shucks' expression spread across his face.

"No. But when the exciting part comes you'd better be ready to deal with it. That's what the training's for."

"I'll bet," Casey nodded. "Makes you appreciate the routine and dull days, is that it?"

"You got it," Cas grinned.

They stopped to have hot chocolate before crossing the line into Marble County.

"Got to keep my business support at home," Cas explained with a straight face as he paid for their chocolate.

"Good idea. Why are you going to Marble County, or shouldn't I ask?"

"I'm going to pick up the back panel of the car that got bumped off the bridge incline out near the cemetery. They used it as part of the evidence against the man who did it."

"How was it evidence, did the damage match up?"

Cas nodded, "That and the paint. The truck left some of its paint at the point of impact. Now that they're through with it I'll take it to the body shop to hammer out the damage and put it back on instead of getting a new one. Keeps our insurance rates down."

Casey thought that over. "That's a good idea. The schools should send students on field trips to the county offices. Or have someone from your department or the city police department from Fort Craig, maybe, go and talk to the students. You know, like they used to have Career Day in elementary school." Casey lightened up, "Look at all I'm learning here. And for free!"

Cas laughed with him. "You'd better quit while you're winning, I might start charging for my tutoring."

"That would scare me if I had any money!" Casey and Cas laughed at their mutual financial condition.

At the Marble County Sheriff's Office, Harlan Glover saw them from his office when they entered.

"Cas," he boomed, coming to meet them. "And who is this handsome young gent? A recruit?"

He eyed Casey and Cas comparing the two of them. "Danged if you don't look like Before and After. Like: don't let Law Enforcement happen to you!'" he guffawed at his own humor.

"Thank you, noble friend," Cas assumed an affronted stance.

"Well, you going to introduce us or are you too mad now?" Harlan agitated, winking at Casey.

"This is Casey Taylor. Casey, this is my sparring partner, Harlan Glover. Meanest mouth in the South to those unfortunate enough to be acquainted with him."

Harlan extended his big paw, paying no attention to the insult or taking any offense as he ushered them into his office.

"We came to pick up the back panel of my car now that the trial's over. Hope they got put away for a long time."

"They did, you can rest easy on that. With the charges for speeding, dope possession and dealing, not to mention the attempted killing of a law officer, neither one of them will even be up for parole for twenty years."

Harlan pulled another chair into the office. "How about some coffee or a cold drink?"

"I'll pass, but thank you," Casey politely declined.

"I'll have coffee, one sugar," Cas ordered.

The receptionist nodded from the door and Harlan turned his attention back to Cas. "You look pretty good for what you've been through. Good thing someone passed by and saw the car go over." He gestured at the mending arm, "That cast getting itchy?"

"That part of it was lucky too. It's not so bad wearing a cast in cool weather." Cas examined the floor beside Harlan's desk. "Where's your brass spittoon?"

"Gone. Had to give up my tobacco," Harlan said through clenched teeth.

"You quit chewing tobacco?" Cas stared in disbelief, wondering if this was one of Harlan's tricks.

"Worse than that. Cold turkey. None of that tapering off stuff. You remember Harry Keller? His son played in the minor leagues and looked like he had a great future, was set to go on to the majors?"

"Yes," Cas thought back. "Haven't heard anything about him or his career in a while, come to think of it."

"You won't, except maybe in the obits. He got sick, ended his career. I don't know if he's still alive or not."

Cas shook his head, "That's tough. He's about thirty-two or so, isn't he?"

"I think that's about right, maybe a little older but not much. He had a wife and two kids."

"Had. Must have been something bad happened to him?"

"He got cancer."

"Was it because he chewed? Seems to me his dad did too. And he got cancer?"

"Yeah. They said it was. I ran across Harry when I was visiting someone else in the hospital. His son was there for treatment."

Harlan's distress creased his worry lines. "I went in to see him, had to, running into Harry like that. But it was rough."

Harlan took a deep breath before going on. "His whole upper lip was gone. They said the roof of his mouth was too. You could see some teeth, roots and gums. It was awful, just awful. He'd have had to stand up twice to cast a shadow, he was so thin. That was the day I quit, Cas. I wish everybody that chews or smokes could get the warning I had."

"That's a shame. He had so much going for him. And two young children. I'm sorry to hear about it."

One of Harlan's deputies came to the door and asked to speak to him before he left and Cas got up, motioning to Casey.

"I won't keep you, Harlan."

Harlan held up a hand. "This won't take long, whatever it is."

"We just came for the car panel, it was a good excuse for a little visiting," Cas smiled.

"It's there in the corner, but wait. It won't take me long to see what's needed out here."

When he came back he and Casey saw to the task of getting the panel in the truck bed safely so it wouldn't rattle. Casey stifled his laughter at their antics and Cas's impossible instructions.

On the way back Casey confided, "I'm thinking about taking criminology. If I ever get to the point where there aren't so many required things and I can."

"Oh, you'll get there. And so much has been learned in the field it will be an interesting subject." Cas's voice was wistful and he was pleased at Casey's choice.

"There's so much to cover and so many related things. Even to the lab work and forensic medicine now. There's a wide choice as well as modern methods and tools we never had before."

Casey nodded, listening to everything Cas told him as they returned to Maryvale.

Connie was surprised to see Missy up so early Tuesday morning. "Hi, Early Bird. Thought you might want to sleep this morning. Dad just left a few minutes ago."

"I heard. I waved out the window but he didn't see me. What's for breakfast? I'll pass on the worms."

"We're out of worms anyway. They really don't freeze worth a hoot," Connie rejoined so seriously Missy giggled. "What about some eggs and sausage?"

"You don't happen to have any of that venison sausage left, do you?"

"Sure do. I made it into patties and froze what we didn't use immediately. It won't take long to fix."

"That's great. I'll have an egg over light with one sausage patty. While you do all that I'll do the toast and get out the orange juice."

They busied themselves with that efficient plan and were soon seated at the kitchen table. Connie enjoyed her second cup of coffee while Missy ate her breakfast. The journal Mary Lou Nelson wrote lay on the table beside her.

"What's that you're reading, mom?"

"It's a journal we found in the library attic. The one I told you about that Mary Lou Nelson wrote in when she was a little girl. It's charming. She talks about getting a new blue velvet dress that's the color of her eyes and a new riding habit."

Missy pictured the little girl in her old fashioned clothes and Connie continued.

"She fusses about all those petticoats, but she's tickled she's going to get to go riding with her Dad. And here, she talks about someone named Addeline. She doesn't like her very much," Connie made a face. "She says she's bossy. She has a music box for her birthday."

She looked up at Missy, "She says she's going to keep the music box and give her hose and a set of combs for her hair." She laughed, picturing the little girls.

"I guess little girls haven't changed as much as the fashions have." Missy was amused as her mother at the little girl's thoughts on her daily life she had written down so long ago.

"I've still got the other one to read. There were two of the journals. The other one was written when she was older but there's not much in it. I haven't had a chance to look at it yet. This is the best one."

"Are you going to town today?"

"Yes, there's so much to do in the attic. And of course I go in and read the material we brought up from the basement every time I get a chance. I want to call the City Beautiful Commission too, after I've talked to Jo Beth. Come with me if you want to."

"I'll ride down with you if you can wait about an hour to go. I want to do a couple of things."

"That's fine. It will give me time to read some of the other journal. I'd only read a few pages when I had to put it down. Just enough to know she was older when she wrote in it. It couldn't be as interesting as the first one."

Missy ran her finger over the spine of the old book. "You can almost see a little girl in an old fashioned dress, hearing some of those passages. Neat, finding all this stuff for the museum to use. And it's nice the Andersons are decorating the old mansion, too. I've missed being home to see all the decorations and look at the shop windows."

Connie nodded. "The Commission has done wonders with the street decorations. Everything looks so Christmassy, even better than last year. The library is the last of the new projects, and the Andersons were paid for some of that. But most of the things like the arrangements, they supplied free to get the advertising."

"Does the Methodist Church still have carolers in costume on Christmas Eve? I don't remember seeing them last year."

"They do." Connie thought back, "I think there was a party or something you went to at the same time last year." She picked up the other journal. "Let me know when you're ready to go."

The second journal was not kept daily, but had random entries neatly dated at the beginning of each of them. Connie read with interest about the daily happenings and special events Mary Lou described. It told a lot about the clothes and the socializing at the time, and the formal way they spoke to each other. She noted there were several mentions of young men. Some of them Mary Lou described as at least sufferable. Or that they had evidently read one or two books not mainly composed of pictures. Connie smiled to herself at Mary Lou's low opinion of most of them.

"Oh! Here's where she met Louis DeVille! At a ball!"

Connie ate it up like a romance novel, which it was. Historic, but true to life in that era and made all the more romantic by the aura of mystery.

"He's the handsomest man I've ever seen, she says. He's a few years older than she is, and from France. How romantic! Mary Lou was fascinated with him and said she could listen to him talk all night, his accent is so pleasing." Connie smiled.

Louie was noted in the journal as being a good dancer, too, and able to do the most modern steps. I guess after meeting him, she thought everything he did was well done. A good looking young man, and a Frenchman, from a prominent family in France.

The following entries though brief, showed the developing affection between them. Several things indicated Nelson's seemingly dislike of DeVille. Connie read on, feeling things were building to a confrontation of some kind. There was not much more, Connie couldn't put it down until she had read all there was. She quickly scanned the last few pages.

"Oh dear, she says it would serve Papa right if I ran off with Louis! She's so upset! I can tell by her writing she's angry. It even affected her handwriting. And there are no more entries." Connie's brows drew together. "That's all there is."

Her fingers traced the sentences scrawled in anger, "It would serve Papa right!"

Connie sat holding the journal and shuddered, feeling like she knew Mary Lou and Louis DeVille and felt their trouble coming. Her unseeing eyes were still on the closed journal when she heard Missy coming downstairs.

"Ready, Mom?"

"Fine. Me too. I'll get my purse."

The phone rang as Connie passed it. It was Cathy Taylor.

"Just wanted to remind you that Della Reubens is coming tomorrow. You're going to be there, aren't you?"

"I sure am. Missy and I were just leaving for the library to do some reading. I mean I am. Missy is going window shopping. What time is Della Reubens coming to your house?"

"That's what I called to tell you. Her daughter thought it would be easier to take her on to the library instead of hunting for my house, since that's where we're going anyway. She said they would be there between nine and ten o'clock. I'm going to be there a little before nine to be on the safe side."

"Good idea, I will too. See you tomorrow."

CHAPTER 14

Connie looked critically at the space on either side of the front walk as she pulled up in front of the library.

"It might be best to put them on each side of the steps that go up to the porch if you're going to run wires to the lights." Missy suggested as they looked at the space.

"Right, and they would look nicer there than out here by the sidewalk. If we can get the size I'd like, they won't grow very fast or very high. They would tie in nicely with the light coming through the doors and the candles in the wreaths. The wreaths already show up well. Of course," Connie reminded herself before she got too carried away with the idea, "I've got to see what the City Beautiful Commission says about it first." She held the door for Missy.

Inside, Missy's eyes went immediately to the stairway.

"Oh Mom, it's beautiful! It's even prettier than I was picturing it. The Anderson sisters must really be good at what they do." Her eyes were dreamy as she pictured the house decorated for Christmas with the family living there when Mary Lou Nelson was a little girl. Her mother's voice broke into her reverie.

"Oh my goodness, there is it again!"

Exasperated, Connie marched to the big red velvet bow on the newel post at the bottom of the stair and began taking it loose.

"Mom! Don't do that, it's perfect right there. Where else would you put it, for heaven's sake?"

Connie released the bow, taken aback at Missy's reaction to moving it. "What? Well, Miss Mayme put it at the top of the stair. She said when there were lots of people moving around in here, it could be seen from anywhere in this big room."

Jo Beth had come to see what they were doing. "I think it looks nice where it is too, if I get to vote." She cast admiring eyes at the stairway and the bow.

"Did you put it there? It does look just as nice there," Connie hastily added so Jo Beth's feelings wouldn't be hurt.

"No, none of us here touched any of the decorations. Only Miss Minnie and Miss Mayme and you. And it all looks wonderful. Just right to give everyone the Christmas spirit who comes in and sees it. Of course, any of us would have helped if we'd been needed and asked to." Jo Beth was puzzled about their concern with the bow.

But Miss Mayme put it at the top of the stair, hadn't she? Connie silently gazed up at the top of the stair again. If it wasn't Jo Beth or some of the library people who moved it, who could have? Connie puzzled about it silently.

Connie got a grip on herself. "Well, no matter. We'll leave it right here where it is and if Miss Mayme wants to move it she can do it when she comes back. She's the professional, after all."

She looked again at the bow. "I don't know why I didn't notice it before, Missy's right. It looks better here anyway."

Missy toured all the way back to the reading room, impressed with the Anderson's arrangements and other work before she left to window shop. "Do you want me to be back here before about three or so, Mom?"

"No, take your time and enjoy yourself. And be careful."

Giggling at that, Missy went back and gave her mother a

hug. "I don't think I could go off on any adventure in life, no matter how fabulous, without you to tell me to be careful." She kissed Connie's cheek.

Jo Beth looked on, her approval obvious. Connie watched Missy go out and turned to her. "Could I use your phone? I'm going to call the City Beautiful Commission and ask if there's any more money left to buy a couple of small holly trees, if you approve of what I have in mind."

"Of course. You're welcome to use it any time. What is this about holly trees?"

"Come let me show you." Connie took her out to look at the front and told her about the Christmas present Cas had bought her. "What do you think?"

"I think it would look really nice and we would enjoy them every year. But the Commission may not have any money left for them in the budget. If we can't get them this year we can put them on our wish list, maybe get them next year. But it won't hurt to ask. I'll cross my fingers."

Jo Beth went back to replacing books on the shelves and Connie reached for the phone.

To her relief, the call was answered promptly by a friendly voice who was the soul of cooperation.

"It so happens there is a small amount of money left in the budget. And the bushes sound like a good idea. I was thinking the library needs something that will show up at night. In fact, someone mentioned it at one of our meetings but we never got around to considering it with all the other things that are going on. And there not being much money left either, it sort of just died like some of our other ideas that involved money," she chuckled.

Connie was already picturing the decorated holly trees when the next question came.

"What size bushes will be needed? Are they called trees or bushes?"

"I don't know. They told Cas they don't grow very fast so I call them bushes most of the time. What I'm picturing is little ones, with the small dark green pointy leaves and lots of red berries. I'm hoping to get some about three feet tall that don't cost too much. They shouldn't cost too much this close to Christmas with all the sales going on."

"Be sure to tell them they're for the library too, that might help."

"I will. We could plant them far enough from the porch and the steps to give them room to grow. It should be years before growth is a problem anyway and they can be kept trimmed like the rest of the shrubs. They will have to be close enough to the porch to hook up the lights, of course." She quickly added, "If we can find some lights, or have enough money left for some. Jo Beth was hoping you might have some Christmas money left?"

"We're in luck there, Mrs. Larkin. Money's scarce as always, but there are two strands of outdoor lights here that weren't used anywhere."

"Wonderful! It was beginning to sound too expensive to me, too, and we've got to have lights of course."

"Well, there's no use these going to waste, if we can get the bushes. I'll go to the nursery myself and see about them."

"Fine. Call me from the nursery when you've had a chance to see what they've got. I'm at the library." Connie gave her the number and replaced the receiver looking pleased.

"Those holly bushes will be pretty. I guess I was eavesdropping." Jo Beth spoke as she came around a shelf. "We do need something out there to brighten up the front at night and it sounds like the Commission thinks so too. Who did you talk to?"

"Oh, heavens, Jo Beth! I didn't think to ask. But she's going to call me from the nursery when she checks on the bushes. I'll be back there reading and separating papers."

Jo Beth nodded and it wasn't long before Connie was engrossed in her work. She doubted something you wanted to do should be called work. She touched the fragile papers carefully as she sorted them into stacks, reading most of the material as she came to it and paying particular attention to pictures and notices in large print.

She stopped, looking closer at a picture. "This is Nelson, I'm sure of it."

Connie reached for her purse and got out the magnifying glass she always brought with her. Peering closer at the picture she found it was Nelson. She recognized him from pictures in the reference books and his name was in the caption. She studied it closely with her glass.

"It must be some kind of to-do here in the mansion. He's receiving people for some event near Christmas, judging by the decorations."

Nelson was standing by the stairway which looked lovely, much as it did now. Her eyes studied the grand sweep of the stairway and the greenery. "But I'll bet all that greenery was real then. More than likely it was gathered by the young people and servants from the grounds. And there's the big red velvet bow!"

She caught her breath, holding the paper up to get the best light.

"It's right there where he's standing. It does belong there on the newel post."

Connie straightened up and shuddered as an eerie finger of cold foreboding traced her spine. "And somebody," she held her breath an instant, peering intently through the magnifying glass again, "Somebody knows it! Oh, I've got gooseflesh. I don't think I'll say anything, I'll wait and when Miss Mayme comes back over here and notices it, I'll show her this picture." She stifled a grin. "If I can keep the secret that long. She and Miss Minnie did promise not to have me committed to the asylum!"

She set the picture aside and tried to get her mind back on her reading and sorting.

At eleven-thirty Connie went to find Hannah.

"If you didn't bring your lunch, would you like to go to the Smithy and get some stew? Or we could go later if you'd rather?"

"I can go now, and I'd like to. I'll get my coat and tell Jo Beth. She likes to go later."

Since it was cold they ate inside, looking out through the steamy windows of the Smithy. "It smells good in here," Hannah sniffed.

"It does. I like their stew. I think everyone in town does." Connie looked around at the early arrivals.

"Look who's coming," Hannah gestured toward the door.

Connie turned and saw Miss Mayme and Miss Minnie. They got up and moved to a larger table, all of them talking at once as they got settled.

"Now, what's new with you, Connie," Miss Minnie asked. Connie had been a favorite pupil of hers and her favoritism still showed. Connie had been a good math student, as had Missy. Doing well in math was one of the surer ways to Miss Minnie's heart.

"New? Let's see," Connie started. "First: Missy is home for the holidays; we've had a lot of compliments on the decorations; I've asked the City Beautiful Commission for two little holly trees to put out in front of the library. They're looking into it and are going to call me back on that if they can find some; Cas's arm is not giving him any unusual problems. I knew you'd ask," She grinned at Miss Minnie. "And I've finished reading the two journals we found in the attic, plus I found a picture of the stairway in some of the old papers."

"Well! I did ask! Whew, what a lot seems to be going on around here. And people think small towns are dull!" Miss Minnie chuckled and broke off part of her roll.

"In the picture you found did the stairway look about like we've got it? You know, the greenery and everything." Miss Mayme asked at once. She wondered how close she had guessed about how it may have been decorated when the Nelsons lived there.

"Yes. Except I'll bet the greenery was real." Connie paused slightly and continued slowly, "The big red bow was at the bottom of the stair. On the newel post."

"Oh," Miss Mayme pictured it. "Now that we know, did you put it back there?"

"No. But I left it there," Connie said quietly.

"Left it?" Miss Mayme's lips formed the words silently, her eyes meeting Connie's. The others were talking about something else, but Miss Minnie glanced briefly at her sister as if sensing she had missed something.

"How is Missy liking college?" Minnie asked.

"She likes it, Miss Minnie. And of course, Casey Taylor is going there too, that's a plus. They came home in his car."

Connie amended that. "His car or his hobby, depending on the condition it's in."

"He's smart to be able to keep it running. He never had any trouble with it that we heard of except the time those club members did something to it."

"You don't need to take up for Casey's car. Cas is vice president of that fan club, I think. He says he doesn't worry about Missy as much as he would if she were going with someone else, even someone with a better car." Connie laughed, "The nut behind the wheel being the scariest part or some such sage sheriff observation."

"What's this about trees and the library?"

"Cas surprised me with two pretty holly trees for our yard for Christmas and put lights on them. They look so nice I thought we'd get small ones, some little bushy ones for the front of the library to give it something pretty that would show up at night."

"The outside is awfully plain. I hope they can find some."

"And Della Reubens is coming Wednesday?" Miss Mayme did not look up as she asked.

"Wednesday morning. She's going to meet Cathy Taylor at the library and go down there where we felt so cold."

"Did Cathy tell her about the crying?"

"Yes. In fact, I think from what she told me that's what made her decide to come. She didn't make any comments or anything, just said she would come."

"I see. I guess she couldn't say anything, not until she sees the place for herself." Miss Mayme studiously pushed a piece of potato around her nearly empty bowl with her spoon until becoming impatient, Miss Minnie handed her a fork to pick it up.

"Can't stand to see you go hungry for lack of the proper tool," she said with sisterly sarcasm.

"You're all heart, Minnie." Munching happily on her potato, Miss Mayme raised her eyebrows, "I wonder if she'll decide to hold a séance. Della Reubens I mean, not Minnie."

Miss Minnie made a face at her.

Hannah hadn't contributed to the ideas about the cold in the basement, but now commented, "I heard the crying too. But I don't think it's anything to be afraid of. It was just so sad. It made the person who heard it sad too, just hearing it. But I didn't feel threatened or anything. Just terribly sympathetic, I guess. "She shook her head slightly, "I don't think it's anything bad or anything to be afraid of." Her voice trailed off, knowing she wasn't going to change any of their minds about holding a séance.

"It won't hurt to hear what she's got to say." Connie pronounced and changed the subject.

"The journal Mary Lou Nelson wrote in when she was about ten years old is charming. It's typical of a little girl who lived back then, and in several places she mentions a Lacey Lynch is coming to play with her. She once said it would be while her mother helps with the baking. I asked Cas to check with Clarence Lynch to see if Lacey was a relative of his but he hasn't had a chance to talk to him about it yet."

About two o'clock at the library Jo Beth called Connie to the phone. "I think it's about the trees," she whispered hopefully.

Connie took the call at Jo Beth's desk and nodded to her as she listened.

"Oh, they sound just right. Is there enough money left to get them?"

"There is, but that's all there is. There's no money left to get someone to plant them for us."

"We'll do that for the library. Cas can get them planted for us. He can call on the same one who planted ours. If you don't mind, will you have them tagged with our name? Cas will come in the morning to pick them up if that's all right with you?"

"I'll do that right now. Thank you, and please thank him too, for seeing to the planting. They will be here waiting for him and I'll have someone drop the lights off at the library."

"Good. We've got it done then. Merry Christmas!"

She turned to Jo Beth, "You heard? She found some that are just right, and she said she would have someone drop the lights by here."

"That's wonderful! You've done your good deed for December," Jo Beth chuckled merrily. "And don't forget to give Cas my thanks too, for taking on the planting job."

"I will," Connie eyed the clock. "I'll get these papers in order or at least a little neater, Missy will be here any minute!"

Cas was sorry to see Casey leave. He had enjoyed his visit and his company on the trip to Marble County. He pulled the phone toward him and reached for the Welemon Lynch file on the corner of his desk. He dialed Clarence Lynch's number.

"I think it's a good idea to keep reminding him I'm here, working on this big as life, remind him that this situation is not going to just go away. And Connie's given me a good excuse."

Clarence answered on the first ring. He managed to sound hesitant and aloof, but civil without saying anything. Cas ignored the negative attitude.

"Connie wanted me to ask you something, Clarence."

"Miss Connie? Ask me?" Clarence was as puzzled as he sounded.

"That's right. She's helping to restore some old papers and things at the library. They're about the Nelsons and the mansion the library is in now. There were some old things in the attic they found. They're going to clean them up and restore what they can and display them."

"What kind of things?" Clarence sounded gruff and not much in favor of the project.

"Some old dresses like the ones worn back then, things like that."

"Old clothes?" Clarence didn't comment, wondering what that had to do with him.

"While they were looking through them Connie found an old journal that Mary Lou Nelson wrote in when she was about ten years old. It mentions several times that someone named Lacey Lynch was coming to play with her. Is this Lacey Lynch some of your kinfolks?"

Clarence hesitated.

"The name is spelled the same as yours," Cas prodded.

"Yes, it's the same. She's my Mama's great Grandmama, I think. Wait a minute."

Clarence laid the phone down briefly, then returned. "She was. She eighty years old when she died, think it was. Here it is, died in nineteen twenty-eight. I got the old tree here."

"Tree?" It was Cas's turn to be puzzled.

"Family tree. It's folded up here in our family Bible. She did die in nineteen twenty-eight. Where you all hear her name from? Something Miss Mary Lou wrote, you say?"

"It was in the journal I told you Connie found. Something like a diary that little girls wrote in. About their everyday lives and their friends."

"Yes, they were friends. I remember hearing the folks talk about it when I was little. About the old days and the family. The Nelsons were good people. Always honest, and treated you right. You can tell Miss Connie, Lacey Lynch was my Mama's great Grandmama. The one here in Maryvale in the nursing home, she's my Grandmother, my Mother's mother. She is Lacey's granddaughter. Is that all she wants to know?"

"I think so. She saw her name mentioned so often in the journal, she wanted to know if she was related to you. I'll tell her, Clarence. Thank you."

That evening over dinner the Larkin family discussed their news. Cas was glad to be able to tell Connie he'd found out exactly who Lacey Lynch was.

"I felt sure she had to be related to him. She and Mary Lou must have grown up together. And before I forget it our new trees are so pretty, I asked if there was enough left in the decorating budget to get two little ones, holly bushes, for the library. There was, but there's ah, one little hitch."

"Why do I get the feeling this one little hitch is going to cost me dearly?" Cas squinted suspiciously at Connie.

Missy's eyes went from one parent to the other like a spectator at a tennis match, dancing with amusement.

"It'll just cost you," Connie reassured him. "But not anywhere like dearly."

"Oh," Cas exclaimed with exaggerated relief. "Thank the Good Lord for small favors. And how much is not dearly, do you think? Or must I figure it out for myself?"

"I'd tell you if I knew," Connie informed him defensively. "The bottom line is, they had enough left in the budget to get the little bushes but no more. There's no money to get anyone to plant them for us. So I told them to tag them with our name and you would pick them up in the morning and see to the planting. They also had a couple of strands of outside lights left for them, so we had it made except for the planting. And I volunteered you."

She lifted her folded hands in a comical plea. "Am I fired, boss?"

"No," Cas's grin was wide enough to be downright suspicious." In fact, you're doing me another favor."

"I am?" Connie and Missy exchanged a surprised look.

"I've told you I don't think Clarence is telling all he knows about Welemon's death. I'm going to sit right on his doorstep until he does decide to trust me or I get something to use as leverage to make him tell me what he knows. Every time I get a chance, I nudge him to remind him I'm here, keeping him uneasy. These things like getting his grandson to plant our trees, asking about Lacey Lynch, and now this, they're good excuses to stay close to him. I'll get his grandson to plant the holly bushes at the library for you."

"Your mind just never quite leaves the office, does it?" Connie laughed at him. "I'm going to peek in some night and see if you're wearing your badge in the shower!"

Missy got up giggling, "I've got to get dressed. You should be on television!" They heard her laughing all the way upstairs.

CHAPTER 15

Cas got out of his office as early as he could the next morning. He got to Clarence Lynch's house and stopped in front. He managed to get to the door without Clarence seeing him this time. Probably because it was so early. He knocked and waited.

Opening the door, Clarence looked surprised as well as suspicious. They faced each other for a couple of silent seconds.

"Yes, there's definitely something on Clarence's conscience. He's braced himself against being found out every time he sees me coming."

Cas smiled, trying to look as if he knew a lot more than he did. "Good morning, Clarence."

"You want to see me about something this early?" Clarence raised his eyebrows.

"It's Terrence I need to see, if he's here."

Terrence had heard his voice and came in. "Hope you've got some more trees, Sheriff Larkin. I could use the money," he grinned at Cas.

"Yeah, I have," Cas grinned back. "That's why I'm here. My wife told everybody about the others you planted and the City Beautiful Commission bought two smaller ones for the library. I came to get you to plant them if you have time."

"Sure do. I'm ready to go."

Clarence had disappeared. He came back into the room and handed Terrence a sausage biscuit.

"Can't plant no trees without some breakfast."

Terrence took the biscuit and kissed Clarence's cheek before following Cas out to his truck.

Cas had pulled in by the shed and Terrence put the shovel in the back. "Same price?" Cas asked as he got in.

"These trees are smaller bushes you said," Terrence reminded him.

"But the holes will be about the same. Same price all right?"

"Fine with me." Terrence swallowed the last of his biscuit and wiped his hands on his jeans.

They picked up the trees at the nursery and got to the library before it opened. Terrence was taking the trees out of the truck bed and Cas pointed to the steps.

Hannah arrived and stopped beside the truck. She looked at the holly bushes where Terrence was carefully placing them on either side of the walk, then turned to smile at Cas. Her glance fell on the shovel in the truck bed. She drew in a quick breath, gasping in shock. The blood quickly drained from her face and she clutched the side of the truck for support.

Cas turned away from watching Terrence in time to see her nearly fall, her face white. He reached out with his right arm to steady her.

"Hannah, are you all right? What is it?"

"The shovel," Hannah murmured softly. "It's bloody!"

Still firmly holding her arm, Cas looked at the shovel. It was only an old worn shovel. There was no blood that he could see.

"Hannah," he carefully released her arm. "Did you see blood on this shovel?"

"Yes," her tormented eyes told him more than her words. "A lot. It was covered with it." She shivered, looking away.

"Stand here a minute and take a deep breath. Don't look at the shovel again." He shut the truck door and went up the steps to the walk with Hannah, holding to her arm.

"I'm all right now. Thank you." Hannah went on up the walk and into the library without looking back.

Terrence looked after her, then at Cas.

"She's all right, just felt a little light headed."

Terrence nodded, "This where you want the bushes?"

"Yes, one on each side just like you've got them. And leave them room to grow."

Cas watched Terrence dig the holes and plant the two holly bushes, thinking about what Hannah had seen.

Just before they got back to Clarence's house, Cas turned to Terrence and asked casually, "Do you think I could borrow that shovel for a couple of weeks?"

"Don't see why not. You're the only tree customer I've had." Terrence smiled at Cas, patting the bills in his shirt pocket. "Probably won't be any more now. Won't be using that shovel again till spring. Keep it as long as you want to."

At the office parking lot Cas parked and lifted the shovel out of the truck with his right hand. Rhodes saw him and came to help. He took the shovel from him and carried it in.

"What are you planning on doing with a shovel?" Rhodes eyed him, grinning. "Connie's right, you don't know how to enjoy poor health." His smile faded at the expression on Cas's face.

"I hope to God I'm wrong," Cas told him solemnly. "But I'm going to send that shovel to the lab to test it for human blood."

Rhodes drew back, swiveling his neck to look at it where he'd stood the shovel in the corner. "Whose shovel is it?"

"It's Clarence Lynch's shovel."

"No." Rhodes looked stricken, the import too unpleasant to take in all at once.

Cas stood beside his desk making no comment.

Wordlessly, Rhodes turned to go. On the way out, he hit the facing above the door a resounding smack with his open hand. The echo of the blow expressed the anguish no words could have.

Cas stood a minute, nursing the arm with the cast on it. "Me too, Rhodes."

He shut all the desk drawers and left as quickly as he could get out.

Cas looked over the rim of his coffee cup watching as Connie moved quietly in the morning silence as if keeping noise to a minimum.

"Missy sleeping in?"

Connie nodded. "She can call me if she wants me to come and get her later." She reminded Cas, "It's Wednesday."

"Oh, it had slipped my mind. Della Reubens?"

"Yes." Connie went on with her work, too busy hurrying to notice Cas was preoccupied too. It didn't take either of them long to get out.

It was a little before the library usually opened for the day when Connie arrived but Hannah knew she was coming and was watching for her.

Through the glass behind the wreaths, Hannah beckoned her around to the side door and let her in.

"Thanks, Hannah. I was planning on getting here a little early anyway, and then there wasn't much traffic to slow me down. Everyone must have their shopping done."

"Oh, I doubt that. Traffic will pick up and be busy later, it usually is. Everyone who can probably sleeps late during the holidays. I hated to leave my warm bed, too."

A little past nine o'clock Jo Beth came to the door of the room where Connie was reading and sorting. She knocked softly to get her attention.

"What is it, Jo Beth?" Connie reluctantly pulled her thoughts back to the present.

"Two of the people working on the museum are here. I took them up to the attic. I thought you might want to go up and meet them, you've been so much help."

"Thank you, I'm anxious to see what they think of the things up there. I know they'll be surprised how much there will be for the museum." She squeezed Jo Beth's hand, looking forward to the reaction the newly discovered things would have.

"The museum's going to be one of the things to see when someone comes to visit, I'm sure of that."

"The dress alone would make people want to come, I think. Lucky we found the one Mary Lou Nelson wore in the portrait. It's like a page of history come to life to be able to see the portrait then get to see the dress as well."

"I returned the journals I read, too. They're up there in one of the trunks."

There were two people in the attic looking at the dress with the hoop and the wardrobe when Jo Beth and Connie came in.

The woman was about sixty or sixty-five. She was dressed in a conservative navy skirt and a white blouse which complemented the white sweeps of hair framing her face. She held out her hand to Connie, "I'm Ellen Toliver and this is Nathan Jessup. We're calling ourselves the Museum Committee, along with one or two others we can call on and anyone else we can rope in." Her smile was open and friendly.

"You don't have to rope Connie in," Jo Beth beamed. "She's already done quite a bit to help and is interested in the museum and the things we've got for it so far."

"I'm glad someone has started working on the museum," Connie gestured at the things around them. "There's so much here that would be interesting to people. All of this is part of our town's history. And you have a place to put it now, don't you? I think I heard Jo Beth say something about a room near the back of the courthouse," she looked from Ellen to Nathan.

"Yes, that's where it is. It's a large room that was once two rooms, so it's a generous space to get started. There's a little half partition on one side. We left that because we haven't really got started on any plans yet. We wondered how we were going to fill even that much space when we finally got it."

Ellen gestured at the dressmakers dummy. "But this dress, It will have to be put in one of those glass displays where it can be seen from all sides and protected."

"That being definite plan number one, it reminds us we don't have much money to work with." Nathan got serious.

He scratched his ear as he looked around, "I thought since the city has given us the room, when we get an idea of what we're going to have we can do the painting and things like that ourselves." He watched to see their reactions to this idea.

"I figured on that," Ellen agreed. "I think the others we've talked to will be willing to help."

"Of course, I'll help with whatever needs to be done."

Connie's agile mind had already gone on to other things, having settled that. "One thing we'd better do first is see how much one of those displays for the dress will cost. Or better yet, see if someone here in Maryvale can make us one."

"I brought a legal pad to make a list of what's here and make notes of what else is needed. The glass display for the dress will be at the top of the list." Ellen started writing.

"We also have that wardrobe the dresses are in. If we get desperate, it would probably bring a good price. But let's not do that unless we have to." Connie felt she had to mention that, praying they wouldn't have to part with it.

"And there are two journals in that trunk right over there. The second one doesn't have much in it, but the first one does. Mary Lou Nelson wrote in it when she was about ten years old and it's typical of what a little girl's life and interests were back then. It might be nice to have it open to an interesting passage in a display case so people could read it but not touch it."

"Better put display cases and shelving on that list of things with the glass display case and start getting some prices on them," Nathan put in as Ellen wrote.

"Well, I'll leave you to your cataloging but I'll be down in the back reading room if you think of anything I can help with. It's so nice to meet you, and I know the museum is going to be something the whole town will be proud of."

Jo Beth went back down with her. "When they first looked in and saw that dress I think right then they knew the museum would be a success. They haven't had much in the way of material or encouragement either up till now."

"They were doing well to get the room, with not much more than hope to go on. Now they've got all this. I sure hope they'll be able to hang onto that wardrobe. But it will be a good museum, with or without it."

Jo Beth stretched her neck, hearing voices. "I guess that must be Della Reubens arriving," she whispered to Connie.

"Must be, that's Cathy Taylor's voice I hear. They must have met outside as they came in. Let's go meet her."

Connie led the way and greeted Cathy, looking expectantly at the woman with her.

Della Reubens was about the same height as Connie and Cathy, very thin, and very straight. Her white hair was short and brushed back in a becoming style. When Cathy introduced them, she smiled sweetly and held out her hand to Connie.

Connie took her hand and returned the smile. "She looks so normal," she thought as she glanced sideways at Cathy.

Della also shook hands with Jo Beth and remembered they had met once.

"A long time ago." Jo Beth was pleased to be remembered.

Hannah stood back a ways, but Della extended her hand to her anyway. Hannah did not move forward or reach out to take it. Della and Hannah regarded each other in silence, then before the silence got too awkward Della spoke. "You won't shake hands?" She raised her eyebrows as if it were a private joke between them.

Hannah stayed where she was and answered, "No." Then she smiled and added, "But I'll come open the door and turn on the light downstairs for you."

When Cathy and Della started down, Cathy turned to Connie. "Would you like to come too?"

"Yes, if it's all right," she turned to Jo Beth.

"Don't see why not, there's no limit posted on the door like there are on elevators." Jo Beth's eyes twinkled.

Cathy laughed with Connie as they followed Della down the narrow stairs. Hannah closed the door behind them. Somehow the closing of the door emphasized the difference in the atmosphere of the gloomy basement, cutting off their laughter.

None of them spoke, Cathy and Connie instinctively knowing it would be best not to interfere with Della's observations. She had come to listen and feel and form her own opinion of the strangeness there. They had reached the back where it was the coldest and stopped, standing silent and still. Della was quiet, her arms crossed on her breast as if for warmth as they listened to the muffled crying.

The sadness of it made them want to cry too. They felt depressed to the point of anguish, but still no one broke the silence.

After Della had listened to the crying for several minutes she said quietly, "I've heard enough. We can go now."

Cathy didn't ask any questions because she didn't know how to ask them. Connie didn't ask any because she knew Cas didn't want her getting too involved in what he called, this business about the basement. But none of that kept them both from being eaten alive with curiosity.

When they got back upstairs Jo Beth came to meet them. She had none of the cautious hang ups the younger women had and asked Della Reubens point blank, "Well, have we got us a spirit or not?"

Already headed for the door, Della Rubens smiled back and answered just as candidly. "Oh, yes. At least one."

Della continued, opening the door. Cathy had no choice but to follow.

"I'll call you," Cathy managed to tell Connie hurriedly as she pulled her coat together, and they were gone.

"Well!" Connie went back to Jo Beth's desk

accompanied by shock and frustration. She wasn't even sure what she should have asked if she'd had the chance.

"You asked and she told you short and sweet and that was it!"

"Della isn't much on small talk. I remember that about her," Jo Beth agreed.

"Not much on small talk?" Connie rolled her eyes heavenward. "I'd say that was the understatement of the year! I'm sure she'll tell Cathy more about it, what she could tell about the basement. It was Cathy who called her after all," Connie consoled herself.

Jo Beth propped her elbows on her desk thinking back. "It's been a long time ago, but seems to me she doesn't mix in much in these things."

"Mix in? What do you mean, not mix in?"

"If someone had a place like our basement or wanted to contact someone, she would try to contact them. But she only tries to get the parties together. She doesn't try to find out anything on her own. I think that's what I'm trying to say. And don't ask me if I believe in all that, because I don't know."

Jo Beth's lips twitched up at the corners. "I guess I feel about it like Della does. If the spirit's happy and the one trying to make contact is happy, it's none of my business."

"That's certainly a strange way to look at it," Connie shook her head. "You'd think a medium would be VERY interested. Oh well, I guess I'll just have to wait until Cathy calls me to find out what she said. If she said anything!" Hannah was nowhere in sight as she went back to the reading room.

At the office, Cas sat with the Welemon Lynch file and its contents spread out before him on his desk. Everything he had including some guesses and thoughts he'd noted was there. But the concrete evidence was very little and the file made it obvious he didn't know where he was going. Gut feelings can't be written down, but one of his unwritten gut feelings was always with him. He was sure Clarence was hiding something. Now this.

He read over his notes. The hospital had called and told him about the wound as they were required to do. Someone had struck Weleman a mortal blow, making this a homicide. He never regained consciousness. Clarence and one of his neighbors brought the victim to the hospital saying they had found him lying in Clarence's back yard with the head injury.

"But I still don't understand why Clarence left. Maybe I missed something that was said. I'll talk to the neighbor again." He got up and left.

"You're Clarence Lynch's neighbor?"

"Yes, sir. I live here next door. This is my house."

The man was a little nervous but otherwise seemed to be cooperative and telling the truth.

"What exactly did Clarence tell you when he came to you for help?"

"He said his nephew, Welemon, had been hurt somehow. Wasn't much to say. He needed help and I went with him."

"You went directly to where Welemon was lying in the back yard?"

"Yes, sir."

"And he was lying there with the head injury. Was he lying on his back?"

"No, sir. On his stomach. I could see the place on his head real good. I was afraid he was dead."

"But he wasn't?"

"No. Clarence said he was still breathing and he did sort of flutter his eyes when we got him up between us to get him into the car."

"Why didn't you call an ambulance?"

"Clarence was afraid there wasn't time, I didn't think so either. He, the boy was just barely alive. I wouldn't have waited either if it had been one of my family."

Cas nodded understanding. "So you took him to the emergency room. What did they say when you went in with him?"

"A man saw us coming and he ran and opened the door for us. Then there were two ladies there. Nurses, I think. One of them, she pushed a wheelchair up behind Welemon. The other one held the double doors open and she pushed Welemon through them, holding his shoulders back against the chair. Then another lady came to us. She was wearing white, the others were in those outfits you see the doctors in when they operate. Green, they was. The lady in white told us the doctor was with him. She got his name and who Clarence was, and asked Clarence what happened to him."

"What did Clarence tell her?"

"Like I told you before, same as he told me. He found Welemon in the back yard with his head all bloody like he'd been hit with something."

"Then you went back and waited."

"No, Clarence said he wanted to go back home. Guess, to tell his mother what happened." He shook his head slightly with a puzzled look, "But I know I saw her at the door when we left."

"So you don't think that's why he wanted to go home?"

"Not unless he wanted to talk to her about it. Explain, you know. She's old and sometimes don't understand."

"But that's when you left, you and Clarence, and went back home?"

"Yes, we went back home then. Later, Clarence came over to my house and said his grandson hadn't come, he'd been expecting him. Said when he came he wanted one of us to come stay with his mother while he went back to see about Welemon. Then it wasn't too long till Terrence came home, so he took Clarence and went back and I stayed there with his mother."

Cas thanked him for his cooperation and gave him one of his cards, wishing he could think of something else to ask.

Back at his office Cas leaned back in his chair to rest his still slightly sore neck muscles and closed his eyes.

"I've got to forget this is someone I know and think of it as any other case. When Clarence went back home, it may well have been to wash the blood off that shovel and put it back in the shed. I've got to face the possibility whether I want to or not. Gut feeling or not."

He sat up, staring into the corner where the shovel had stood.

"The lab report will tell us about the blood, but if it turns out it's not Welemon's blood Hannah saw, what then? I don't see how it will help. My number two problem was shot, not bludgeoned with a blunt instrument. There are too many unknowns in these two cases, I've got to get some help from that bloody shovel. It's all I've really got." Cas pictured Laurence Fields defending Clarence.

He resolved to find some way to use the shovel to pressure the truth out of Clarence in case it wasn't Welemon's blood on it. He couldn't think of anything it would be worth Clarence's effort to hide. That was the heck of it. It was obvious Welemon was a user, so there was not any point of trying to hide that. His thoughts turned to Terrence, but Terrence hadn't been home so he wasn't protecting Terrence.

"And I've been with Terrence several times lately. I'd stake my badge there's nothing on that young man's conscience. Nobody's that good an actor. There would have been some negative reaction when I asked to borrow the shovel. No, he not only didn't do it, he doesn't know anything about it. The soil samples place Sellczk in Clarence's yard, but he was shot, not hit with a shovel."

Cas put his hands on both sides of his forehead as if that would relieve some of the pressure building inside.

"I wish I could be sure the lab results will ease the headache I'm getting. I'm going home and try to forget it for a few hours. I may have even more problems when the test results get back."

CHAPTER 16

Connie looked at her watch as she pulled into the driveway. It was only four o'clock. She decided to call Cathy Taylor when she got in.

The kitchen door opened before she reached for the knob. Missy met her sporting a big grin. She was wearing an apron and the kitchen was full of a delicious and familiar scent.

"Hmm," Connie sniffed the aroma. "Something smells wonderful and you look mighty pleased with yourself for some reason."

Missy stepped aside and gestured proudly toward the chocolate chip cookies cooling on the table.

"I used your recipe for these, Mom. They turned out pretty good, didn't they?" She waited for her mother's opinion as she helped herself to one of the cookies.

Connie tasted one. "They sure did turn out good! I've got to have another one right now, two won't ruin my supper. These are great, Missy, they turned out just right."

They hadn't heard Cas open the door. "What's great? Oh, I see. Did you make these?" Cas looked pleased. "I'm impressed."

"She took the recipe and did everything on her own. She didn't need any help as you can see, and taste."

Connie helped herself to another cookie. "I highly recommend them, but I've got to stop. Right after this one."

Missy watched as Cas bit into his second cookie. "I approve. You're a good cookie baker," he smiled around the remains of the cookie.

"There's just one thing," Missy observed gloomily, plopping down in a chair by the table full of cooling goodies.

"What? These taste great to me."

Missy's sad eyes looked up. "I forgot to save myself some chocolate chips."

Cas and Connie laughed at Missy's disappointed expression. "I guess you have to be a Mom to be able to remember that." Connie got that small comfort out between giggles.

"Based on my personal investigation I'd say these look good, smell good, and taste good. You have now earned the title, Very Good Cookie Maker. Make that Baker." Cas bestowed a kiss on Missy's forehead as a reward.

"That makes it official," Connie declared, seconding the motion to bestow the title.

"Aren't you home a little bit early?" Connie turned her attention to Cas.

"Things were so quiet it was downright dull and I haven't taken much time off for sick leave so I left a little bit early, aided and abetted by Gladys."

"Good old Gladys. Next time I see her I'll give her a big hug. Since it's early and we're cookie rich, I'll make us some coffee and bring it in the den."

"Good idea. I'll get my boots off and meet you there." Cas left the kitchen.

Connie watched Missy as she went about cleaning up and putting some of the cooled cookies into the cookie jar.

"I'll take some of the warm ones and put everything on the tray so I won't have to take two trips. The cookies are good, Missy, I'm glad you made them."

Missy smiled at the compliment from someone who was an authority on cookie baking. "Is there anything you want me to do while I'm in here? For supper?"

"You could slice some tomatoes if you want to but there's plenty of time. I'm going to make beef Stroganoff."

"Beef Stroganoff," Missy's young face lit up. "Let me start it, please?"

"All right, if you want to. Remember to put the meat on low."

"I will, I've watched you so many times. Do we have any mushrooms?"

"They're in the refrigerator. Let me know if you need me or want to ask about anything."

Cas was already settled in the den and Connie set the tray down on the table to his right.

"Our daughter is showing an awful lot of interest in cooking."

"She seems to be doing pretty well at it too. I hear noises in there, what's she up to now?" He smiled like the proud father he was.

"I said I was going to make beef Stroganoff for dinner and she wanted to do it. I think she's watched me enough to know how and I'll be here if she needs help."

"That's sort of ambitious, isn't it," Cas said uneasily. "Maybe we should remind her she and Casey have three more years of school ahead of them."

"Cas, you're a world class worrier. But this time, I agree. We'll remind her at dinner. Think of something subtle," she suggested. "So she won't think we're BOTH world class worriers.".

"Whatever we think of probably won't fool her. She's already got a good idea what kind of worriers we are. By the way I never did get around to telling you, but I asked Clarence Lynch about the Lacey Lynch you said was mentioned so often in that journal of Mary Lou Nelson's."

Connie set her cup down, interested in what he had learned from Clarence.

"She was a relative of his. He had a paper he called his family tree folded up in the family Bible. Lacey was Mary Lou Nelson's age and they spent a lot of time together. He said he could remember the old folks sitting around talking about them and the Nelsons and all their family. Lacey died at the age of eighty about nineteen twenty-eight, he told me."

"So, was she an aunt, or great grandmother. Did he say what relation to him she was?"

"She was his great grandmother. He told me the lady who's in the Maryvale Nursing Home is Lacey's granddaughter. Her name is Daisy Walters."

"Must be her married name, Walters. But this Daisy Walters in the nursing home is Lacey Lynch's granddaughter?"

"Right. Clarence says she's ninety-six now. The reason she's in the nursing home is her mind comes and goes. He said they were afraid she would wander off or fall, or hurt herself some way. Sometimes she's all right but other times her mind is back in her childhood or somewhere in the past. I think he feels bad about her being there, but it's the safest place for her."

"I'm sure that's true," Connie said thoughtfully. "So, she's Lacey Lynch's granddaughter and she's ninety-six. Let's see, she would have been born I guess when Lacey was in her fifties or maybe sixties."

"You sound like Clarence's family tree. When I talked to him he read me parts of it while he guessed at what wasn't written down."

"It was practical to write down some of the dates like that. Evidently, they're a very close family. It's too bad what happened to Welemon. I don't guess anything's come up to shed any light on what could have happened to him?"

"We don't have but one concrete clue. It's not much like crime investigation on television, is it?"

Cas didn't mention the shovel, hoping help would come from some other direction. But Hannah's vision worried him. He would wait until he had the lab report on it in hand.

"With Welemon's being on drugs there's not much telling what happened. He'd been away so long, he may have been in some kind of trouble the family knew nothing about."

"I suppose. And not yet thirty-six years old." Connie shook her head at the tragedy.

Cas didn't comment. He finished his coffee as Connie went to check on Missy's progress with the Stroganoff.

"I'm about ready to add the sour cream," Missy reported brightly as she set the table.

"Good, looks like it's going to be good."

As Connie passed the phone, it rang. She stopped to answer it.

"I completely forgot about calling Cathy," she thought as she picked it up.

"Hi!," Cathy's voice greeted her.

"I was just about to call you. I couldn't believe it when Della Reubens just left like she did. She came to the basement, looked everything over, and she was gone without a word. No, that's not quite right. I remember when she left Jo Beth asked her if there was a spirit down there or not and she said, yes, at least one. What a place to leave someone hanging!"

Cas came to set the tray and cups on the table, made a cursory check on dinner, and retreated to the den. Connie threw him a silent kiss on his way out, still listening to Cathy's report on Della Reubens.

"I thought she was so normal looking when I saw her, it was hard to believe she's a medium. Maybe she didn't see anything wrong with leaving us hanging. Jo Beth told me later she isn't much on small talk. Isn't that the understatement of the decade?"

"No, Connie, I don't believe she did see anything wrong with it. Or maybe she didn't think she left us hanging. She did say there was a spirit there, which is what we wanted to know. She didn't say anything else until we got back out to my car. It was like I was tongue-tied or something, trying to phrase any intelligent questions to ask and find out more. She said she had told her daughter she would meet her at the Smithy and asked if I would mind driving her there.

Then she laughed when she saw how close we were to it. That sort of broke the ice, and I finally got up the nerve to ask her what she thought about the spirit she said was in the basement."

"Did you find out if it's more than one?"

"She said there was a spirit there and there was, she felt, more than one. But one was more restless."

"She must mean the one who was crying."

"I'm sure that's what she meant. I told her we thought it must be a girl or a young woman, since that's how the voice sounded to us."

"Yes, Hannah heard it too. She hasn't been back down in that basement since." Connie drew a deep breath, "And another thing, you know I told you about the bow we found in the attic and put at the top of the stairs? The one we kept finding back down on the newel post?"

"Uh-huh. I remember our laughing about it because it sounded like a Three Stooges plot."

"Well, I was wrong about Jo Beth moving it. She didn't. None of the people at the library did. Then among the old newspaper issues we bought upstairs I found a picture of the stairway decorated for Christmas and guess what? The bow was right there in the picture, big as life, on the newel post at the bottom of the stair."

"You mean?" Cathy held her breath.

"I mean that's where it belongs, where they had it when the family lived there. It gave me a weird feeling looking at that picture of Nelson standing there beside it. I guess you know we left it there, too. Missy said it looked better there to her anyway."

"Goodness, that would give anybody a weird feeling," Cathy's voice went soft with wonder. "Do you think the spirit, whoever she is, moved the bow?"

"I don't know. All I know is none of us or the library people moved it. And according to the picture, that's where it belongs. They may have had it made for the newel post for all we know."

"That's one more thing that needs an explanation. The cold, the crying and now, who moved the bow."

"Maybe we'll get some answers if Della Reubens holds a séance. Did she say she would? Or did she say anything about finding out who the spirit is?"

"She said it's been a long time since she held a séance but there is a spirit there, and she would hold a séance if we, I mean if I want her to. I know how Cas feels about all this."

"He's left no doubt about that. But if Della holds a séance, I would have liked to go. How much does she charge to hold a séance?"

"She doesn't charge, but rather, takes donations. She said ten dollars apiece and we need twelve people. Who do you think I should ask, or will they think I'm crazy if I ask anyone to a séance? That it's a crazy idea?"

"I don't know. I've got cold feet too, but my cold feet want to go ahead and see if Della Reubens can shed any light on this. How about you?"

"I don't think it will do any harm to ask. And I'm not being forbidden from anything but going to the séance, we can ask anyway." Connie laughed. "Just be glad you don't have to run for sheriff."

Cathy laughed with her. "And you know I'd be there too if Cas hadn't put his foot down. And if people think we're nuts we'll live it down before too long even if a few people do wonder what we're using for brains right now."

"I don't know. I'm beginning to appreciate Cas's point of view, now that it comes down to asking people. Maybe they will laugh at the idea. We'll have to be careful how we go about this, about who we ask, to keep from being considered mental cases whether we ever want to run for public office or not, Connie."

"The ones I've mentioned it to, the ones who already know something about it won't think we're mental cases. They want to be there." Connie's tone was positive.

There was a brief silence as Connie remembered the reactions of those she had mentioned the séance to. Cathy listened as she continued.

"Let's see, Lisa Randolph and Jill want to come, they've already told me so. And Dick's a lawyer, it would be a feather in his hat to have helped raise the dead as Cas calls it," Connie laughed.

"Oh, Connie, what if he decides Lisa shouldn't come either?"

"He won't. And he's definitely going to come. He said so. His wife and Jill want to come and I'll ask Miss Minnie and Miss Mayme. Miss Minnie may not, but I'm almost certain Miss Mayme will want to come."

"Let's see, that's me; Lisa and Jill; Miss Mayme; my next door neighbor and her cousin who's visiting said they want to come; and possibly Jo Beth, since she's gone along with us this far. How many's that?" Cathy tried to count them.

"That's seven. And Cathy, let's make sure of those seven before asking any more since all we need or want is twelve. I doubt that anyone who wants to come will want to come alone, would you?"

"No, come to think of it, I wouldn't. Okay, That's seven. And she didn't say we had to have twelve. She just mentioned there were twelve at the last one. Really, ten might be more comfortable. I was only going to try to get twelve since that seems to be the number she wants. I'm going to use my drop leaf table at the end of the living room."

"Okay, I'll get started calling and talk to you tomorrow. Oh, when do you think it might be? Did she say? I need to give them some idea."

"We talked about that. Me and Della, I mean. Unless you have some objection, we both thought a week from tomorrow. I don't know why Della Reubens picked that time, but it will give us time to get it together and get it over with before Christmas. Maybe that's what she had in mind."

"Good idea. That's the date we'll give them. What time?"

"Eight o'clock."

"Fine. I'll get back with you as soon as I can talk to everybody."

CHAPTER 17

Connie started making her calls with Miss Minnie and Miss Mayme at the top of the list. She listened, holding her breath until she heard Miss Mayme's cheerful voice, relieved she had been the one to pick up the phone.

"Hi, I didn't know if you'd answer the phone before opening time or not. I wanted to catch you before you get too busy."

"What's too busy?" Miss Minnie's voice chimed in. "There's no such thing."

"I put the speaker on," Miss Mayme explained.

"Oh, good. Then I won't have to explain everything but once."

"Right. And we can get our money's worth out of this phone equipment we splurged on." Miss Minnie agreed, practical as always.

"I don't know if you'll think this was worth the splurge or not." Connie sounded dubious. "You may hang up on me," she began. "But I thought you would be interested to know that Della Reubens is going to hold a séance."

"A séance? And try to contact the spirit at the library?" Miss Mayme's voice rose with excitement.

"That's it. And before I forget it in the rush I've got something to tell you. You remember the bow that wouldn't stay put at the top of the stairs? Well, Miss Mayme, you didn't move it, and I found out that no one at the library touched it or any of the decorations. So that's another thing besides the crying to find out about."

Miss Minnie broke up, laughing heartily. "You mean we had help from the basement with the decorating? That's all we need, competition from the spirit world!"

"Aw, Minnie! You're an unbeliever," Miss Mayme scolded. "What about the séance, Connie? Where, when, and I'm sure I'd better ask, how much will it cost us?"

"It will be at Cathy Taylor's house. In a week, on Friday at eight o'clock. And it will be ten dollars each. She says it's not a charge but a donation, don't ask me what for. It could be spooks without castles for all I know. But that's the bottom line, ten dollars. And I think there will be twelve people. That's the number Della Reubens suggested."

"I want to go. What about you, Minnie?"

"Yes, I'll go. I wouldn't miss it. And we'll have our fee or donation as she calls it in our hands and ready." She stifled more laughter. "I wouldn't want goblins or demons to come trying to collect," a giggle escaped.

"You mean you do want to go? After all the fun you've had at our expense about it?" Miss Mayme said sounding grumpy. "You've already got your ten dollars worth of entertainment out of it."

"Of course I want to go. It's not very often you get to go to a séance. And besides, every séance should have a skeptic or two."

"Then we'll both be there. Should we call and tell Cathy we're coming?"

"No, I'll just check your names as coming. We're calling the people who have already said they want to go first. I can't go but I'm helping with the calling . You can just guess how Cas feels about it. If it weren't for that, I'd sure be there." Connie's voice grew wistful.

"That's all right, dear. We'll tell you everything that goes on. And I know Cathy will keep her eyes open for both of

you so you'll be posted immediately about what happens."
Miss Mayme made it a promise.

Connie called the library next to talk to Jo Beth.

"Connie!" Jo Beth's voice greeted her. "What are you
doing, taking the day off? I've got so spoiled to your being
here I forget you aren't on the payroll."

"I'm calling some people to tell them about the séance
Della Reubens is going to hold," Connie started cautiously.

"Oh, she's going to do one then? I wondered if she was
joking when she said there was at least one spirit here.
Though she's not one to joke, I'd think."

"No, she wasn't joking. She told Cathy she feels the one
spirit very clearly. She said there are probably more, or at
least one, but the one crying is more restless. Restless is the
word she used. One is more restless or maybe what she
means is more distressed than the other one or others if
there are more. And remember the bow we thought
someone moved? You know, or at least when I told Miss
Mayme about it, none of us moved it to the bottom from
the top of the stairway. Then you remember I found that
picture of the bow on the newel post."

"You mean the spirit must have done that? Moved it back
to where they used to put it?" Jo Beth gave it a second's
thought. "Maybe it wasn't the one who was crying who did
it, maybe it was Nelson." She grinned at the phone. "He did
have the reputation of being hard headed!"

"All I know for sure is none of us did. That's one thing
Della could ask about if she runs out of questions. But what
I called for, Jo Beth, would you like to come to the
séance?" Connie crossed her fingers.

"Yes, I'd like to. If I remember right, Della just accepts
donations. I'd always sort of wanted to go to one, a real
séance. When is it going to be, and where?" She hesitated,
"I guess we could have it here. I don't know. But it would
take a while to get permission and all that. I'm not too sure
how to go about it."

"Oh, that's no problem. Cathy is going to have it at her
house. It will be a week from tomorrow, Friday at eight

o'clock. And you were right about the donations. Della suggested ten dollars each for the donations."

"Put down my name and also my niece. You remember Joy, don't you?"

Connie thought back, unable to place her.

"She comes in and helps sometimes. Just put down two by my name and I'll pay her donation so she can drive me. I don't see too well at night and I know she will want to go."

"All right then, I've got you both down."

"Will you be there?"

"No, since Cas doesn't want me to go, but I'm going to hear all about it. You can bet on that."

Next on Connie's list was Lisa Randolph. "I'm sure she will want to go, but there's no telling what Dick Randolph will think about it."

Connie wiped the nervous perspiration from her hands before dialing the number.

Lisa was delighted as Connie expected when she heard the particulars about the séance.

"I definitely want to go. Wait a minute, I'll check with Dick."

At the other end of the line, Connie cringed, wondering if he would trust her with any more of their statements after this.

Lisa came back laughing. "Yes, Dick and I will both be there. He said every séance should have a skeptic there to keep the operation honest!"

"That's what Miss Minnie Anderson said too," Connie giggled. "She and Miss Mayme are both coming."

"Wait a minute."

Connie heard voices and thought she recognized Jill's and the word 'séance.'

"Connie?" It was Jill's voice.

"Yes, Jill?"

"I wanted to catch you and tell you I want to come too. Me and the man I'm dating. If you haven't got too many already."

"No. We're only asking twelve and I was going to talk to you next to check with you about coming."

"Put me down for two places. I'll get the directions et cetera from Lisa."

"Okay, great. I've got the two of you down. See you there." Connie hung up the phone, elated at her success.

"This is wonderful!" Connie rechecked her list as she dialed the phone again. "That's eight people. I'll see how Cathy is doing."

"Connie," Cathy's voice trilled. "I'm glad you called. My next door neighbor and her husband and niece are coming. That's four when you count me."

"That's perfect. I've got eight, so that's our twelve. Exactly what Della Reubens wanted. Dick and Lisa Randolph are coming; Jo Beth and her niece; Jill and her boyfriend; and Miss Mayme and Miss Minnie."

"That's it then. You know, I think we could have got as many as we wanted. Everyone seemed so interested. I didn't know what to expect when we started."

"Even our skeptics sounded like they were looking forward to it. Dick Randolph and Miss Minnie will be on the lookout for anything they think might be a trick of some kind. A lawyer and a school teacher should be pretty hard to convince. Darn, I wish I could be there. They may get their education broadened," she laughed.

"I'm sure they'll be all eyes and ears. But Connie, I think she just might be able to do it. To really contact the spirit world. You remember the way she looked in the basement?"

"I do. And I heard her when Jo Beth asked her if there was a spirit there. She didn't hesitate to tell her in no uncertain terms there is a spirit, and perhaps more than one. She was definite about it."

"I wish Cas hadn't decided you shouldn't come."

"Oh, I can see his point. I'd like to go, but I can understand his feelings about it."

Connie was resigned to it. "I'll make up for it some other way. He was really good about planting the trees at the library."

"I'd feel the same in your place, I know."

"I'll bring some chocolate chips over to pass the time while you wait for Della to start."

"Thanks. We'll enjoy them if we aren't all too nervous to taste anything. I'm going to make coffee and set out some chips and cheese, nothing elaborate."

"How is Della going to get there, is her daughter going to drive her?"

"Yes. She said she's going to visit someone here while Della does the séance."

"Okay, let me know if there is anything else I can do."

After dinner that night, Missy went out with Casey and Connie took a coffee tray into the den.

"You've not said anything lately about the two murder cases. I guess that means there's nothing new?"

"Yes and no."

Connie raised her eyebrows at that.

"There's nothing concrete, is what I'm saying. I'm still running tests, asking questions, and whatever looks like it might help. No one in town seems to have known or ever heard of this Peder Sellczk. It's like he was invisible before he got shot between the eyes," Cas said with unaccustomed bitterness.

"But that's not all, is it? You look like you've thought of something negative or got something to worry at. As Miss Mayme says, fess up, what is it?"

"I don't like the way things are pointing and the only thing I'm sure of is that Clarence isn't telling me all he knows."

He lifted his eyes from his cup of coffee and looked miserable as a politician with his hand shaking arm in traction. His dark brows drawing together.

"I like Clarence. I don't want to suspect him. He's a good man, a family man. Not one who would do something like this to anyone, much less a member of his family. But why won't he tell me what he knows if he's got nothing to feel guilty about?" Cas gave a sigh, searching for answers in the cold coffee in front of him. "I hope the way things are pointing right now is wrong but I don't know how to get at what seems to be stuck between Clarence's ears for the life of me. All my staying close to him has got me nowhere. And he is holding something back. I don't have to hear him admit it to know it. I've known him too long."

"I know what you mean about unsaid things, "Connie's eyes focused on another scene. "I was at the library when Della Reubens came to see what she thought about the cold in the basement. I shook hands with her, so did Jo Beth and another person there. But when she held out her hand to Hannah she didn't."

"Hannah was there too?"

Connie nodded. "She was working that day and standing in back of everyone else. After she'd shaken hands with everyone else, Della held out her hand to her anyway and Hannah wouldn't take it. She didn't move forward or hold out her hand or make any move at all. Then Della asked her as if a little amused by it, if she wouldn't shake hands. And Hannah said no. Just plain, flat NO. Then before anyone could say anything or find fault with that, Hannah said, but I'll come open the door and turn on the light for you, and moved away."

"I guess she thought as long as she had to move, she'd move in a necessary direction." Cas looked down at the coffee tray, not meeting Connie's eyes.

"I guess that could be it," Connie admitted doubtfully.

"But Cas, when she and Della were just standing there face to face, I had the feeling they were communicating or at least understood each other. And on a level the rest of us couldn't reach. It was strange. Like they were reading each other's minds, or witchcraft or something."

"WITCHCRAFT!" Cas's head jerked up. "I can't believe you said that! My own wife!"

Connie stared at him, startled at how upset he was.

"That I said what? What on earth is the matter?"

"What you said, that's what's the matter! Like you thought Hannah is a witch. She's not the one claiming to be a medium or call up spirits or whatever they are."

"That's ridiculous, I don't think Hannah's a witch. Calm down for goodness sake. I just felt she and Della Reubens understood each other somehow."

"That's exactly the kind of thing that started all the witch hunts in Salem. Imagination, superstition, and just plain meanness in more than a few cases. Pretty good way to get rid of someone you don't like or is in your way, just accuse them of witchcraft and let ignorance and superstition do the rest. People say they can't understand how all that could have happened, but I can. I see it every day. It's too easy to hurt someone with rumors."

He looked sternly at Connie. "You see why it's so important not to say anything until you're sure what you're saying is true?"

"Of course I see what you mean. But Cas, I'm not going to tell anyone I think Hannah's a witch. What a thought! I told you about it because it was strange she wouldn't shake hands."

Cas didn't answer and Connie stubbornly added, "And I had the feeling Della KNEW why Hannah wouldn't shake hands. I can't explain it, but that's what I felt when they were standing there looking at each other."

"Well," Cas relented a little. "Maybe Della's encountered that before. People who wouldn't shake hands with her or showed their suspicions some other way." He gave her one of his sideways looks. "Her profession is a little more unusual than freelance typing, for one thing."

"Can't argue with that." Connie laughed, at ease again. "But I shook hands with her. And I was thinking how normal she looked, not at all like someone who could do something like call up a spirit to talk to. If she can really read minds, I hope that didn't hurt her feelings."

"Don't worry about it. If she can read minds that was probably one of the better opinions she's run across. There's bound to be skeptics around who would do her ego a lot more damage than thinking she looks normal. Let's forget about mediums and spirits and have some more coffee. Mine's as cold as—never mind," he grinned.

"Okay, I'll start my bath running first. Be back in a flash."

Connie poured scented bubble bath into the tub and set the water's temperature just right. As she watched the scented bubbles grow she amused herself wondering if Dick Randolph would shake hands with Della at the séance. She gazed at the Roman tub which had been her one luxury item when they bought the old house to fix up. Cas got the fireplace he wanted.

Downstairs Cas and Connie avoided talk of the supernatural as they finished their refreshed coffee. "Want to share my bubble bath? Might be easier than standing with that cast out the shower door."

Cas smiled and returned the kiss she bent down to give him. "No, I'll struggle with the shower. I don't want to face Rhodes and Gladys tomorrow smelling like a rose sachet."

Connie grinned as she went out, "Chicken!"

CHAPTER 18

"It's a good thing we didn't have long to wait for this, I'd have been a nervous wreck." Cathy fretted as she worked to get things ready Friday night, checking the refreshments on the buffet again. Everything was ready but her. She glanced out at the dark night. Only half an hour to go and so far no one had shown up early.

A few minutes later realizing she was pacing like an expectant father she popped one of Connie's chocolate chip cookies into her mouth and went to stand before the fireplace.

People began arriving at Cathy's about a quarter of eight o'clock.

All of them arrived about the same time, not wanting to be too early. But they certainly didn't want to miss anything. All of them seemed to feel a bit edgy and self-conscious now that the time for the séance was actually at hand. They greeted each other and each new arrival nibbled on the snacks Cathy had provided, and drowned any stubborn misgivings in fruit punch or coffee.

Miss Mayme and Miss Minnie were the last to arrive. It was five minutes till eight and Della Reubens had not yet come.

Between sips of coffee Miss Minnie and Dick Randolph scoffed at the very idea a séance could be regarded as anything but an evening's entertainment.

Miss Mayme knew well her sister's attitude and turned her attention to more important things.

"Ah, Connie's cookies. Cathy, do tell her I missed her but I recognized her chocolate chip cookies. I never can resist them!"

"When did you ever try?" Miss Minnie couldn't resist the input.

It had no effect on Miss Mayme's appetite or obvious enjoyment.

"I can't resist them either," Cathy joined her. "I wish she could have been here. She made me promise to be her eyes and ears tonight so I'll call and tell her all about it, never fear." Cathy looked up at the clock.

Promptly at eight o'clock the doorbell rang. Della Reubens was there.

Opening the door, Cathy glanced behind Della as she welcomed her in. But she couldn't see her daughter's car on the dark street. It gave her an eerie feeling.

"Why do I feel like she got here by broomstick?" She thought uneasily as she closed the door and watched Della's straight, black back as she approached the others.

Cathy had each of them introduce themselves as they finished up their snacks.

Della nodded, acknowledging each one. Cathy had the feeling Della knew each one's attitude about what she was about to do as well as their names. Some were there for a lark, Jill and her boyfriend and the neighbor's niece. Some were hardened skeptics, Dick Randolph and Miss Minnie. And the rest, if not believers at least had open minds.

Cathy slipped away and moved the table out a little so everyone would have plenty of room when they were seated.

Dick and Lisa Randolph saw what she was doing and went to help her arrange the chairs.

Della Reubens chose the seat toward the bay window where she sat with her back to it, framed by the long drapes.

The others drifted in and took their seats at the table, conversation giving way to watchful curiosity.

Miss Minnie sat on one side of Della and Miss Mayme on the other. Cathy was directly across from her.

As soon as everyone was seated Della asked, "Has anyone here ever attended a séance?"

No one present had and Della smiled around the table to put them at ease.

"What a séance is for is to contact the spirit world and ask what we want to know of the spirit we contact. In this instance, we know there is a presence at the library."

Dick Randolph self-consciously cleared his throat.

"We want to contact it and ask what it wants of us. I don't know if we will be successful in contacting it, but I will try."

Della's eyes sought Cathy. "Please turn off the lights. The firelight is quite enough. Spirits are shy and don't like a lot of light."

Cathy obediently turned off the lights and was glad she had had the gas logs put in after she became a widow. Glad to have at least a little light, she wondered briefly if they would have used candles or something if they hadn't had the gas logs. She returned to her place at the table.

"Now, will you all join hands." Della joined hands with those at her sides, bent her head, and closed her eyes.

In an expectant quiet like the opening of a play, Della began to speak. She exhorted the spirit in the library to come to them.

"We have felt your presence in the library and invite you to come to us. To tell us how we can help you." Della paused a few seconds then continued. "If you are here, let us know you are here with us." She repeated the invitation twice in a soft voice, pausing each time, with no visible or audible results.

Cathy's heart sank. "Nothing's going to happen." She was disappointed and knew Connie would be. Before she could feel any worse, Della started speaking again.

Della's voice was quiet and soothing as if trying to reassure something wild and afraid to come to her. Cathy thought briefly of a cat she had tried to lure out from under a bed when Casey's dog had scared it.

Della repeated the invitation. No one stirred. Her voice was soft and comforting in the near dark, silent room.

As she continued to speak, suddenly there came a rush of wind around the table. It swirled the drapes behind Della and as it passed Cathy, she shivered in its coldness.

All the hands around the table gripped each other harder in anticipation and not a little fear. They held tightly to the reality of the warm and known friend beside them.

Cathy peeked at Della. She sat with her head up, attentive to something, her eyes still closed. Without moving her head, Cathy glanced at Dick Randolph. He was watching Della intently.

"I feel your presence." Della spoke calmly, not raising her voice. "Let us know you are here by rapping on the table."

The cold rush was felt again but there was nothing else. Della still exhorted, "If you are here with us rap on the table so we will know you are here with us. That you can hear us."

Della paused and suddenly the silence was broken by a loud rap on the table. The circle of hands again tightened on each other. Some of the eyes around the table opened then quickly shut again. Dick Randolph still watched Della, his hands linked with Lisa's on one side and Jill's on the other.

"Are you the spirit from the library?" Della asked slowly and distinctly. "If you are, rap twice. Once for no, and twice for yes."

There came a loud rap on the table. Then a heartbeat later, a second rap.

"Yes!" Miss Mayme and the other believers thought exultantly. Cathy wished again Connie was beside her.

"Are you a member of the Nelson family?"

"Oh, now we'll know!" Cathy hardly breathed. Her heart was racing.

There was a loud rap on the table. Though all of them seemed to expect it, no other rap was heard.

"Then it's not one of the Nelsons." Cathy felt so let down a little doubt crept in that this really was the spirit from the library basement. But Della was speaking again.

"Is there some reason you are still at the library?"

Two raps answered Della.

"We want to help you. We have come here to try to help you," Della said. "Is there some reason you are here and not at peace, are you bound to stay here?"

One rap was heard. All of them listened intently now, hardly daring to breathe as they held the hands beside them.

Della paused only a few seconds, listening. "If you are not bound, are you here to help someone else?"

Two raps came quickly, as if the spirit was cooperating with Della and answering promptly, trying to communicate.

"We've heard someone crying. Someone needs help. Are you the one who is crying?"

One rap answered just as quickly. No.

Della paused and another rush of cold air surrounded them. It billowed the drapes behind Della and fanned the gas logs, settling to a uniform coldness embracing all of them as if waiting, trying to be understood.

Della's head fell forward on her breast.

Without raising her head or opening her eyes, Della spoke. But it was not Della's voice they heard. It was a young and feminine voice, breathless as it spoke quickly.

"Help Miss Mary Lou! Please! Help Miss Mary Lou!"

The voice tapered off as if that was all the strength it had.

Quickly, Cathy leaned forward and asked, "Are you the one who moved the Christmas bow?"

"Yes," Came the puzzled answer, soft as a sigh. Then it was gone and the cold with it.

Della raised her head, blinking her eyes as if she'd been asleep. She looked at the faces around her.

"I see we were successful." She looked at Cathy for a report on what happened.

"Was it the spirit from the library?"

"Yes, just as she said. But we still don't know who it is." Cathy shook her head, "It's not one of the Nelsons."

"I know. The answer was no when I asked if it was one of the Nelson family. But contact was made, what did it say?"

"It told us to help Miss Mary Lou. And it repeated it. Help Miss Mary Lou. That was the message. So it must be somehow connected with the Nelson family."

Della rose and they drifted back for coffee and punch. No one said very much. Dick Randolph peered down into his cup of punch as if he wanted to ask questions but wasn't sure he wanted to hear the answers.

Miss Minnie and Miss Mayme were saving their comments to each other for a more private place.

Lisa and Dick were the first to leave, Dick still not commenting. As they left, Cathy saw a dark car double parked in front of the house.

"There's my daughter," Della Reubens said behind her. She kissed Cathy on the cheek. "I'm glad there was contact made, sometimes it takes longer." She slipped the envelope with the donations in it into her coat pocket and was gone before anyone could think of anything else to say or to ask her.

After everyone had gone Cathy put everything away before sitting down to call Connie, getting her thoughts together about the brief contact that had been made with the spirit.

It was nine-thirty when Connie picked up the phone. "I knew it was you! Tell me all about it! She made contact, didn't she?"

"Yes, she did."

"I knew it! I knew it!"

"We were all there in the dark with only the light from the fireplace for light, our hands joined. And we did make contact with a spirit from the library. But Connie, we don't know any more than we did."

"But, how could that be? What do you mean? You must have found out the spirit was from the library from what you said. Start at the beginning, when Della Reubens came in. Don't leave out a single thing," Connie insisted.

"Okay. Everyone introduced themselves to Della and we had a little punch and coffee and took a few minutes to get acquainted. Then we went in and sat around the table. Della asked me to turn off the lights. But I'll tell you right now, I was glad to have the light from the gas logs. Anyway, we sat down at the table and she told us to join hands. She closed her eyes, so we did too, and Della invited the spirit to come to us. It was so eerie sounding. Her voice sounded, I guess the only way to describe it is soothing. It was like she was trying to coax some animal, a wild thing, not to be afraid."

Connie listened, picturing everything as Cathy told it, down to opening the door and seeing Della's daughter waiting for her.

"I'm glad you thought quickly enough to ask the spirit if she was the one who moved the bow."

"And she said yes, as if of course the bow should be where she put it. Funny, isn't it?"

"And the voice said to help Miss Mary Lou, said it twice." Connie mused.

"That's it, word for word. It wants us to help Miss Mary Lou and it moved the bow, that's what we know for sure from the contact as Della Reubens calls it. It sounded like a young girl's voice, like the crying, so I guess I had about decided it had to be Mary Lou Nelson. But it's not, she wants us to help Mary Lou."

"And it sounded like a young girl, like the one crying." Connie worried at it trying to find some explanation. She wondered without voicing it to Cathy if spirits could lie. She dismissed the idea, blaming it on being married to her personal and up close arm of the law so long.

"Oh, and when Della asked it if it was bound there, it said no. But when she asked it if it was there to help someone else, it knocked twice for yes. I would still have thought it might be Mary Lou Nelson, if she hadn't said to help Miss Mary Lou."

"Cathy!" Connie's voice exploded in Cathy's ear.

"What? What is it?"

"It's LACEY! It's got to be. Lacey Lynch, her friend that she talks about in the journal. She knew the mansion because she and her mother were there so much and she and Mary Lou were friends. And the voice, they were the same age. Don't you see? It must be Lacey Lynch," Connie's voice held conviction.

"If Lacey and Mary Lou are both at the library and the spirit that answered asked for help, it wasn't the one doing the crying."

"It's Mary Lou who's crying."

"You're right, that must be it. But we still don't know how we can help her, or why she's there. Strange, they must have been very good friends."

"And you said Della asked if the spirit was bound there and it answered no, isn't that right?"

"That's right, it rapped once for no."

"So Lacey must still be here trying to help her friend somehow. But she can't. So she wants us to help her."

"That's what it sounds like, but how? I do know one thing. That bow's going to stay right there where it is, right?"

"Right," Connie laughed. "We'd already decided that when I lucked up on that picture of it. And Cathy, the séance is what I'd call a big success. Della Reubens contacted a spirit from the library and we do know more. At least a little more than we did. Enough to make some good guesses. But we've got even more questions now."

Connie paused briefly then stifled a laugh. "Tell me, how did Miss Minnie and Dick Randolph take all this?"

Cathy giggled. "Well, from the way all of them looked there were more open minds going out than there were coming in."

"Made some holes in the concrete ideas, did it? I remember some of the remarks that were made."

Cas came in hunting more coffee as Connie said goodbye to Cathy. She got a plate and a tray, reaching for the cookie jar.

"I guess that was a news bulletin about the séance?"

"Yes it was, and it was really something! Wait till you hear."

He turned, heading for the den. "Aren't you the least little bit curious," her voice followed him.

"Yeah, a little," Cas admitted when she caught up with him.

"Okay, I'll tell you—a little," Connie set down the cookies with a grin and went upstairs to run her bath water.

"All right, all right," Cas ate humble pie when she came back. "I give up. Tell me about it. What happened at the séance? Did Della Reubens really conjure up a spirit, I think they're called?"

"Yes, she did. And she refers to them as spirits." She told Cas all Cathy had told her and about Dick Randolph and Miss Minnie's doubts being shaken.

He looked everywhere but at Connie. His expression suggesting he had a vague and embarrassing pain somewhere.

"I guess it was a real sacrifice for you not to go to that séance." He was feeling guilty hearing her talk about the séance like it was a party she'd missed. "But I did get the bushes planted at the library." he reminded her.

"You certainly did and that and our new ones in front are worth a lot of points."

She stopped to kiss him on the forehead on her way upstairs. "And anyway I know everything that happened, thanks to Cathy."

"Telephone; telegraph; tell a woman." Cas was smart enough to keep the observation to himself, thinking of Connie all warm and rose scented after her bubble bath.

* * *

The next day Cas got a call from Clarence Lynch.

"Clarence," Cas was glad he had answered the phone. "Do you have some news for me? Heard someone mention this Peder Sellczk?"

"No," was the too quick answer. "No, nothing like that. I just wanted to know, did Terrence leave the shovel in your truck?"

"No, he didn't forget it. I asked him if I could borrow it for a couple of weeks. Are you needing it?" Cas fished for information, listening for something in Clarence's voice.

"No, no. I was out at the shed and noticed it wasn't there and wondered about it."

"I'll take good care of it." Cas stopped there, not wanting to lie to him or give him any more information.

"All right, then." Clarence spoke slowly. "I won't be needing it any time soon," he added softly before breaking the connection.

Cas frowned as he replaced the receiver. Clarence hadn't wanted to say any more than Cas did, but he sounded worried about that shovel. Clarence didn't ask why Cas had the shovel and Cas remembered Connie telling him about the communication she felt went on between Della Reubens and Hannah. He had a healthy respect for unspoken messages.

"I hope to God I'm wrong." Cas shook his head, refusing to think any more about it until he got the lab report he was waiting for.

His next call was from Connie. She apologized for bothering him at the office. "I forgot what relation you told me the woman in the Maryvale Nursing Home is to Lacey Lynch. You said Clarence looked it up in his family tree he had in their Bible."

"He said she's Lacey Lynch's granddaughter. She's ninety-four or six I think he said. Her mind is a little addled, lives in the past a lot. Sometimes she's all right, he said. But they were afraid she'd wander off or hurt herself." He went on as if talking to himself, remembering their conversation.

"Clarence's mother is awfully nervous too. She was scared to death when she first saw me after Welemon was killed. And there's no reason for me to make her nervous that I can see."

"It's the uniform," Connie grinned. "You always look so starched and efficient."

"Is that right? Thanks. I think. Is that all you wanted to know?"

"I thought you said she was Lacey Lynch's granddaughter. I just wanted to make sure. And I did write down her name. It's Daisy Walters. I meant to check with you last night but I forgot about it in the heat of the moment," she smiled into the phone. "See you later, I love you."

Cas was still lost in the memory of the heat of the moment when he heard the dial tone. He put the phone down and looked around to make sure there weren't any witnesses to the self-conscious flush on his cheeks, brief or not. He sat a few minutes, enjoying pleasant thoughts: Connie smelling like roses; the feeling he had turning in the driveway at home; Missy baking chocolate chip cookies; and Casey coming to visit him. Then unbidden, there was Hannah's pale, horrified face looking at that shovel.

"It can't be," he muttered to himself, "It just can't be."

CHAPTER 19

Cas was surprised when the lab report on the shovel came in. It was one report he wasn't all that anxious to get. This was one time it didn't bother him to think that considering it was the holiday season, he probably wouldn't get his report till the first of the year. He eyed the yellow envelope with mixed feelings.

"Doug picked the report up for you," Gladys called as she passed the door. "I've got a fresh pot of coffee made, want a cup?"

"Yes, but I'll come and get it." Cas knew he was killing time. He came back and sipped his coffee slowly, looking at the shovel in its cardboard carton standing in the corner.

He had about half a cup left when he heard Rhodes come in. Rhodes stopped at the open door, looking at the expression on Cas's face. They had worked together so long it was almost like being married when it came to unnecessary conversation. Rhodes's eyes went to the corner where the shovel stood.

"Got the report on the shovel?"

"Got it. Haven't opened it yet."

"I'll get me a cup of coffee. Be right back."

Cas finished his coffee and waited until Rhodes set his cup aside.

"Well," Cas pulled the report toward him and opened it.

As Rhodes waited Cas glanced through it to the sections which were of interest to him. Then instead of going back and reading it thoroughly he laid it aside and his eyes met the worried ones across the desk. The little hope still left on Rhodes's face was fading fast.

"It was the shovel that killed Welemon," Cas put it into words. Flat and cold and damning. "They found blood under the metal pieces on the back of it and the blood is Welemon's type."

Rhodes didn't comment. He just sort of wilted in the chair, looking gloomy as rain on a picnic.

"Of course that doesn't tell us who hit Welemon with it. Whoever did it could have thrown it back into the shed as he left."

"Yeah," Rhodes spat out the words. "This nice, neat stranger could have washed it off, too."

"It's official now, like it or not. May as well stop dragging my feet hoping for a miracle or an excuse of some way to bail out of this mess."

Rhodes groaned, "It's Christmas! Hell of a time to get arrested for murder."

"I'm not going to arrest him for murder. Not yet. I'm going to bring him in and talk to him."

"Shall I go and get him?"

"Yes, but wait a minute. I'm going to call him."

Cas had dialed the number so many times he didn't have to look it up and Clarence answered on the first ring.

"Clarence, this is Sheriff Larkin."

Clarence took note of the use of the title and something dead serious in his voice. "Yes?"

"I need to talk to you, Clarence. Rhodes is going to come and bring you in to the office here. I wanted to let you know he's coming. He's coming now."

A few seconds of silence passed. "All right. I be ready when he gets here."

Cas looked up as he broke the connection, agony drawing his dark brows together. "He said he'd be ready.

He didn't even ask why."

Clarence was waiting at the door when the car got there. He came out as soon as it pulled up at the curb. Rhodes reached over and opened the door for him.

"Evening, Mr. Rhodes."

"Good evening, Mr. Lynch."

Of all the discomfort and pregnant ache of questions in both minds, those greetings were all that made it to the lips of the sufferers. They rode in silence to the courthouse.

As Rhodes parked the car in the lot beside the office, he said, "Some days this is a good job. Some days it's not."

"Been that way most everywhere I ever worked," Clarence replied solemnly. They walked in together.

Gladys looked up, surprised to see them. Cas came out of his office to meet them.

"Clarence, would you like a cup of coffee?"

"Yes, thank you. I believe I would."

"I'll be right there," Gladys volunteered when she heard the question. "Would you like another cup?" She asked Cas, wondering what was going on.

He nodded. "Just warm it up," he handed her his cup.

Cas and Clarence got their coffee fixed just right with the things Gladys brought on the tray and Cas got up to close the door.

"Gladys, hold any calls. Don't put anyone through even if you have to tell them I'm not here."

Gladys nodded, wondering if there had been some kind of break in the murder case.

"Clarence," Cas began. "I've got to ask you some more questions about Welemon's death. There's been some evidence come to light that needs explaining."

"Is that my shovel in that cardboard box over there?" Clarence nodded toward where it stood.

"Yes, that's it. It's just come back from the state lab with a report of their findings." He waited, hoping Clarence would start explaining, that there could be some explanation.

"They find out it had Welemon's blood on it?" Clarence bowed his head. "I washed it the best I could."

"You washed it? You?"

Cas gripped the edge of the desk with his right hand. "Do you know what you're saying, Clarence?"

Clarence's sad eyes met his. He suddenly looked every day of his age. "Yes, I know."

"Clarence," Cas's misery showed on his face. "I'd have bet my badge you wouldn't hurt Welemon or any other member of your family. I couldn't believe you'd hit Welemon with that shovel."

"And you'd been right." Clarence declared emphatically.

Hope leaped in Cas's heart, there must be an explanation.

Clarence's voice was positive and sadly solemn. "You'd been right, but I'm guilty."

Cas's brows drew together. "I'd have been right but you're guilty? You can't have it both ways, Clarence. Did you, or didn't you?"

"No, I didn't. I didn't hurt Welemon. It was that other one. The white one I killed."

"You mean Peder Sellczk? The one you told me you didn't know?" His eyes pierced Clarence, reminding him he'd lied, searching for the truth. Clarence sadly nodded.

"He's the one. The white one."

"Clarence, start at the beginning and tell me what happened. Did Welemon bring the white man to the house? Take your time and this time, tell me the truth. The whole truth."

"I's settin' out in the back yard enjoying the sunshine since the weather was good." Cas remembered the two old lawn chairs.

"I had my eyes closed and I heard someone coming. I opened my eyes and saw Welemon coming and this white man was right behind him. I got up and met them by the shed. I'd been raking leaves 'fore I set down to rest a little. He didn't tell me who the man was and I didn't ask. Didn't want to know him. Welemon wanted money to buy dope with. He never lied to me, he knowed I wouldn't 'low it. I told him I didn't have no money and I'd not give him any to buy dope with if I did. I could tell the white man was the one wanted the money, anyway. I looked at him and he knew I knew what he was. He pushed me, the white man. And I fell back and set down hard on the ground. Welemon pushed the white man away, Welemon was bigger than he was. Then Welemon bent down to me to see was I all right. And Welemon asked me if there wasn't anything I had they could sell and get money for, and I said no. He asked about an old carpet bag he'd heard I had in the shed and I shook my head. Then I saw a shadow pass behind him. The other man was going to go in the shed to look around for himself and I hollered at him. Welemon waved him back and he bent back down, trying to calm me. Then I saw something move and I looked up. The man had the shovel in his hands and he hit Welemon and he fell. He hit him again but stumbled and turned on me. He looked crazy, holding that shovel in both hands. I got up and run in the house and got my little pistol to run him off. I got it and it was loaded and I run down the back steps holding it behind me and looking at Welemon. I could tell he was hurt bad but he was still alive. Then the man run at me and swung that shovel up to hit me with it and I raised the little gun and shot right at him! He and the shovel just sort of fell down together, and Welemon, he was bleeding so. I jerked the door of the shed open and pulled that little white man in and threw the shovel in after him and run got my friend to help me get Welemon to the hospital."

Bit by halting bit, all of it came out. Cas saw it all like a movie playing in his head. This was the whole story, all that Clarence had been holding back. Cas knew he was hearing the truth at last about the two deaths and his heart ached for Clarence and Weleman too.

"Mom, want to go shopping or looking, or whatever you want to call it?"

"I do, but there's something I want to do first."

"What? We've got all day even if it does rain." Missy

stretched, looking out at the gray day. "We can have a snack here and not have to stop for lunch. It's about time anyway, isn't it?"

"Must be," Connie smiled. "My second cup of coffee's gone. I'll fix us some tuna salad. And I'm waterproof, I don't care if it rains either."

"I'd already decided I'm going to wash my hair when I get home. What is it you want to do?"

"I'm going to visit someone at the Maryvale Nursing Home. How about dropping me there and coming back for me in about an hour?" Connie finished mixing the salad as she talked and set crackers out to go with it.

"Who are you going to see?"

"I'm going to see Mrs. Daisy Walters. Mrs. Daisy Lynch Walters. She's a member of Clarence Lynch's family. She's Lacey Lynch's granddaughter."

"Oh, the Lacey mentioned in the journal. Do you suppose she remembers much about Lacey Lynch?"

"I would think so. Lacey was her grandmother. The only thing is when your dad asked Clarence about her for me, he said Mrs. Daisy's mind sort of wanders. It may be one of those times when she won't remember anything. Or maybe everything if we're lucky. Sometimes the past is clearer to older people than the present. I'll have to wait and see. And I'm going to take her a plate of cookies. I know she'll enjoy those and having someone to spend a little time with her."

"That's a nice thing to do, I approve. It's a good way to celebrate Christmas."

Cas and Clarence were still talking when Gladys tapped on the door. Cas raised his hand for Clarence to wait. "What is it, Gladys?"

"I had asked for the rest of the afternoon off to go do some last minute shopping but if you want me to, I'll stay."

"No, that's all right. You go on. Hook up this phone and I'll answer it until Rhodes or Doug gets here."

Gladys nodded and left quickly.

Cas turned his attention back to Clarence. "So that's the way it happened. He tried to hit you with the shovel and you shot him? Then you drug him into the shed. You didn't try to help him or?"

"No, I knowed he was dead. Wasn't anything anybody could do for him."

"And you and your neighbor got Welemon to the doctor, to the emergency room?"

Clarence nodded. "They took him in as quick as we got there. They could see he was in a bad way."

"You knew he was in a bad way but you didn't stay?"

"I knew they were doing all they could do and Mama had seen that man, and wasn't nobody with her."

"What else did you do?" Cas pressed.

"I'll tell you, I just hadn't come to it yet. The first thing I did after seeing to Mama was I saw the bag was still there."

"What bag? Did Welemon bring a bag with him when he came back?"

"No, the bag they asked about. The one in the shed that man was going to look for. It's a bag I've had for a long time. Welemon knew I didn't have any money, but he thought there might be something worth money in the bag."

"You've lost me, Clarence." Cas was perplexed.

"Oh, it don't matter about the bag. Welemon was desperate, him and this Peder as you called him, for money. They were trying to think of anything they could use or sell no matter how slight a chance they had, of finding any money or anything worth money."

"I see, that's where the bag comes in. So you checked on the bag. Then what did you do? Is that when you washed the shovel? Tell me all of it."

"The man in the shed, he was a little wiry man. And he was dead, nothing was going to change that. And I washed the shovel and locked the shed. Then Terrence come home and I got my neighbor to keep an eye on Mama and he and I went back to the hospital."

Cas waited, letting Clarence tell his story in his own way.

"After dark, I waited till after dark. Then, Terrence had parked the car in the driveway when he got back and went to the park with some friends to play football before he went home. I backed the car up as close as I could get to the shed. I dragged him, the man you said was named Peder. I dragged him out and propped him up and managed to get him in the trunk and close it."

He looked gravely at Cas. "I took him to the river. It wasn't far, and I rolled him out and pushed him into the water."

Connie drove, Missy carefully holding the heaping plate of cookies covered in plastic wrap. It was dark and gloomy but still wasn't raining when they stopped in front of the nursing home.

Missy got out and came around the car to drive. She tossed her long hair, giving it a pat as she watched Connie straighten the plastic wrap over the plate of cookies.

Getting in behind the wheel she called, "I'll see you in about an hour, Mom." She drove away thinking what a nice thing it was to take the cookies in and visit at the nursing home.

Inside, Connie asked at the front desk to see Mrs. Daisy Walters.

The nurse glanced at the paper plate of cookies and smiled at her. "She's sitting in her chair in the television room."

She hesitated, knowing Connie wasn't a regular visitor and added, "She has good days and bad days when things are a bit hazy. So don't be too disappointed if she doesn't react much. She's really in pretty good shape for her age and she's a very sweet person."

The nurse pointed, "The television room is through that door you can see from here."

Connie walked slowly, wondering if she would know which one was Mrs. Daisy if there were several in the room. "And how will I bring up Lacey if I get a chance and start asking the questions I want answered? I guess it will just come naturally if I tell her Cas knows Clarence. Hope so anyway, and I know she'll like the cookies."

As Connie entered the television room she realized at once which lady was Ms. Daisy. There were only two others there, both of them elderly white women. One of them left taking tiny little steps, and the other was sound asleep.

"Ms. Daisy?" Connie spoke softly so she wouldn't wake the other woman.

Ms. Daisy was not looking at the television set, but over it, out the window at the gray day. She turned her head when Connie spoke her name. "I saw Miss Mary Lou," she told Connie with a confidential smile.

"You did?" Connie seized the opening. "That's nice, I came to talk to you about Miss Mary Lou. And I've brought cookies," she hastily added when a shadow of suspicion crossed Ms. Daisy's face.

Looking away, Connie draped her coat on the back of the chair she had pulled up. She took the plastic wrap off the cookies and with a smile, placed them on the table beside Ms. Daisy. "I hope you like chocolate chips."

"Why, you sweet chile!" The old woman was delighted. She picked up a cookie, looking it over. "Chocolate. Chocolate candy. I like chocolate candy."

She peered at Connie, a bit puzzled. "I don't remember your name, chile, I don't remember much anymore."

Connie's heart sank at the admission but the way she enjoyed the cookies made her smile.

Ms. Daisy was enjoying the cookies, chewing on the front teeth she had left, a pleasant expression on her face now.

"I'm glad you like them. So you remember Miss Mary Lou?"

"Oh my, yes! Well, that's not quite right. I remember my Granny telling me about her and the good times they had playing together. Miss Mary Lou, she so good hearted. Poor thing. Poor thing."

"Poor thing? Why do you say that?"

"Why because," Ms. Daisy peered at her again, suspicious again. "I can't tell you that. My Granny told me and my Mama before she died. Can't tell no one else, not unless Miss Mary Lou comes herself and tells me to and that sure ain't likely." The white head nodded and bobbed repeating, "Poor thing, poor thing."

Connie watched her from the corner of her eye. "She knows why Mary Lou's spirit is crying. She's determined not to tell, but her grandmother Lacey told her, she knows, all right. She and Lacey were best friends and there's something, some secret she told them before she died."

"Have another cookie, Ms. Daisy. And don't you worry about telling anything you aren't supposed to. We'll just talk about the good times Lacey that your Granny had. Her and Miss Mary Lou."

"Oh, they did have fun all right." Ms. Daisy enjoyed talking almost as much as the chocolate chips. "They were born the same year, eighteen forty-eight. And they played in the house and in the attic, and under the stairs, and in the trees and the tree house in the back. Wasn't no tree those two little girls couldn't climb," Ms. Daisy chuckled.

"They were friends a long time, weren't they?" Connie prompted.

"A long time, yes." Ms. Daisy's eyes seemed focused on the past, picturing the times her grandmother had told her about. "Long time. All the time she had, poor thing, poor thing."

Talking slowly Connie told her, "There are some things in the attic. The attic of the old Nelson mansion, where the Nelsons lived, where Mary Lou and your Granny Lacey played together," she explained carefully. "We're cleaning and restoring them so people can come and see them. All the pretty things from so long ago."

"What things you talkin' about?" Ms. Daisy's dark eyes snapped.

Taken aback at her tone, Connie explained. "There are two or three of Miss Mary Lou's dresses that we found. They are so pretty," Connie said gently. "And there was a journal she kept when she was a little girl. She talks about your Granny in it. She says real often, that Lacey is coming to play with me today. And we found a pretty little trinket box with roses on it. Things like that are what we found in the attic."

Ms. Daisy nodded slowly, remembering her Granny Lacey.

"I was hoping there would be a picture of her young man, but there wasn't. Not a good one, anyway. I found one in an old newspaper -"

"Mr. Louis DeVille. Mr. Louie, he a handsome one, all right." The black eyes on the past turned dreamy. "My Granny say he can charm the birds right out of the trees. But he no empty hearted flirt. He loved Miss Mary Lou. She loved him too, poor thing. Poor thing."

Connie sighed to herself. "Well, she pronounces it Louie too, I guess that's all I'm going to learn from her. I wish the old papers were in better shape."

Connie broke a cookie in half and nibbled a little of it. "So that was his name, her young man?"

"Yes, Louie DeVille."

"It was this Louie that she ran off with?"

"Humpf!" Ms. Daisy snorted. "Run off! Poor thing. I can't talk no more about it. Only if Miss Mary Lou come and say it's all right, my Granny told me."

She gave Connie a sly look, "You come back and bring Miss Mary Lou with you, I'll tell you."

Connie mentally resigned herself that was all Ms. Daisy was going to say. "She'll keep her Granny's secret till she can't remember it anymore."

Trying to shake her depression, Connie raised her head to look out the window and saw Missy pull up in the car outside. The rain was falling heavily now and the car lights went out as she watched.

"She's already got her umbrella up, I'll just wait in here a few minutes, Ms. Daisy was sure enjoying these cookies till I mentioned Mary Lou running off with her Louie."

She offered her another cookie and pushed them closer to her on the table.

"Miss Mary Lou run off without telling her Papa, humpf!" Ms. Daisy was still indignant.

"That's what everybody thinks, Ms. Daisy." Connie couldn't resist prodding, feeling that Ms. Daisy wanted to say more. But her Granny Lacey had fixed that, telling her not to talk about it unless Mary Lou herself came and told her it was all right. Connie knew there was no hope of finding out anything else.

"Can't tell you any more." Ms. Daisy's sly look was back with a child's simper, "No, not unless?" She stopped, staring. "MISS MARY LOU!!"

Ms. Daisy's eyes stared past Connie. They were full of pleased surprise but afraid at the same time, in awe of something or someone.

Connie turned and looked across the long room to the arched door that led into the hall. Looking out of the dimness of the television room, the hall light was like a spotlight on Missy as she stood there, waiting to get her mother's attention and let her know she was waiting for her.

Missy had on her rain boots and had put on her Dad's raincoat. He left it in the car half the time. The coat was royal blue and hung to her ankles.

Connie watched the water dripping on the floor from the coat and the umbrella she held at her side.

When she saw Connie turn, Missy smiled and waved, glancing back toward the nurse's station.

"Miss Mary Lou! Miss Mary Lou herself! She come and smile at me!"

The look on the beaming old face made the hair on the back of Connie's neck stand up, and a little shiver danced along her spine like an icy butterfly.

Connie hardly dared to breathe, looking from one to the other.

Ms. Daisy smiled and chuckled to herself. Missy stood waiting for some sign from her mother that she was ready to go.

Time seemed to stand still as Connie gazed at her daughter. Missy's fair face was framed by her long dark hair and the blue of the coat accented still more her dark blue eyes. Feeling strange inside, Connie beckoned to her to come in.

As Missy came toward them, Ms. Daisy watched her every move. When Missy pulled up a chair near them, Ms. Daisy spoke.

"Your eyes just as blue as my Granny says, Miss Mary Lou. Yes ma'am, they the bluest eyes I ever did see." Ms. Daisy nodded her head, smiling fondly at Missy.

Missy shot a concerned look at her mother.

Connie gave a small but emphatic shake of her head.

"Where my manners? Will you have a cookie, Miss Mary Lou?" Ms. Daisy pointed to the plate of cookies.

"Thank you," Missy said politely, and took a cookie. She smiled at Ms. Daisy.

Connie spoke up. "This is Lacey Lynch's granddaughter. You remember, Lacey, who used to come and play with you." Connie spoke slowly, willing Missy to understand.

"Oh," Missy nodded slightly at her. "You're Lacey's granddaughter." Missy bit into the cookie, not knowing what else she should say.

Ms. Daisy chuckled. "This lady, she want to ask about you but I say no. Not unless you bring Miss Mary Lou with you." Ms. Daisy beamed at both of them. "I'm glad I can tell at last," Ms. Daisy sighed. "Been too long, too long. Something should be done, poor thing. Poor thing."

She brightened, "But you be here with us! You come to me and I can tell."

"Tell about the night she ran off?" Connie pushed her, trying to keep her mind on track.

Missy bridled, giving Connie a sharp look for prodding the fragile old woman.

Ms. Daisy saw the look and laughed a rich, contralto laugh. "Don't you fret, Miss Mary Lou. I tell her. I tell her right now."

Connie and Missy sat enthralled, listening to the poignant recital of all the secrets that tumbled out of those loving, friendship bound old lips that could let them go at last.

"Storming that night it was." Ms. Daisy made a contemptuous gesture at the window. "This just a little downpour. The lightning walk around that night, and the thunder loud as cannon fire." The old eyes saw the scenes her Granny had described to her and her mother so many times and so many years ago.

When it was over Connie and Missy got up slowly, moving as if mesmerized. Connie pressed Ms. Daisy's hand in both of hers. "Thank you, Ms. Daisy. I'll see that this is taken care of. I promise you, I will." Connie patted her hand and walked toward the door.

Missy knelt down, tears welling into her eyes, and put her arms around the thin shoulders, holding Ms. Daisy close.

"It's all right now. It's all right. She said she'd see to it."

"Yes," came out on a relieved sigh. Ms. Daisy's smile would have made the angels glad. "Now you be at peace. Miss Mary Lou Nelson and Miss Lacey Lynch can play together again in Heaven."

Outside, it was still raining hard. Connie paused at the door, touching her daughter's arm. "Missy, don't say anything to anyone about this, not even Casey. I'll tell your Dad about it. He'll know what to do, how to handle it."

CHAPTER 20

It had been a mostly silent drive. As Cas entered the narrow driveway beside Clarence's house it was an uphill fight to keep his feelings from showing. He was taking Clarence home because he trusted him and he hadn't actually been charged with anything yet. Clarence's trust lay heavily on him. He trusted Cas to do what he knew had to be done.

Clarence broke the silence. "I appreciate you bringing me home. Will you pull back there by the shed?"

Cas obligingly pulled into the back yard, thinking Clarence wanted to go in the back door.

"Wait here a minute," Clarence asked as he got out. He headed for the shed. He came back with something wrapped in cardboard and put it on the floor of the truck.

"What is that, Clarence?"

"This is the bag Welemon thought might have something worth money in it."

Wondering what the connection was to the actual case, Cas asked. "Is there?"

"I don't know. I surely don't," Clarence answered honestly. "I think it most probably is old clothes. Maybe a locket or some small keepsake like that, but mostly just some old clothes."

"You think it will be needed for evidence?" Cas sounded doubtful, not seeing any useful connection to the thing.

"It's what Welemon wanted to look in to see if he could find something to get some money for, for that white man. It's what that man hit him with the shovel for."

"All right." Cas gave in, humoring him. "Do you want a receipt for this, this bag?"

"No, don't need no receipt. It won't bring Welemon back. But no one else needs to die for it. Way I see it, you got my life in your hands. What difference an old carpet bag going to make?"

"Well," Cas managed a weak smile, "You've sure got your priorities straight."

More seriously he added, "Mind what I told you. Stay here and don't do anything or talk to anyone about this until you hear from me. I'll do my best for you."

"I know you will." Clarence smiled then, "I told you, I voted for you."

Pulling into the driveway at home couldn't lift his spirits this time. Cas tried to grin as he came in the back door but it was a pretty weak effort that didn't quite make a happy face.

"Tough day? We're having banana pudding for dessert," Connie tried to cheer him up. "It's waferless though, I forgot to stop and get them."

"That doesn't bother me long as you didn't forget the bananas. You know what a banana freak I am. If you have to forget something, just make sure it's only the wafers."

"Good," Connie brightened. "That's a much better grin than the one that came in on you." She came and traced the corners of his mouth with her fingertips.

Cas took both her hands in his and kissed her, feeling better.

"If you two can spare the time?" Standing in the kitchen door, Missy did her best to look prim. "Casey will be here soon, and I want to eat."

"Everything's ready. If you don't have time for dessert you can have it after you come home."

"If there's any left," Cas pointed out, getting even. "You know how it is with dessert around here."

"I know how you like bananas. Casey can wait!" Missy made mincing, fast steps into the kitchen.

Cas's humor had improved almost to normal. "I like Casey, he's dependable."

"I like him too, if anybody cares." Connie started putting things on the table as Cas and Missy continued their conversation.

"He told me about going to your office to visit and see how your arm was," Missy said. "He told me he went over to Marble County with you."

"Yes, he did. Harlan likes him too. Harlan's the acid test," Cas chuckled. "They got along. Harlan's quit chewing tobacco, but he's got a long way to go to be the ideal role model." Cas laughed at the thought.

They moved their conversation to the table as Connie set out hot rolls and butter.

Missy managed to finish dinner and dessert before Casey came, and Cas walked to the door to watch them out the driveway.

Connie heard the car go up the drive and called to Cas, "Why don't you come in here and sit while I finish up. I've got something to tell you."

"Okay." Cas glanced at his cast, "I guess I'd better not try to dry."

"No. I'll let you off kitchen duty until you get that cast off. Probably save a fortune in broken crockery." She made a face at him.

"You're the one who said I should learn to enjoy poor health," he reminded her. "What is it you want to tell me?"

"I went to see Mrs. Walters at the nursing home today. She's Daisy Lynch Walters. Remember you told me she's Lacey Lynch's granddaughter?"

"That's what Clarence told me." He looked away, his mind going back to Clarence and the problems he and Cas had before them.

"I took some cookies and told Missy to come back for me in about an hour so I could talk to Ms. Daisy. She talked about her Granny and her mother and about the Nelson family and being acquainted with them for years. About the times back when her Granny was a little girl."

"Clarence told me her mind's a bit off. Comes and goes, is the way he put it. It's not surprising she would talk about things and people she remembers from years ago."

Connie nodded, "I didn't know what to expect. But when she talked about the Nelson family and the things her Granny told her about, her mind was clear as a bell. I could almost imagine I was there, seeing the things that happened the way she told it."

Something in Connie's voice made him think picturing some of those remembered events was unpleasant. "Clarence said they were friends, Lacey and Mary Lou."

"They were. They grew up together and played together, and did all the things little girls do, sharing their feelings and secrets and fun. Ms. Daisy told me about what happened at the Nelson mansion so plain I could see it in my mind."

Cas braced himself, remembering Hannah's words when he had asked her about the basement. But she had said she didn't feel any danger. He clung to that and he braced himself for whatever was coming.

"The way she told it," Connie continued. "So carefully word for word in places I know it was repeated just as her Grandmother Lacey told the story to her and her Mother so long ago. Before she died she passed the secret on."

"Secret?" Cas got up and poured coffee for them both, glad to have something to get his mind off what Clarence had told him.

"Yes, secret. The true story. About the two little girls and what fast and good friends they were. I asked her if they were still such good friends up till the night when Mary Lou ran off. But every time she got up to that night she'd just say, Humpf, can't talk about that, and wouldn't say anything else."

"The black edged item you found in the old newspaper said Nelson died by his own hand that night. The night Mary Lou ran off with this Frenchman. Isn't that right, according to the date on the paper?"

"He died that night and the Frenchman's name was Louie DeVille. That much is true."

"And because of that, Nelson put a bullet through his head. That's the story."

"That's what everybody thought because Mary Lou and Louie were gone and they found Nelson with the gun still in his hand."

Cas sipped his coffee, relaxing. It seemed to him all the pertinent facts were already known.

"Mary Lou did threaten in front of other people to run off with Louie, and Nelson was pretty loud about his disapproval. Everyone in town was aware of the situation. They had seen Mary Lou and Louie together and you could see they were in love even looking at their pictures in the old newspapers, whether Nelson approved of it or not."

Connie took her cup to the sink to wash. "But why then, in all those years has no one ever heard from them? And who is it that's crying in the library basement? And the séance, Cas. Why is Lacey still here?"

"I don't know." Cas shook his head and pushed his cup aside when Connie glanced back at the pot.

"I'd about given up. Decided that was all I was going to get from Ms. Daisy, about her Granny and Mary Lou playing together. It was about time for Missy to come back for me anyway. Ms. Daisy looked like a sly little girl with a secret when she told me if I'd bring Miss Mary Lou with me next time she'd tell me what her Granny told her. She said it about three times. Like it was a game she knew, and she could keep the secret her Granny told her."

"So you didn't learn much that you hadn't already guessed from reading the journal."

"Yes, I did. I'm getting to it. I'd just given up learning anything else when Missy came back. It was raining hard then, really coming down. When Missy came in to let me know she was there she had on your raincoat which hung to her ankles, and the big black umbrella dripping as she waved to me from the hall door."

Cas smiled. "I'm glad somebody's getting some use out of that raincoat, I usually forget it."

Getting excited now, Connie tossed the dish cloth aside and sat down opposite Cas. "Ms. Daisy looked up and saw her standing there. I wish you could have seen the look on her face! She looked at Missy in her boots and that long coat, water dripping off of it, and Missy's long dark hair and blue eyes. Ms. Daisy thought she was seeing Mary Lou Nelson!"

Cas raised his eyebrows but didn't interrupt.

"She was so pleased, it just wrung my heart. I beckoned to Missy to come in and Ms. Daisy told her how her Granny had told her how blue her eyes were and smiled and offered her a cookie. I shook my head and Missy went along with it, and didn't startle her. It was so strange, it gave me gooseflesh. Cas, she was talking to Mary Lou, her Granny's friend."

Cas frowned a little, "And Missy didn't say anything?"

"No, I didn't want to startle the poor old thing though I wasn't really sure whether I should feel guilty about it or not. And she seemed to be relieved to be able to tell what her Granny had told her because now, Mary Lou wanted her to."

"Mary Lou wanted her to?" Cas questioned that, looking puzzled. "A thing that's been secret so long, why would Mary Lou want her to tell?"

"Because we can HELP her! Now that we know, we can do what needs to be done."

"Help her do what? Nelson did kill himself, we know that. Nothing's going to change that now. What did she tell you?"

"She told me what really happened that night. Why it was covered up and never told. Louis DeVille and Mary Lou went and got their union blessed by the new young priest at St. Anthony's. Mary Lou packed her bag, and Louie was to come for her that night. They would go to Nelson, wearing their wedding rings, and together ask for his blessing. Then if he still would not approve, they were going to tell him they loved each other. The union had been blessed and they would leave and live their lives together somewhere else." Connie drew a deep breath, "I'll tell you the way she told me and Missy, in her words."

CHAPTER 21

"It was a terrible stormy night. The rain come and lash the trees, and the thunder and lightning. The lightning so bad it showed in big streaks and look like it walk around. The thunder loud as cannon fire. Seem like the feelings in that house caused a war in Heaven, the way that storm rage. Lacey, my Granny, she was there when Miss Mary Lou and her Louie came before the priest and she know he was coming to take her away after they talked to her Daddy. Miss Mary Lou, she still thought her Daddy would come around. But my Granny, she know how proud and stubborn he is. She afraid he break Miss Mary Lou's heart and she never come back. My Granny slip into the house to listen that night, and see what Nelson do when they come to him. She heard it all and saw what happened. It carved on her heart, she told me and my Mother, what she see that night. The door was open up there to Mr. Nelson's study. She slipped up the stairs because she could hear voices. Miss Mary Lou and Mr. Louie, they up there with him. They must have just come in, 'cause Miss Mary Lou was talking to her Daddy. She told him she loved Louie and he loved her. He didn't say a thing. My Granny could see them from where she hide. And Mr. Nelson, he just look at Mr. Louie DeVille with contempt. Miss Mary

Lou told her Daddy much as they hoped he would give them his blessing and be happy for them, they were going to be together. Mr. Nelson didn't say too much at first. He treated Mr. Louie like he wasn't worth worrying about, so contemptuous of him he was. Mr. Louie didn't say anything except when Miss Mary Lou asked him something or say something to him. Granny told us she thinks he knew Nelson would never change his mind. Mr. Nelson let Miss Mary Lou finish about going somewhere else to live, then he told her Louie had no way to support a wife and family. That he had no expectations and if she was foolish enough to run away with the likes of him, neither would she. He would cut her off entirely and she would have no home or anyone to go to when she needed help. He said she didn't know anything about hardship. He said nobody could live on rainbows and promises for more than a few weeks. He talk to her like she in school and he trying to teach her something. He said she didn't know what she was asking for. And make no mistake, he say, he would cut her off without a cent. He told them when Louie seemed set on trying to gain himself a comfortable life by marrying his daughter, he had changed his will to leave his house to the city and he would see to it that they had nothing but each other if that's what they had their hearts set on.

"Mr. Louie, he spoke then. He said it was true he could not keep Mary Lou in the style she was living in. But that he could make a comfortable home for them, and he would love and take care of her without any help from Nelson.

"Then Miss Mary Lou held up her hand with the gold ring on it and said, Tell him, Louie."

"And Mr. Louie, he held his hand up too, to show the wedding ring. He told Mr. Nelson, we have had our union blessed by the priest at St. Anthony's. In the eyes of the church, we are wed."

"Granny so scared! She looking through a crack 'tween the study door and the wall. She see Mr. Nelson open his desk drawer and get out his gun. He get up and he point the gun at Mr. Louie. Then so quick no one can rightly see what's happening, Miss Mary Lou throw herself in front of Mr. Louie and the bullet meant for him hit her in the back. My Granny cry out then and run to the door. She see Miss Mary Lou lying there on the floor, her Louie kneeling beside her.

"Mr. Louie's face so pale. He look up at Nelson and say, "You've killed her!'"

"Mr. Nelson stand up there over them. Granny say he look like one them ugly gargoyles under the church roof, he so full of hate. He raised the gun and shot Mr. Louie and he fall back."

"My Granny cry out, but can't hear nothin' but the angry thunder. She run and put her arm under Miss Mary Lou's head, crying, begging her not to leave them, but she gone. She gone, poor thing, poor thing. MISS MARY LOU GONE! My Granny, she set there on the floor holding her friend to her heart and crying. Mr. Nelson standing over them, seeing what he done. My Granny scream when she hear another shot. She looked up to see Mr. Nelson fall. He can't live with what he done in hot blood. He shot Miss Mary Lou and her Louie and he shot himself."

"My Granny sittin' there crying, the storm raging, and death all around her. She jump up and run to get her young man, my Grandpa he was. He see her coming in the storm and crying and blood on her bosom. He run out to meet her and go with her to the mansion. My Granny didn't want it known that Nelson killed his own flesh and blood. Between them they got the young couple down to the basement where they were working on a wall and put them in there, in the wall. My Granny got a comforter and a quilt and they wrapped them in those. My Grandpa was fixin' on the wall and he put up the rest of the wall braces so no one could see behind them. He tell Granny he seal up the wall the next day and no one would know what Nelson done."

"Then they went back upstairs and put Nelson where all the blood was, his fingers still fast on the gun, and left him there for someone to find the next day. Then as they started back down to leave, hurryin' to get away from there, Granny saw the bag Miss Mary Lou had packed. She cry when she touch it, and hold it 'gainst her heart. She took it with her and hid it so people wouldn't know. Then she hurt, all the rest of her life 'cause her friend couldn't be proper buried and people wouldn't know her and Mr. Louie were proper married in the church. She carry that in her heart as long as she lived. She kept the family from the biggest scandal, but she say Nelson is the one should not be buried in hallowed ground. She always mourn that Miss Mary Lou might not be at rest."

Cas sat spellbound as Connie had been by the old woman's story seeing it in his imagination as Connie and Missy had, feeling the pain and horror of it.

"That's bad, worse than what people thought they knew," Cas frowned. "His own daughter. Nelson killed his own child."

"And Cas, Mary Lou is NOT at rest. I think, and Cathy does too, it's her we hear crying in the basement. And now we know why," a shiver ran through her. "They are there, her and her Louie, in that wall. They're sealed up there, that's why she's crying. Cas, what can we do? And where do you suppose that bag is? Ms. Daisy said Clarence knows, but does he? After telling all that, that she's kept in her heart and memory for so long, maybe she's confused about it."

"No," Cas said slowly. "I think she knew what she was saying. I've had to question Clarence again about the two murder cases and he gave me some kind of a bag. He told me some things about it, but I didn't understand what he was talking about. He told me they, Welemon and Peder, wanted to look in some kind of a bag he had to see if they could find anything valuable to sell and buy drugs. He insisted on giving it to me to use, for evidence, he called it. It seemed to me he just wanted to get rid of it, just wanted me to take it away from there. So I took it even though it didn't have all that much to do with the case. It's out in the truck. I've got the whole story now. My two murders were connected, Clarence has confessed."

"Clarence? Oh, not Clarence. Clarence? No, not his nephew. His dead sister's child?" She put her hand over her mouth, shocked.

"No. No. Clarence didn't kill Welemon. But he did kill the other murder victim. I had to send for him when I got the report back on his shovel, the one we used to plant the holly bushes here and at the library. It had Welemon's blood on it. And we had mud from the dead man's shoes that was the same as the mud in Clarence's back yard. He knew we had about all the pieces of the puzzle when he found out I'd borrowed that shovel from Terrence."

"And Clarence confessed? But how in the world did all this happen? Can you tell me?"

"Welemon was looking for money to buy drugs, being pushed by Sellczk, of course. They went to Clarence's house. Clarence refused to give them any money, and there was a scuffle. Sellczk pushed Clarence and he fell. Welemon leaned down to see about Clarence and it was then Sellczk hit Welemon with Clarence's shovel. He hit him hard twice and Clarence ran to get his gun he kept for protection, to scare Sellczk off. When he ran back to chase him away and help Welemon, Sellczk raised the shovel to hit Clarence, and Clarence shot him."

Connie shuddered, "He would have killed Clarence too."

"There's no doubt about that. I think anyone can see it was self defense, but it's got to be cleared up. Clarence went back home and washed the shovel. Then he took Sellczk's body to the river and pushed it into the water, trying to hide what happened."

Connie sighed, thinking about Clarence and Terrence who had planted the trees, and the rest of the family. "What's going to happen to him?"

"It's self defense, no doubt about that. But putting Sellczk in the river and washing the shovel, that's got to be dealt with. I wish he'd told me. I had the feeling from the beginning the two cases were connected but until I found Welemon's blood on that shovel, there was no tangible proof."

Connie sat back down opposite him. "I guess this is a classic example of the dead having to wait on the living, isn't it? You've got all this to finish up on the two cases and Clarence's confession before you can do anything for the poor, dead lovers at the library. Do you have any idea how to begin when you get around to taking the bodies out of the basement?"

"The most time consuming thing about that will be taking care of all the paperwork and permits involved. I know how to proceed on some of them, but I'll have to check on others. Just don't say anything about it to Cathy or anyone else, until I can get a chance to get to it."

"And this bag you said Clarence gave you. Is it the bag Mary Lou Nelson packed that night?"

"He didn't tell me that in so many words. He said things I didn't understand then. All that came across to me was he wanted me to take that bag away from there. But from what I remember and what you said Ms. Daisy told you, this must be it. The one Lacey took away with her that night and hid. I'll call and ask Clarence about it, he won't mind."

Connie pictured Clarence wanting to get rid of the bag his poor nephew was killed for. "No wonder he wanted to see the last of it. Poor Mary Lou and Louie, and now this. What a lot of sadness there is packed in this one bag, if it really is Mary Lou's."

Cas dialed Clarence's number, glancing at Connie when he answered. Clarence was more interested in making it clear he didn't want that bag anymore than supplying any other information. "I told you, I've had it a long time and I don't want to keep it any more. Not since Welemon was killed."

"Yes, I understand. But where did you get it, Clarence? Whose bag is it?"

"My Grandmother, she gave it to me. My Mama didn't have a place to keep it, and come to live with me not long after that. So I took it and hid it out there in my shed."

"Whose is it, Clarence?"

"Why you want to know, Sheriff?"

"I want to know because Connie went to see Ms. Daisy at the nursing home today and Ms. Daisy told her what her Granny told her happened in the Nelson mansion so long ago. About Mary Lou Nelson and her Louie DeVille. She said that night Lacey and her young man, they overlooked the bag Mary Lou packed, so Lacey took it home and hid it so no one would know what happened that night."

"So you know all about what happened," Clarence sounded resigned. "It was a burden to keep a secret like that, all these years."

"Yes, I'm glad Ms. Daisy felt relieved to tell it. And this is Mary Lou's bag. It's the bag brought home from the mansion. As you can see, it's probably not in too good shape as old as it is, is why it's wrapped up."

"I haven't taken it out of the cardboard, Clarence. I wanted to know if this was the bag Ms. Daisy was talking about first. Also, if you want to be here when it's opened I'll understand and wait."

"No, it's all right for you to open it. You're the one in charge and I guess someone will have to open it. I don't even know what's in it. It was brought home and hid and passed from one to another and no one has opened it that I know of. Just wrapped it up and kept it. I guess it's got Miss Mary Lou's clothes in it, things she'd need to go away. I doubt if there's anything that's worth anything in it. Welemon and that thieving doper was just lookin' for something, anything, they could turn into money to buy dope. But if there was anything in it, it was Miss Mary Lou's anyway, not any of ours."

"You don't mind if I open it, then?"

"No. I'm glad to get shed of it. It's not going to do me or mine any good if I'm hanged."

"Clarence, You are not going to be hanged. You shot a man who was trying to kill you. I would have done the same in your place."

"Hmm. Well, I be here when you want me for anything," was the dubious reply.

"Listen to me, Clarence. There are certain things I have to do, things that have to be taken care of. The judge is out of town right now. I need to talk to him, the Attorney General's Office, and do some finishing up on these two files which have turned out to be the same case. You just stay right there and keep your hopes up. We'll get this straightened out. And don't talk to anyone about it."

Connie had been hanging on every word of his conversation. "So this is Mary Lou Nelson's bag. Just think! After all these years."

"I'll go out and get it."

CHAPTER 22

Connie had cleared the coffee table and Cas laid the bulky cardboard shrouded package on it. Cas came around and sat in the chair nearest the table and Connie pulled up a hassock on the other side, holding her breath in the excitement of having found the bag. Mary Lou Nelson's bag.

"Or is it Mary Lou DeVille's bag?" Connie's romantic heart questioned silently. She watched, everything seeming in agonizingly slow motion, taking too long.

Cas began by carefully removing the cardboard. It had been tied with heavy twine to keep it in place. Beneath the cardboard was a plastic trash sack, a large one that had been gathered at the top and secured with wire.

"This is twisted so, maybe you'd better get the scissors or my wire cutter."

Connie hurriedly brought her sewing box, the scissors on top, the wire cutter and the pliers.

"Taking no chances?" Cas grinned at the tools.

"No mere wire is going to stop us now, after all these years." Connie watched as the stiff old wire broke in two pieces and Cas cut off the rest.

Beneath the plastic sack there was a large cotton pillow case wrapped around the bag and simply gathered at the top. Though Cas was careful, he made two rents in it which followed the weave of the cloth as he removed it. Coming away, it revealed a carpet bag whose colors were still surprisingly bright and gay. The double clasp was fastened securely between the polished wood carrying handles, but it was not locked. With Connie's help, Cas cleared away the things it had been wrapped in and the gaily colored bag sat there before them looking much as it must have when it had been packed and made ready for leaving. For Mary Lou and Louie's elopement.

"It's sad, isn't it?"

Cas nodded. "Packed a long time ago for a trip that was never made. I'll open it and reach in," Cas grinned at his wife's anxious face. "And if nothing bites me you can have the fun of seeing what there is in it."

"If you think it's inhabited by something that may bite you'd do better to turn it over on its side instead of running your hand into it."

"Probably be able to see in without reaching in, the way it opens."

He opened the double clasp and pushed the bag open as far as it would go. "There you are."

Connie began carefully removing things from the bag. A scarf had been laid over the top before the clasps were closed.

"I guess that was to protect things from dust."

Cas nodded, more curious than he would admit.

Most of the bag's contents were camisoles and other underclothes. There was a silver mirror and brush set, a small wooden box that played music when the lid was raised and held some small jewelry items. Wrapped in a piece of muslin were two bars of soap scented with attar of roses, some of the scent still lingered, or perhaps the picture of a rose and romantic imagination made it seem so to Connie.

There was an item wrapped in another silk scarf which turned out to be a jeweler's box. With a wide eyed glance at Cas, Connie raised the lid and gasped at what she saw.

"Emeralds!"

Cas touched the necklace lightly. "Must be worth a fortune. What's that under it?"

"Looks like something silver."

Connie gently put aside the emerald necklace and carefully drew out the piece beneath.

"Oh! It's beautiful. This is platinum, it must be!"

"What are those blue stones?"

"Blue topaz, I'm sure. Sapphires would be a lot darker than that, and these are the color of her eyes. Cas, I think this is the necklace Mary Lou Nelson is wearing in the portrait in the courthouse. And to think, these and her personal things have been hidden away all these years."

Picking it up delicately with her fingertips Connie held a delicate lace camisole to her heart. "They thought they were going to go away together and live happily ever after, in spite of Nelson. Oh, Cas," a tear welled up and spilled over.

"It happened a long time ago," Cas reminded her gently. "No one could have known how it would end. Nelson, hardhearted and stubborn as he was, he suffered too. It was a scandal, all right. But a lot worse than anybody knew."

Connie bowed her head over the fragile lace. "We've got to do now what should have been done then. The only thing we CAN do for them now, get them properly buried."

"Look on through that and unfold everything that's folded or wrapped up," Cas ordered, peering into the bag from where he sat.

"I was going to anyway but what is it you're trying to find?"

"That piece of paper Ms. Daisy said they had from the priest."

"Oh, so everyone will know they were married?"

"Yes, but we may not need it if we can find enough witnesses, references to it. We might be able to mark their graves as husband and wife."

"Oh Cas," Connie's eyes were bright with hope they could do something more for the ill fated young lovers. "Could that be done, do you think?"

"I don't know. Right now, I've got to find the proper paper route to go to just get them out of the library basement much less to where they belong. But I'll try, I promise I'll try. There's still some room in the old area up on Peaceful Ridge where Nelson is buried that we can use for them. Then we'll have to arrange for the stone, or stones."

"I hadn't thought of that. How can we get the money for the stones? Who, how will we pay for them?"

"The old skinflint himself will pay for them." Cas said grimly.

"When Nelson left the mansion to the city he left an amount to be used for an income to take care of it. We'll take it out of that, is what we'll do. As soon as we know how to go about it." His eyes gleamed, "How's that for making the punishment fit the crime?"

"You always get the bad guy, don't you?" Connie laughed. "You're a genius! Now that you bring it up, what could be more fitting?"

"Haven't got it done yet, so just hold on. It may take a while to get everything done and properly legit."

"But you will, I know you will!"

"Clarence Lynch is the first thing on my priority list now. I've got to get all my information and evidence together in presentable order before I can talk to the powers that be on his behalf."

Cas brooded over the problem before him. He listened as Connie went about starting coffee, glad she couldn't see how concerned he was.

As it happened, he need not have given his worry lines such a workout. His success surpassed his hopes and he was able to give Clarence good news in a matter of days to set his mind at ease.

As Cas had told him, having shot the man in self defense, he was not charged with murder. After he had presented his case, he brought Clarence in for the prosecuting attorney to question him, and stayed with him.

Though Clarence was not charged with murder, there was no getting around the facts he had washed the shovel, hid the body and put it in the river, and did not tell the whole truth when he gave his statement about Welemon's death. As he listened to those things Cas remembered Clarence's face when he had told him he was guilty of shooting the man who tried to kill him, who had already killed Welemon. In spite of Cas trying to help him, Clarence saw no hope at all and sat looking as if he was already condemned to spend the rest of his life in prison.

When they went to court Clarence hung his head as he stood silently before the judge, knowing he had done wrong. His conscience of all his own wrong doing and his grief for Welemon weighed heavy on him.

Judge Carpenter heard all that was presented to him. He listened with solemn patience to what Clarence had to say, making notes on the withholding of evidence and other things Clarence sorrowfully but honestly admitted he did. The worst of it being hiding the body then putting it in the water.

Tim found him guilty of that breach of good judgement and the law and one or two other offences he managed to make sound minor, winking at Cas over Clarence's bowed head. Then keeping in mind Clarence didn't have any money for a fine and Christmas was near, he pronounced the sentence to be imposed.

"One hundred hours of community service to be served within the coming year and a year's probation."

Connie was delighted when she heard about it.

"Yeah, I'm glad he got community service instead of a fine." His eyes narrowed, "But you've got something in mind, haven't you?" Cas fixed his suspicious Sheriff's look on his wife.

"As a matter of fact, I do. Tim didn't specify what the public service would have to be, did he?"

"No. But he will have to approve it," Cas quickly reminded her.

"We need Clarence at the museum. He can help us get it all done up and ready."

"Are you sure? He's not going to be able to do much building and remodeling if that's what you've got in mind."

"No, we've got some stronger and younger backs for that. But he can paint and sort and arrange things and," her eyes twinkled. "While all of us work, he can tell us about what he heard the old folks in his family talking about when he was a child at home. About his family and the Nelsons and how things in general and everyday life were back then. We'll be glad to have him and I think he'll enjoy it as much as we will. I know you can't send someone his age out to do hard physical labor of any kind. And work at the museum would be community service, wouldn't it?"

"It isn't me you need to convince of that. But I think it's a good idea, even if you did think of it first," he teased her. "I was wondering what could be found for him to do. You'd better call Tim and make sure it's all right before you say anything to Clarence. And remember, Tim said the sentence could be carried out any time in the next year."

"That's good, since we don't know exactly when we'll be needing him. I'll talk to the Museum Committee, then to Tim, then to Clarence."

"By the way, I asked around and found out where to go to get the permits and paperwork to take the two bodies out of the basement."

"Is it going to be complicated?" Connie asked, looking worried.

"I don't think it will be. I had to be pretty cagey. I didn't say what I had in mind or where the problem might be, just asked hypothetical questions and let gossip and speculation do the rest."

"Hypothetical questions?" Connie was horrified, "In a town this small? And nosy?" Her eyebrows flew up, incredulous.

"Yeah, I know," Cas grinned. "But it was a calculated risk. By the time I tell them what it's for, they'll be so relieved it's not some new murder case, they may gift wrap my permits for me."

"See, I told you you're a genius," Connie laughed with him. "I'm proud of you!"

"Well, I should hope so, after all my conniving and trouble. Because I'm not a devious person by nature." He paused trying to look noble and open.

"No," Connie snorted. "You're just suspicious as all get out, thinking everyone else is! Devious, I mean." She laughed at his reaction to that.

When Connie approached Tim Carpenter with her idea about Clarence doing the museum work he listened with interest to her plans for Clarence Lynch's community service.

"Sounds good to me. I'll be glad to put my paw print on that. Of course one good turn deserves another, as the saying goes." He managed to get a cunning nuance into the old cliché.

"You think it does, do you?" Almost sure of what he was going to ask, she grinned into the phone. "What do you have in mind? Judge Carpenter?"

"I've finally got moved, if you can call it that. You should see this office. No, on second thought, you shouldn't. There is one woman who comes in every day and does all the routine things. I don't even know what routine consists of yet, or what other categories are lying in wait for me."

He heard a stifled giggle, but continued.

"There's a part-timer who comes in on Friday afternoon and mostly files and works on her nails, filing seems to be as rough on them as the alphabet she uses. I'm not too sure it's English. She should probably go into cosmetology, concentrating on manicures and pedicures."

"Judge Carpenter, you're going to make me cry," Connie let the giggles out.

"Then there's the Office Manager who is also the judge's secretary according to her job description. She has her hands full without my correspondence but so far, it's gotten done. Right now, she's taking vacation days and if I'm not mistaken, she's thinking seriously of retiring when her sister retires from teaching in a year or two."

Connie didn't tell him he was right about Muriel. He already felt outnumbered in his new office.

"I want to be put at the top of your list when you go back to work after the holidays. I know it's early to ask, but do we have a deal?"

"We've got a deal if I can. I mean, if the museum committee can have Clarence whenever we want him and he can come to work for us whenever we need him?"

"Fine with me. Consider it chiseled in stone. You let me know the hours he puts in and handle it any way you want to. He's a nice old fellow. To tell the truth, I didn't know what in the world to do with him."

"We've solved each other's problems then. I'll call you soon as I get through entertaining and celebrating. You're my number one job next year."

"Hallelujah! I'm hanging up before you get to thinking it over and weasel out. Bye!"

Connie was too elated to keep still after talking to Tim. She knew Clarence would be happy about the work at the museum and she had work lined up for after the holidays. All the practical instincts she'd cultivated living with Cas rejoiced. She hurried upstairs for her coat and drove into town to visit with Miss Mayme and Miss Minnie.

"What good is good news if you can't tell anybody?" She put what Cas called her lead foot on the gas pedal.

There were three customers in the shop when Connie went in. She looked around while Miss Mayme waited on them. She was admiring the scent of a new potpourri item when Miss Minnie called to her from the office.

"Come on back and help me watch the coffee perk," the cheery voice invited.

Miss Mayme still had one customer. She gave her a small wave and went back to the office to help Miss Minnie watch the coffee perk. She pulled a chair up to the desk to get comfortable.

"Let's have the latest bulletins." Miss Minnie noted her pleased expression as she gathered up cups, "What's going on?"

"So much, I don't know where to start!"

"Don't start without me, I deserve better after making those three good sales." Miss Mayme hurried in and sat down looking proud of herself.

"Now. You were saying?"

"I'm trying to figure out where to begin. Everything sort of is, I guess you'd say, linked up together."

"That's life," Miss Minnie laughed. "Linked, connected, scrambled, what else is new?"

"That sounds like a lot. Maybe we should ask questions." Miss Mayme suggested helpfully.

"Have you learned any more about the spirit Della contacted and the crying in the basement?"

"Yes. Cathy and I figured out it must be Lacey Lynch Della contacted since she said she's the one who moved the bow. And the one crying in the basement has to be Mary Lou Nelson. You know, she said to help Miss Mary Lou twice. So it must be Mary Lou who is crying."

"All logical. And?" Both Andersons raised eyebrows hopefully.

"And Cas is working on a way to help her but I can't tell you about that yet."

"Cas is? Cas the unbeliever in the occult and match making—not necessarily in that order?"

"How did he get involved in this anyway?" Mayme demanded indignantly. "He didn't even want you to go to the séance!"

"I know, but Clarence Lynch is Lacey's great grandson and he's given Cas an old bag that used to belong to Mary Lou Nelson. It has some things in it we can use in the museum and I think Clarence is going to come and help us get the museum set up too. I haven't talked to him yet, but I think he will. I'll tell you more when I know more."

"Cas got a bag that belonged to Mary Lou Nelson? How did he happen to have it? I guess Mary Lou gave it to

Lacey?" Miss Minnie answered herself.

"It had been in Lacey's care, yes." Connie admitted carefully.

"And I've got some work already lined up for after the holidays. I'm going to work for Tim Carpenter at least a day, maybe more. Anyway, it makes me feel good to know I've got some work lined up."

"We know how that is. It was good to know we would have this business when we had to retire. We didn't know if we'd make it or not, but it was still good to have something to work for."

Miss Minnie got on with the questions, "Missy's still dating Casey Taylor I suppose?"

"Yes, and Cas and I are still glad they're going to the same college. His old car is still safe enough to come and go in. His guardian angel must be a mechanic," Connie giggled. "It runs right along like it doesn't know how old it is."

Connie set down her cup. "Before I forget it, when we finally get the museum ready to open would you like to bring some of your arrangements over, besides the one we will buy for the front? You could set them around like you did at the library. I guess we'll put one at the front, what do you think?"

"Probably one big showy one at the door will be really effective, you're right. And we could put the arrangements around inside. Let us know when."

Miss Mayme looked at Miss Minnie. "I forgot to tell you, Minnie, Hannah McLaughlin came by early this morning and bought a small bouquet. She had me fix it one sided. Must be going to hang it beside her desk or something."

"The customer is always right." Miss Minnie shrugged, not concerned about it.

Connie finished her coffee and got up. "I'm going by the library for a few minutes and make sure everything is where I left it. I hate to waste time going back through papers and things I've already looked at." Connie pulled on her coat.

She left her car at the flower shop and walked to the library. There didn't seem to be anyone there but Jo Beth.

Connie waved and went on back to the reading room. She selected some papers which hadn't yielded any useful information and brought them back out with her.

"I'm going to stick these back downstairs, Jo Beth. They don't seem to need any work on them or have anything about the Nelsons in them so I'm through with them."

Jo Beth nodded, busy stamping cards. She put the key on the corner of the desk for her and went on with her work.

Connie turned on the basement light and went downstairs.

It didn't take her long to walk to the last shelf and put the papers back with the others. There on the back wall was the small bouquet of carnations Miss Mayme had so accurately described. The sight of it touched Connie's heart. It made a pretty island of color in the gloom of the basement. The blue of the carnations matched the blue of Mary Lou's dress in the portrait.

Her hunch about where it was had been right, too. Hannah had bought them for Mary Lou and hung them about eye level on that grim looking concrete wall with library tape. Connie stood wide-eyed, as if assuring herself the carnations were real. They were beautiful, blue and white stripes the same color as the generous blue ribbon at the bottom of the small arrangement. So blue and perfect they almost looked artificial. She lightly touched the library tape.

"Hannah knows," she said aloud. Her voice was firm with conviction, "I don't know how, but Hannah knows."

She touched the cold concrete wall, realizing there was no crying now.

"Mary Lou, if you can hear me, help is coming. My husband Cas, he's the Sheriff here now. And he's working for you and Louie DeVille right now. There's a lot of paperwork and arrangements to be made but he's working on them and Hannah has brought you these beautiful carnations." She lightly touched the ribbon. "It won't be long, Mary Lou."

She turned and hurried back up the stairs, half afraid of getting an answer.

CHAPTER 23

At home, Connie called and talked to Ellen Toliver about Clarence coming to help them set up the museum. She explained about his family's ties to the Nelson family.

Ellen was delighted to have his help and was sure the others on the committee would be too. She was anxious to talk with him when she learned about the friendship between Lacey Lynch and Mary Lou Nelson. "This is really wonderful to find someone like this who really knew the family. Knew the people who are all part of Maryvale's history."

"He's doing some community service right now so I know he'll be glad to come help us. I'll let you know definitely after I talk to him, but I'm sure he will."

"Good, let us know as soon as possible. How interesting it will be to hear about the families and the early times from someone who was so close and knows about them, like a page out of history. It will be good to have his help, too. We'll be glad to have him."

Next, Connie called and talked to Clarence. She told him she had asked Judge Carpenter if he could help them at the new museum for his community service, if he wanted to.

"He gave his permission if you were agreeable. We sure could use your help, if you're interested."

"I'd be pleased to come and help whether I get any credit for it or not. Do you have much to put in the museum?"

"Oh, yes, we do. I think you'll be impressed how much we have and how nice it's going to be."

She told him about the dress they'd found with the hoop in it. "And you know about the journal Cas told you about that has Lacey Lynch's name in it. We're proud of it and all these things for our museum as we can be already and haven't even got off the ground yet!"

Clarence chuckled at Connie's enthusiasm. "I be pleased to be part of getting it started. You let me know when to come in to work, and I be there and help any way I can."

Christmas day Cas went in to work and relieved Doug from ten until two o'clock so he could enjoy dinner at home with his family. Missy was having dinner with Casey and his mother. Connie enjoyed sleeping late Christmas morning and had planned their turkey and trimmings for seven o'clock.

Cas dressed as quietly as he could. He looked around the kitchen and picked up a couple of sweet rolls on his way out, hoping coffee would be made when he got to the office.

When he came home about two-thirty, Connie fed him cheese toast and coffee with a big piece of pecan pie to go with his second cup of coffee. She bustled around waiting on him, pouring more coffee when needed and bringing his pie when he finished with the cheese toast.

Somewhere between finishing his cheese toast, a masterpiece of cheese, onion, and crisp bacon, and having his pie placed in front of him, Cas realized Connie wasn't talking.

"That's not a normal condition for her, certainly not during a holiday season and with all that's going on."

He paused, studying her from the corner of his eye. He wondered if she was upset about something but her expression was placid. She didn't seem worried, just quiet.

"Well, I don't guess I have to start confessing across the board not knowing what I've done to cause this. She's not mad at me but there's something wrong or must need fixing somewhere."

"Want seconds on anything?" Connie picked up his plate and cup.

"No. I just want to know what's wrong."

"Wrong?" Connie went on washing dishes and didn't look around.

Cas got up. "Yes. Wrong." He took the sponge out of her hand and threw it into the sink.

"You haven't said three words that weren't necessary since I came in. There's either something wrong or there's something on your mind. What is it?"

"All right, nosy. But you may wish you hadn't asked. I went by the Anderson's flower shop and heard Miss Mayme tell Miss Minnie that Hannah McLaughlin had come in and had a small bouquet made up."

She studied his face as she answered. "The arrangement was small and beautiful. It was one-sided, like it was going to be against something or hung up someplace. I went by the library on a hunch and took some papers down to the basement. The little flower arrangement was hanging on the back wall."

Cas didn't say anything, waiting.

"Cas, Hannah knows what's behind that wall. I don't know how she knows. But she knows."

Cas shrugged, turning away. "Most of you suspected it, why shouldn't she?"

"That's not the only strange thing."

"Whoa! We haven't established it's a strange thing unless feeling compassion is a strange thing. I doubt Hannah makes very much at the library. It was a sacrifice for her to give a ghost flowers for Christmas." Cas smiled at the thought, obviously approving the good deed.

"Um, well, it seems strange to me. And too, there's the way she acted when Della Reubens came. You remember I told you how she acted and wouldn't shake hands with Della?"

"I remember that. The only strange thing about that was your attitude. You had made up your mind based on not shaking hands that Hannah was a witch and could read Della's mind." He rolled his eyes heavenward at such a far out idea.

"You'd have to have been there to know what I meant. They stood there after she said no, she wouldn't shake hands, and you could tell there was some kind of communication going on between them. They understood each other all right."

Cas chuckled uneasily, not meeting Connie's eyes. Glad she had turned her attention back to the dishes.

"Connie, if I had a case with nothing but that in it, I'd close it and give up. Putting flowers on a wall where someone's been heard crying and refusing to shake hands with Della Reubens," he stated the case. "That makes you think there's something strange about Hannah?"

Cas raised his eyebrows in disbelief as she turned to look at him.

Connie sighed. "Well, when you put it like that," her conviction was fading. "I guess everybody did think there was a spirit down there." She stifled a giggle.

"What now?"

"I don't think Dick Randolph would have shaken hands with Della either."

"There, you see how silly all that suspicion is?"

"Oh, you're probably right. But it seemed strange when I saw those flowers hanging there."

"Did you hear crying this time?"

"No, I didn't. I wondered if it was because Mary Lou knows we are trying to help her." She looked hopefully at him. "When Hannah went down there and hung those carnations on the wall, blue like Mary Lou would have liked, do you think it's far out to think she knew somehow we're trying to help her?"

"I don't know. I don't know much about any of that. But we've started the ball rolling to do what needs to be done and we're not going to help anybody or any spirit, by hurting each other. I do know that." He put his arms around his wife. "We'll get it done. I promise. We'll get it done."

Casey swung by Cas's office to say goodbye before he went to pick Missy up and head back to school. Cas walked out to the parking lot with him and watched as he drove away. The old car would never win any beauty contests or races, but Casey kept it in good condition and it was safe.

He chuckled as he watched it pull out into traffic. Talk about tired iron!

Back in his office he got his papers together and called Clint at the coroner's office. "Do you have that crew ready?"

"Yes, are you ready for us?"

"Yes. I've got the papers and I'm leaving now."

Cas entered the library and went straight to Jo Beth's desk. She glanced up smiling. She paused when she saw the expression on his face, her hand with the rubber stamp in it stopped in mid air.

"Is there something wrong?"

"No," Cass assured her. "Nothing that can't be fixed."

He laid the papers on Jo Beth's desk. "This is an order allowing us to open a wall in the basement."

Her mouth slightly open, Jo Beth scanned them. "It is? The wall in the basement? You think then?" She stopped, looking a bit scared.

"We've come across some information recently that indicates there may be two bodies there in the wall."

"Two!" Joe Beth gasped, cringing back from the desk. "Two bodies in the wall," she repeated softly her eyes going to the men with him. She was too stunned to think of more questions to ask.

"We had to give a reason for breaking into the wall. It's written right there," Cas explained, putting his finger on the line. "It might be as well if you didn't tell anyone about it. Everyone will know about it soon enough."

"All right." Jo Beth nodded, still looking uneasy.

Cas followed the men downstairs and Jo Beth soon heard the noise of the wall being demolished. She flinched at the noise.

It didn't take long to get through it. As Jo Beth listened to what sounded like pieces of concrete falling the crew from the coroner's office came in, pulling on their gloves.

Clint looked around. The cold draft from the open door to the basement hit him as Jo Beth pointed in that direction.

Clint called down the stairs, "Cas?"

"I'm here, that you, Clint?"

"Yes, we're here. Are you ready for us?"

"Yes, soon as the other crew gets up there."

Clint stood back and watched as the crew with their sledges and axes came out. Then he and the men in white scrubs went down with one of the two stretchers they had brought.

Jo Beth watched from behind her desk, staying out of their way without missing anything that went on.

Great care was taken with the contents of the old comforter and quilt as they were lifted from their cold tomb. After more than a hundred years, they were kept intact and disturbed as little as possible as they were carried up the stairs one after the other.

Jo Beth and Hannah, who had come from the back, stood quietly by Jo Beth's desk and watched.

Cas was the last to come up, turning off the light behind them. His eyes met Hannah's and he handed her the small bouquet of blue striped carnations.

Jo Beth looked from them to Hannah, understanding at once.

"I, I just thought maybe it would make her feel better," Hannah explained softly.

Jo Beth smiled affectionately at Hannah, then as Cas turned away she asked, "So there were two as Della

Reubens said. Can you tell us any more than that?"

"Not officially just yet. But we can soon."

Cas went back to work. Four murder cases had been solved, two of them more than a hundred years old.

EPILOGUE

Clarence was holding court. He was sanding off a shelf getting it ready for painting, talking as he worked.

Nathan, Ellen, Connie and the other volunteers who were constantly coming in and out, listened to him as he talked about the things he heard from the old folks when he was a little boy playing near them. By now, all of them knew he was Lacey Lynch's great grandson and an integral part of the history of Maryvale.

"Oh, Cas," Connie reported at home, "It's going so well! We'll have a gala opening when everything is ready, with two young ladies in dresses with hoops to show everyone around and point out the exhibits."

"Hoops?"

Connie nodded, "Two seamstresses came in to look at the dresses and make copies. Missy will be one of our guides, we'll have the grand opening when she can be here, and the other will be Terrence's sister, Clarence's granddaughter."

"What was decided about the jewelry in the carpet bag?"

"Almost everything is being kept, certainly Mary Lou's blue topaz necklace. I was ready to fight for that if need be. And we are keeping the beautiful old armoire we found the dresses in. Turns out it was made in France. The only thing that will be sold is Mirelle Nelson's emeralds. The emerald necklace is the most expensive item anyway. And the money from that will be handled very carefully for things we can't get donated or manage for somehow."

"How is Clarence taking his so called punishment?"

Connie laughed. "So well, we may charge him for coming in!"

The next day, Connie went out to Peaceful Ridge Cemetery.

She wanted to see for herself where Nelson was buried and look around at what space there was for Mary Lou and Louie DeVille.

She slowed as she neared the bridge, remembering how Cas had been pushed off the road when he broke his arm. She gave an involuntary shudder. Out here in the dark, hurt and unconscious. "It's a good thing someone saw the car." She looked back as she passed over the bridge. "It's a wonder anyone did see it."

Something not clear enough to grasp at the edge of her mind worried her as she looked down, unable to see over the railing. She shook off the uneasy feeling, just glad Cas was all right now.

Leaving the car parked halfway up the slope, she walked to the top of the ridge where the older graves were. She stopped to look at several of them before finding Nelson's grave. He had been buried beside Mirelle, Mary Lou's mother. The stones were both beautiful gray granite with the dates on them and nothing else. Connie stood looking down at Nelson's grave.

"I'll bet you had a lot to explain and answer for when Mirelle and St. Peter got hold of you, you MONSTER!" She kicked a few leaves over him, looking around.

Cas had been right, there was plenty of room left for Mary Lou and her Louie. Enough to give them a choice when the committee had to make a decision.

Clint was the first person Cas saw when he entered the coroner's office.

"Hi, I had the feeling you'd turn up," Clint greeted him.

"I didn't want to call, I wanted to come see for myself, about Mary Lou Nelson and Louis DeVille. You were able to establish their identities, weren't you?"

"We were," Clint nodded, "But forensic science wasn't as clear as what we found with them."

Clint beckoned Cas into his office and pointed to a box on his desk. "This seems clear enough to me."

Cas pulled the box toward him to look at the contents.

"The gold watch has Louis DeVille's initials on it and a picture of himself and Mary Lou inside it. The little heart shaped locket has a picture of Nelson and Mary Lou's mother in it. There was a picture of Louie and Mary Lou with their hands together showing off their wedding rings and also the wide gold band and smaller one that had belonged to the couple ."I've heard some of the rumors that are going around, and there was a bullet in each of them about where the heart would have been, though there are only bones here now. What exactly happened, or do you know?"

"Yes, I know. The story was handed down through the years, from the only witness there was. DeVille and Mary Lou confronted Nelson, told him they had been married by the local priest and had their rings on. Nelson lost control of his anger and tried to shoot DeVille, but Mary Lou threw herself in front of him and took the bullet. Nelson, still in a rage, then shot DeVille. Lacey Lynch, the witness, had been watching from the hall, afraid of what Nelson might say or do. She ran in and sat crying over Mary Lou, then Nelson, realizing what he'd done, shot himself."

Clint grimaced, his arms folded across his chest as he listened. "What an unholy mess, shot his own child. Then it was Lacey Lynch and someone else who hid them so no one would know what happened, is that it?"

"That's it. Lacey Lynch got her boyfriend, Clarence's great grandfather, to help her. He's the one who sealed them up in the wall. Lacey told her granddaughter and it was the granddaughter who finally told the truth about what happened. She said Lacey Lynch worried about it as long as she lived, grieved over her friend not being buried in hallowed ground."

"What about this crying in the basement business," Clint pinned Cas down. "Anything to that rumor?"

"I'm not going to make any speeches and I don't pretend to understand it. But I heard the crying myself. And I guess you heard about the séance and Lacey's spirit asking someone to help Miss Mary Lou. She was trying to fix that not being buried properly in hallowed ground business."

"I took it with a grain of salt till I could ask you, and I don't think I'm going to comment either."

"And you also know," Cas grinned. "If you tell anybody I said all that, I'll be forced to say you lied!"

Clint shrugged. "Of course, I'd feel the same way. But we can fix that burial problem now. I guess Mary Lou will be buried up there where the rest of the Nelsons are?"

"So will he. They were married, you know."

"I don't see any point in keeping them or doing any more tests, whenever you want them released."

"Give me a couple more days. A place in Fort Craig will have the stone ready by then. He wants the publicity and gave us a dirt cheap price on the pink marble stone."

"You're going to bury them side by side as man and wife?"

"Yes. That's how the stone will read. I'll take these things in the box and give them to the museum committee if it's all right?"

"Sure. Take them. Mine is not exactly a career where you want to keep souvenirs." Clint looked mischievous, "I wonder if it will get old Nelson's goat, having them buried up there with him as man and wife?"

"I HOPE so, Clint," Cas ground his teeth picturing the grisly murders. "I just really do hope so. I hope it GALLS HIS HATEFUL BACKSIDE!"

Clint laughed, holding the door for him. "Me too. Just give me a holler when you want them released. I've got to get back to some more recent meanness."

The day of the funeral there were quite a few people who came to see Mary Lou and Louie DeVille buried. The papers hadn't left out a single romantic nuance or now known fact about the tragedy and there were people there from the surrounding areas as well as Maryvale and Fort Craig.

Clarence and his family had come. Ms. Daisy too, with two of the nurses from the nursing home who had brought a folding chair with them for her.

Connie stopped to speak to her and pointed out the pretty pink marble stone.

"My Granny and her friend, they at peace now," she smiled up at Connie as she turned to rejoin Cas.

The minister gave a brief but beautiful eulogy about love and forgiving, and there were more than enough tears and compassion to put troubled spirits to rest.

Connie and Cas joined Jo Beth and Hannah to walk back down together. Hannah seemed preoccupied.

"I think Hannah is hearing music or something we don't," Connie smiled at Cas.

"No," Hannah looked puzzled. "Not music, it sounds more like two little girls, laughing and giggling...."

*Turn the page for an
excerpt from*

RECIPE
FOR
TROUBLE

A Maryvale Cozy Mystery

Book Three

———◆———

Jackie Griffey

Miss Minnie looked worried as she poured the last of the coffee into their cups.

Even the scent of good coffee didn't improve Cas's mood. "I've got bad news," Cas began. "Yesterday, I went up to check on Mattie, to see for myself how things were. I wanted to see if she was still feeling better or might need anything. It's a good thing I went. She was nearly gone."

After a few seconds of shocked silence, Miss Mayme drew an anxious breath. "Gone. Nearly gone. Cas, you, you don't mean?"

He tried to smile. "I think she'll make it. She's pretty tough, and always has been healthy from what she and the rest of you have told me. I called the drugstore for the name of the doctor up there. There's a Dr. Kelso who has a clinic up there near the crossroads, a nice one. It's a small hospital, actually. That's where Mattie is now, at his clinic."

Miss Minnie's hands pressed against her heart, "At the clinic! What happened? What's wrong with her?" She looked puzzled, "She seemed to have an upset stomach and was tired, but I thought she'd be over it by now. She seemed so much better when I left."

"She's holding her own, Dr. Kelso is keeping a close eye on her and there's a nurse with her around the clock. He was still doing lab tests the last time I talked to him."

"Tests." Frightening thoughts showed on Miss Mayme's face. "Oh, you mean, he thinks she may have cancer or an ulcer or some disease?" Miss Mayme clasped her shaking hands in dread. Minnie reached out to her.

"No, not a disease," Cas corrected. "Poison."

"Poison?" Miss Mayme nearly upset her cup, her hand hitting it as she reached to grasp the edge of the desk. It clattered in its saucer. "The doctor thinks Mattie was poisoned?"

"But," Miss Minnie gasped, "that's ridiculous!" Her eyes met Cas's. "There was no one there. She's been up there by herself!"

---◆---

RECIPE FOR TROUBLE

available in print and ebook

THE
MARYVALE COZY MYSTERY
SERIES

The Devil In Maryvale
The Nelson Scandal
Recipe For Trouble
The Mardi Gras Murder

Cozy mystery author Jackie Griffey likes to read as well as write mysteries and romantic suspense. She and her family, two cats, a Chihuahua, and a couple of wild bunnies live in Arkansas.

Jackie loves hearing from her readers. You can contact Jackie through her publisher at:

JackieGriffey@epublishingworks.com